THE KEY

A seemingly worthless book, it held the answer to an ages-old mystery—which would grant omnipotence to the one who discovered its secret and damn all others to merciless death.

THE PUZZLE

A friend's brutal murder brought the book into Alex Warner's possession, and at once he was besieged by threats of a sudden and violent end. For a secret religious sect and a magician with incomparable powers would do anything to gain mastery of the invincible force. Warner and the sorceress Valerie Lancaster had to solve the mystery first if they hoped to live.

THE QUEST

Following a trail of clues from Chicago's back alleys to an impregnable Swiss fortress, and into a hidden history filled with Nazi atrocities and vampire legends, Alex and Valerie drew ever nearer to a horrific battle with the forces of evil. If they lost, all mankind would suffer at the hands of the most diabolical tyrant ever known.

THE ARMAGEDDON BOX

Robert Weinberg

Two-time Lovecraft Award Winner

Other *Leisure* Books by Robert Weinberg:

THE DEVIL'S AUCTION

ROBERT WEINBERG

LEISURE BOOKS NEW YORK CITY

To Stefan R. Dziemianowicz—
fellow traveler among unnameable horrors

A Leisure Book ®

November 1991

Published by

Dorchester Publishing Co., Inc.
276 Fifth Avenue
New York, NY 10001

Printed in the United States of America

THE
ARMAGEDDON
BOX

That there are creatures in existence, neither man nor beast, but strange, unearthly creation born of the nefarious passions of distorted minds, you will not deny.

from *Alraune*
by Hanns Heinz Ewers

Prologue: Dachau, Bavaria: Winter 1944

The pain and the cold kept him awake. Shivering, Howie Rosenberg uncrossed his arms off his chest and let them fall to his stomach. There was no other place to put them. Bodies hemmed him in on both sides. On his right, Jacob Nash muttered a few inarticulate words in his sleep and huddled closer. Howie stifled a groan as ripples of pain shot through his legs. Even after a half-year, his lower limbs were still incredibly sensitive to any sort of pressure.

There were four of them pressed together like chunks of firewood on the narrow bunk, desperate for the little warmth that their combined body heat provided. These four skeletal men were dressed only in rags in the dead of winter, four among the thousands of inmates in the Nazi concentration camp at Dachau, Bavaria, men condemned to a living hell on Earth.

Outside a fierce blizzard raged. The wind howled like a hungry wolf, looking for prey. Wordlessly, Howie prayed for the snow to stop before morning. Herr Doktor Rascher had bizarre ideas about human survival in freezing cold weather. With the consent of his friend, Reichsfuhrer-SS Heinrich Himmler, the Commandant often used the camp inmates as human guinea pigs.

Three weeks ago, in the midst of a storm much like the one tonight, Rascher's guards had pulled a dozen inmates from their beds in the middle of the night, forced them to strip and then herded them outside. Howie, unable to move without assistance, had not seen what happened, but other prisoners had provided the grisly details.

The naked victims had been buried up to their necks in snow and left there for a half-hour. One man, braver than the rest, had tried to resist. Two guards had methodically clubbed him to death with their rifle butts. His body, skull smashed to a bloody pulp, was left on the threshold of the dormitory as a testimony to the price of disobedience.

After half an hour in the intense cold, those prisoners still alive were pulled from the snowbanks and removed to one of Rascher's infamous labs. Of the original dozen, only three made it that far. None of them was ever seen again. Survivors of the Herr Doktor's experiments were rare. The Nazi officer considered the inmates of the camp as experimental animals, not human beings. Whether they lived or died was of little consequence. All that mattered was the scientific result.

Howie grimaced with the thought. Everyone in the camp knew that Sigmund Rascher had no training in either medicine or science. He was a Nazi toady with the right connections, whose insane theories served as a thin excuse to perform the most diabolical acts of torture, all cloaked under the name of humanitarian research.

Rascher enjoyed testing humans to the limits—and then beyond. His cruelty knew no bounds.

Experimenting with the results of high altitude on the human anatomy, the mad doctor had used decompression chambers in a way never dreamt of by aerodynamic engineers. He placed his victims inside the rooms and killed them slowly by lessening the air pressure. According to rumor, Rascher spent hours fiddling with his switches, carefully studying the expressions of his subjects as their internal organs exploded. No one was sure how many inmates died before Rascher tired of his study, but it had to be hundreds.

"Nein, nein!" Jacob whispered, his body gripped by a powerful dream. Shaking all over, the man lashed out with both feet, catching Howie with a glancing blow across his ankles.

Caught by surprise, he screamed, a high-pitched shriek of intense pain. No one stirred. They were inured to such screams in the night. It was part of life and death in Dachau.

Outside, the wind growled, and Howie's body shook from the cold. It had to be well below zero tonight. The thin walls of the dormitory provided minimal shelter from the fury of the blizzard. The building, which had little heat and no insulation, housed 500 prisoners. Oftentimes, after bitter cold snaps like this, not all of them woke the next morning. They were the lucky ones, those who died in their sleep.

The frigid temperature made the pain in his legs worse. His bones throbbed in constant agony, and he knew that there would be no sleep for him this night, like many other nights during the past six months.

Six months previous, Howie, along with ten others, had been the subject of a Rascher experiment in natural healing. Howie was still recovering from its effects.

Early one morning, he had been roused from sleep and taken by ever-silent guards to the gleaming white surgery of the laboratory. He barely had time to wonder what was going to happen. Two male orderlies strapped him down to an operating table. No one talked of anesthetics or pain killers.

A team of surgeons, under the watchful eyes of Herr Doktor Rascher, did the actual work. The doctors, each one armed with a steel-headed mallet, broke every major bone in

Howie's legs and ankles, only sparing his knees. However, striving for perfection, they smashed all the bones in his toes.

Mercifully, he passed out from the pain soon after they began. Afterwards, they wrapped his broken limbs in bandages and brought him back to the barracks. Of the eleven men chosen, only six survived. Three died the next day. Another two succumbed to fever a week later. Somehow, Howie survived and slowly healed.

One of the other prisoners who once worked as a doctor tried to set the bones but without much success. The Nazis didn't care. Each day, one of the orderlies visited and studied his crushed legs. Howie's agony and suffering meant nothing to them. Only Herr Rascher's mad pseudo-scientific studies mattered.

A half-year later, he still could not walk without assistance. The unrelenting pain made his every waking hour a nightmarish ordeal. During the day, he hunched over a table and made uniforms like all the other prisoners. In Dachau, you worked or died—and Howie Rosenberg was not yet ready to die.

At night, he dozed fitfully, rarely sleeping for more than a few hours at a time. Hundreds of prisoners were crammed into buildings designed for one-tenth that number and slept four to a bed. After a time, he learned to remain motionless, so as not to disturb those around him. His broken legs acted like anchors, trapping him to the cot until morning, when his companions awakened.

All around him, the barracks were silent. Only the howling of the wind and the creaking of the walls disturbed the quiet. Closing his eyes, he tried to blot out his surroundings, gradually letting his thoughts drift back to the days before the war, before Hitler's rise to power. But he was unable to sleep.

Hours passed. It was just after midnight when Howie felt an unnatural lassitude sweep through him. It was as if his head was filled with cotton. Yawning deeply, he shifted groggily, trying to get comfortable. Sharp needles of pain darted up his legs, shocking him fully awake.

Fearfully, Howie raised his head a few inches off the bunk and looked about. All around him, the breathing of his comrades had grown shallow. Not a man stirred in the entire dormitory. Suddenly frightened, Howie dug an elbow into Jacob Nash's back. His friend didn't move, didn't even grunt. He slept the sleep of the dead.

Tightly wedged between two unconscious prisoners, Howie was trapped. His dead legs worked as shackles, pinning him to the bed. He suspected the Nazis of some new atrocity, perhaps nerve gas, but he was at a loss for an explanation. There was only one way to find out. Carefully, he closed his eyes to mere slits and sank back on the bed. Matching his breathing to that of his fellows, Howie pretended to sleep.

A blast of arctic air alerted him when the door of the dormitory opened. Cautiously, he raised his head a few inches—and found himself staring at madness.

Three figures stood in the doorway. Only one was human. He stood over six feet tall and wore only a pair of army trousers as protection from the cold. The weather didn't affect him. His skin, the color of weathered ivory, glowed with an unnatural luster. Beads of sweat glistened on his naked chest.

His short blond hair and pale blue eyes proclaimed him the perfect Aryan. Muscles bulged in his arms and chest. His every move spoke of great strength, yet, despite his size, his features were those of a young boy. The mind of a child commanded the body of an adult.

He entered the barracks arrogantly, his head thrown back in a childlike pose of command, as if he owned the building. The Nazi guards were nowhere to be seen. Behind him were two horrifying beasts.

Glowing like hot coals, the creatures' blood-red eyes nestled in thin, narrow faces of dead white skin. Two black airholes and a thin gash were all they possessed for a nose and mouth. Each hissing breath revealed a maw full of needle-sharp yellow fangs. Their pointed ears pressed up tight to hairless skulls.

In size and shape, they resembled men, but their arms stretched down nearly to the floor, and their clawlike fingers ended in inch-long nails. They wore no clothing. The darkness hid most of their torso and legs, but Howie knew that the huge black humps on their backs had to be folded wings. The monsters were a grotesque mixture of man and bat.

They shuffled along stiffly behind their leader, distinctly uncomfortable walking on their stumpy legs. Their heads swung from side to side, as if seeking something. A primal fear whispered to Howie that these things hungered, and instinctively he knew on what they fed.

Trembling, Howie uttered a prayer for deliverance. The Undead, the Nosferatu, hunted for human life. Eaters of flesh and drinkers of blood, their presence had haunted Yiddish folklore for generations. Howie's mother often threatened him in his childhood with stories of such creatures stealing away bad little boys for food. She had called them the Very Old Folk, and her tales had never failed to terrify him. Now, those very monsters walked only a few feet away.

Horror paralyzed him. He lay on the bunk with his eyes pressed tightly shut, his ears straining to hear the slightest noise. Helpless, trapped by dead legs, he waited. Inhaling and exhaling regularly, he tried to feign slumber.

Even the wind no longer howled outside. From somewhere in the room, the man-child giggled loudly as the claws of his companions scraped along the floor.

Finally, the boy spoke. His voice echoed through the silent barracks, sweet and clear and innocent. His words burned into Howie's brain. "Let these Nazi fools learn the folly of threatening me. After tonight, they will realize that no one, no place, is safe from my wrath. Feast, my friends, feast."

The Nosferatu obeyed. At first, the muted sounds Howie heard puzzled him. The noise reminded him of Friday night dinner at his parents' home many years before. Visions of anxious children scrambling for chicken drumsticks raced through his brain. Then, when the truth struck him, he almost lost control of his senses. The monsters were gorging themselves on the helpless bodies of the sleeping prisoners.

Howie could hear their teeth ripping human flesh. Powerful jaws crunched into bone and muscle. After each kill came a terrible loud sucking noise that filled the room. Yet, all through that macabre feast, no one stirred.

Victim after victim fell to the vampires' lust. The creatures only spent a few minutes on each kill. From time to time, their companion pointed out a healthier-than-average sleeper they had missed. He delighted in discovering tasty finds for their hunger.

Slowly, the trio made their way across the room. Dozens of men died beneath the monsters' fangs. Gradually, as they moved farther and farther away from Howie's corner, his tense muscles relaxed. He risked one deep breath, settling his shaken nerves. Cautiously, he opened his eyes.

Without warning, a white hand shot out from beyond Howie's line of vision and seized him by the chin. Strong fingers dug deep into his flesh and jerked his head around. Howie gasped in terror as he found himself staring deep into the eyes of the Nosferatu's master. The boy grinned nastily and laughed insolently like a spoiled child.

"I caught you listening to my friends," he said, shaking his head from side to side. "We don't like eavesdroppers. We don't like them at all. You need to be punished. The only question is what we should do to you. Something special, perhaps?"

The boy's speech brought his two companions rushing over. Blood still glistened on the vampires' fangs, their red eyes blazing with unholy fire. The monsters hungered for more victims, but they remained quiet, waiting for their master to speak. This unnatural child controlled their every action.

He stood there for a moment, concentrating. Howie, positive death stared him in the face, felt strangely at peace. In seconds, his suffering would be over. He was not afraid of dying but almost welcomed its embrace.

"Aren't you going to beg for your life?" the boy asked. "The guards outside pleaded on their knees before my friends finished them." He laughed again, a frightening sound. "I might be merciful this time."

Howie shook his head, sending a painful spasm rippling down through his legs. "Kill me and be done with it," he declared through gritted teeth. Tense muscles made his agony almost unbearable. Light-headed, he barely knew what he was saying. "Finish the job your Nazi friends began."

"Finish the job?" the boy said, glancing down at Howie's legs. Frowning, he examined the grotesque lumps of bone and knotted muscle. His brow wrinkled in annoyance.

"Suicide would have put an end to your suffering long ago," he said, half-questioning.

"Never," Howie said. No matter how great the pain, how intense the agony, he refused to yield. He would not, could not, give up. It was part of him, part of his soul.

"A fighter," the boy said, grinning. "How convenient." He leaned closer, so that his face was only inches away from Howie's. "I need a messenger. You will be that man. When those in command of this camp want to know what happened here tonight, you will tell them. Tell them of the Very Old Folk who made a mockery of their defenses. Of how they feasted on both prisoners and guards alike. And when they ask you who lead this attack, who invaded their sanctum, speak my name. Remember it well, little man. Tell them all the gates and all the guns and all the guards in the world cannot protect them from the power of Dietrich Vril."

He turned to his two followers. "We want to make sure our friend here does not forget his lesson," he said in a voice as cold as the darkness itself. "He needs some sort of reminder. I know. Feast well on his companions."

The vampires needed no further urging. Howie squeezed his eyes shut, but he couldn't close his ears. Teeth tore into flesh, sending hot blood spurting across his face and chest. Bones cracked as powerful jaws bit deep. And then came the sound of that monstrous sucking.

Howie screamed and screamed, until finally madness engulfed him. He sank into a black pit of unconsciousness, the high-pitched laughter of the unholy child ringing in his ears.

Chapter One

"That's an incredible story," Alex Warner said, staring across the table at his old friend, Howie Rosenberg. Cautiously, he sipped at the glass of schnapps he held in one hand. It was quite potent. "You've kept it secret all these years?"

"It took place nearly half a century ago," Howie Rosenberg said with a shrug. A short, elderly man, a sparse white beard covered his lower face. A black satin skullcap rested on his bald head. "I tried hard to forget those days. More than once I doubted the truth of it myself."

They sat in the back room of Rosenberg's Book Emporium on Chicago's far South Side. Alex had arrived an hour earlier, summoned there by an urgent call from the owner. Howie had refused to say over the phone what troubled him, but the desperation in his voice made it clear that it was no idle invitation. He started telling his tale soon after Alex arrived.

Alex took another sip of his drink. A tall, muscular man in his late thirties, he was a university professor specializing in medieval history. He had known Howie Rosenberg for more than 20 years. Alex considered the elderly bookstore owner one of his closest friends.

Outside, a major snowstorm was in the process of dumping a foot of snow on the city. The snowplows were out, but they battled impossible odds. Already, most streets were nearly impassable. Alex had been forced to park over a block away from the bookstore and walk the rest of the way.

"Then I look at this," Rosenberg said, raising one arm to reveal the concentration camp numbers etched into his flesh, "and all of my doubts disappear."

Alex shivered, not just from the cold. His gaze wandered across the huge stacks of books that filled every nook and cranny of the storeroom. Other than the card table and chairs, the only piece of furniture in the room was a battered old refrigerator in the corner. On top of it rested an inch-thick platform. Covering the raised surface was a heavy velvet cloth, decorated with a silver Star of David. Two multifaceted glass tumblers, half-filled with white wax, sat on the dark fabric. These were the Sabbath candles, and for all the years Alex had known Howie, he had never seen them anywhere but in the front room—until that night. A slow-burning wick in each candle sent strange shadows creeping through the room that increased Alex's sense that something unusual was going on.

"I never delivered Vril's message," Rosenberg continued, rising to his feet. Face contorted with pain, he shuffled his way to the rear entrance of the store. Carefully, he checked the two deadbolt locks and the chain on the door. Alex wondered what was going on. He had never seen the bookseller so jumpy.

"My mind snapped. However, instead of shooting me, their usual treatment for madmen, the Germans nursed me back to sanity. They transferred me to a prisoner-of-war camp where I was treated quite well. Evidently, according to my captors, a very high party official wanted to personally question me about the attack, but he never got the chance. The war ended while I was still recovering."

Alex leaned forward, his relentless curiosity aroused. "Who was that official?"

Rosenberg shrugged. "I never found out. Only a few men in the Reich held such power—Hitler, Himmler, Goering. It matters little now. They are all long dead."

The book dealer shuffled back to the table. Pouring himself another glass of liquor, he gestured to his friend's glass. "No more for me," Alex said.

Rosenberg tossed the drink down with a flick of the wrist. Alex felt uneasy. Rosenberg was scared, very scared. His fear permeated the very air of the room. A miasma of evil hung over them like some dark cloud, and a feeling of impending doom held Alex in a grip he could not shake.

"I hate asking you for help," Rosenberg said, "but of all my friends, you are the only one I can trust. The modern world laughs at evil. Only a handful are wise enough to realize the truth. From our many discussions over the years, I know you are one of those few."

Alex remained silent, his features grim. He saw no reason to mention his recent adventures tracking down the murderer of his wife's father, Jake Lancaster. That quest had brought him face to face with the forces of black magic. Those experiences had converted him from skeptic to ardent believer in the supernatural.

"I turned up an unusual book a few weeks ago," Rosenberg continued, his voice trembling. "Morris Levine, the antique dealer down the block, brought it into the store one afternoon. He recently bought a small collection of Nazi war memorabilia and found the book at the bottom of the crate.

"Levine owed me a few dollars and asked if I would take the book in payment. I didn't examine it closely, but to be charitable to an old friend, I agreed anyway."

"Who was the original owner?" Alex asked, not sure why Rosenberg was telling him this story. The book dealer was acting very mysterious.

"I checked with Levine as soon as I noticed the inscription on the fly. The box came from an old warehouse being demolished on the west side of town. It was one of a number of containers that Levine bought from the manager of the building for ten bucks. Years ago, the place had been used for personal storage.

"The original owner must have been a soldier who left the box there and forgot about it. No one remembered a thing about him. All of the other items in the box were war souvenirs, the usual things soldiers brought home after World War Two. The volume had probably languished in that crate since the late forties."

"A rare book?" asked Alex.

"Unique," Rosenberg answered. "At least, the inscription inside made it thus. Realizing the value of the volume, I decided to list it in *The Bookman*. The ad appeared nearly two weeks ago. I received two calls on it, the first coming soon after the ad appeared. It was from a priest, Brother Ambrose Haxley of the Order of Circumcellions. He was quite anxious to obtain the volume but wanted to wait until he saw it in person. The second response came late last night."

"Another priest?" Alex asked, guessing. Rosenberg shook his head, his eyes reflecting a nameless dread.

"The other call—"

Bang, bang, bang. The whole store vibrated with the sound of someone pounding on the front door of the showroom. Rosenberg's face turned dead white. Trembling with emotion, he clutched Alex by the shoulders.

"He told me he would come tomorrow," Rosenberg gasped, his expression ghastly to behold, "but I suspected he would not wait. That was why I called you."

"What are you talking about, Howie?" Alex asked, rising to his feet. The air shook again with the violent hammering outside. "We'd better answer the door before that lunatic breaks it down."

"I hid the book the one place he would never think to look," Rosenberg whispered, as Alex pushed open the door to the front room. "Remember that, Alex."

It was freezing cold in the showroom. Two huge picture windows fronted the store, facing the street. Outside, the wind swirled the snow about, cutting visibility down to a few feet. Little traffic moved on the street.

A lone figure stood framed in the doorway. It was a massive figure who Alex instantly recognized from Howie Rosenberg's story. Incredible as it seemed, this intruder had to be Dietrich Vril.

Vril looked as if he had stepped out of the pages of a comic book. Alex estimated the man stood six-foot-six and weighed around 300 pounds. However, his proportions matched so perfectly that he seemed gigantic only when compared with the normal world.

Powerful muscles rippled beneath his shirt. Despite the raging storm, Vril held his head up high. Alex shook his head in astonishment. He could not see the man's eyes, but his blond hair glistened almost pure white, complementing the ivory color of his skin. Vril pulsed with energy. His body almost glowed with electricity. In below-zero windchill, he wore no coat or other protective garb.

His face resembled a carved slab of ice. A wide forehead bridged down sharply over his eyes, giving his entire face a shadowy and sinister look. A powerful hook nose and large, slanted cheekbones added to the impression of unlimited strength.

Alex wrenched open the door. A gust of freezing cold wind escorted the giant into the room. For a second, flakes of ice and snow covered Alex, and he shivered involuntarily.

Vril stalked to the center of the room and took in the entire store with a sweep of his head. Satisfied with the layout of the room, he lowered his head and met Alex's gaze. His bright blue eyes were as cold as arctic ice.

"Dietrich Vril?"

"Correct," the giant answered, in a deep guttural voice that grated on Alex's nerves like sandpaper. He spoke perfect English but with a thick, German accent. "I called last night about a book. You are Rosenberg?"

"Not me," Alex said. "I'm Alex Warner. A friend."

Howie had seated himself on a high stool behind the cash register. "That's him over there."

Rosenberg said nothing for a moment. Conflicting emotions flashed across his face. He opened his mouth to speak, but for a few seconds, no sound emerged. Finally, he managed to stammer out a few words.

"You told me tomorrow over the phone."

"My flight arrived this evening. I could not wait another day. Forty years I searched for that *verdammte* book. I traveled throughout the world, spending thousands, tracking down one false lead after another. Once you read me the inscription over the phone, I knew my quest was finally over. I had to get my hands on the book tonight."

"Normally, I close the store at six," Rosenberg said, staring down at his hands. He seemed afraid to look directly at Vril, as if fearing the giant might recall him after all the years.

"I suspected you might be here tonight," Vril said, his mouth curling into a slight smile. "A hundred thousand dollars works wonders."

Rosenberg took in a deep breath. Raising his head, he stared directly at Vril. Alex, watching the German closely, saw no evidence that the giant recognized Howie.

Alex gnawed on his lower lip in annoyance. Rosenberg's experiences in the concentration camp took place nearly a half-century earlier, and the German had mentioned hunting for the book for nearly 40 years. Yet Vril appeared to be Alex's age, perhaps a few years older—definitely not 60 or 70. It made no sense.

"Your offer was quite generous, Mr. Vril. Please sit down." Howie's voice still trembled with emotion as he motioned to a large chair near the front windows. "You look somewhat flushed."

"Excuse me if I prefer to stay on my feet," Vril said, pacing back and forth by the windows. "My metabolism plays tricks on me from time to time. A childhood disease that reoccurs during times of extreme tension. I cannot remain still."

Sweat dripped off the giant, as if his entire body was on fire.

"When I indulge in intense physical activity, my body burns calories at an incredible rate. When I relax, that speed drops down to safe levels. From time to time, that slowdown does not take place as quickly as I prefer. During that period, I suffer these spells."

Vril clenched his hands in huge fists. "Medication controls the problem. Being in a rush tonight, I left my pills at my hotel. Of course, the one time I find myself without them, an attack occurs."

"A terrible calamity," Rosenberg said, his tone anything but concerned. "Perhaps it would be better if we postpone our business to another evening as originally planned."

"No!" Vril's voice stayed calm, but somehow that one word carried more than a trace of menace. "The fever will pass in a few hours. It always does. I must have that book tonight. After all these years of searching, my health hardly matters. I want that book now, Rosenberg."

"You collect rare books, Mr. Vril?" Alex asked from the corner.

The giant turned and stared at Alex, as if suddenly remembering him. After a few seconds, Vril chuckled humorlessly.

"I have no time for reading, especially the type of drivel written by Ewers. The real world contains more horror than any writer could inscribe on paper. History drips red with blood. I want this book for sentimental reasons."

"Dr. Warner is here at my invitation tonight. Alex teaches at the university nearby."

Vril dipped his head in a short bow of acknowledgement. "Enough small talk. I did not fly all the way from Germany for idle chitchat. Where is the book?"

"I am not—"

"I want that book *now,* little man," Vril said, his tremendous hands curling into fists. He took a step forward towards Rosenberg, then another. "I offered you a hundred times its worth. No more stalling."

The book dealer's face turned ashen with fear. Without thinking, Alex stepped between the giant and his friend. "Calm down, Vril. No reason for threats."

"I take what I want, Warner," Vril said with a sneer. "No one stands in my way." He raised one huge hand, as if to brush Alex out of the way. "Move aside or suffer the consequences."

Alex tensed. He had fought many enemies in his life, from the Vietcong to powerful sorcerers, but never one the size of Dietrich Vril. The giant personified brute force. Alex knew that any struggle with this man would be for keeps. There would be no quarter asked or given.

"There are fifty thousand books in this store, Mr. Vril," Howie Rosenberg said softly. "Do you think you could find the Ewers books without my assistance?"

Vril scowled. For a second, his lips drew back from his teeth in an expression of animal-like rage. Then, with a snarl of anger, he swung away from Alex and stomped back to the center of the room.

"You must excuse my temper," he said, his breath coming in deep, labored gasps. "I am not used to bargaining." His tone softened. "At least let me examine the volume to insure its authenticity."

Alex glanced over at Rosenberg. If Howie gave Vril the book, Alex was positive the giant would never surrender it. Nor was Alex convinced the big man intended to pay for the volume, whatever it was. Vril struck him as a man who played by no rules other than those to his advantage.

The sharp ringing of the telephone caught all three by surprise.

"Excuse me," Rosenberg muttered, more to himself than to the others. "I can't imagine who would be calling at this time of night."

Rosenberg walked slowly and deliberately to the phone at the other end of the counter. His breath came in deep, painful gasps with each step. Twisted legs shifted treacherously as he moved. Alex shook his head in despair. It was incredible that Rosenberg could walk at all, suffering the way he did.

Alex frowned. He disliked surprises of any sort, and there had been too many this evening. He wished he knew more about the first caller Rosenberg had mentioned and a great deal more about this mysterious book worth a small fortune.

He desperately wished his wife, Valerie, was with him here. As a practicing sorceress, she intuitively understood a great deal about the unexplainable. Those gifted with the power, the ability to practice real magic and sorcery, recognized all other masters. Alex suspected Vril was a master of arcane sorcery, but he couldn't be sure.

With a shrug, Rosenberg hung up the receiver, looking puzzled. "Odd," he said reflectivly. "The person on the other end first checked with me to make sure he dialed the right number. Then he asked if he could speak to you for a moment, Mr. Vril. When I asked him to hold for a second, he told me not to bother and hung up."

When Rosenberg finished speaking, Vril reacted instantly, moving incredibly fast for a big man. He launched himself forward, his arms held together in front of his head to form a battering ram of bone and flesh. With a crash, he smashed through the nearest plate glass window and went hurtling out into the blizzard. Landing in a tumbler's roll, Vril came up into a crouch, his arms extended from his body in a karate stance. In a second, he disappeared into the blinding snowstorm.

"What's going on here?" Howie exclaimed, half-rising from his chair. He appeared stunned by Vril's sudden actions. "Alex—"

"Get down! It's an ambush!" Alex shouted as he charged across the room to his elderly friend. Rosenberg stood motionless, his eyes wide and uncomprehending. Before he could say another word, the roar of automatic weapon fire filled the shop.

Instinctively, Alex dropped to the floor as the other plate glass window erupted in a hail of bullets. Machine-gun fire raked across the front of the store. Rosenberg's body jerked convulsively as a dozen shells tore into his flesh. The old man dropped to the floor like a puppet cut from its strings. Alex knew his friend was dead.

The hard lessons of Alex's years in Vietnam came rushing back. No reason existed to rescue a corpse. The dead didn't care. Nor was this the time or place for mourning.

Long-buried survival instincts took control of Alex's senses. Keeping low to the floor, he scuttled between the tables of books to the back of the bookstore.

Outside, heavy caliber guns roared. Another round of machine-gun fire blasted the shop. Hundreds of books leapt off the shelves and into the air. Though other guns chattered, none of their fire was directed at the store. Alex guessed why. The hunters wanted Vril. That phone call had placed the man at the bookstore. He and Rosenberg hadn't mattered one bit to the nameless assassins. Civilian casualties often paid the price for being at the wrong place at the wrong time.

He doubted that the ambushers had achieved their objective. Poor execution of the trap had given Vril a few seconds warning. The man reacted with such speed that Alex felt sure he had escaped the first hail of gunfire. In the blinding snowstorm, it seemed unlikely that Vril would be caught. All Alex hoped was that the search for the man would draw the attackers away from the store.

Cautiously, Alex pushed open the door to the back room and crept inside. He wanted that book, but where could it be? Howie had said it was in the one location Vril would never think to look.

Suddenly the room exploded with gunfire, but Howie Rosenberg's precautions earlier that evening saved Alex's life. Two dead bolt locks and a chain held the back door shut. The upper bolt made the difference when a round of machine-gun fire shattered the lower panels of the door.

Alex scrambled desperately to the back wall as a second burst blew the wood to kindling. A short man, clad in black, forced his way into the room. Angrily, the intruder smashed the remnants of the frame out of his way, using the short barrel of his gun to push the wood away.

Deep inside, Alex flinched. A true professional never treated his weapons as tools. Guns were used to kill people, not to break down doors. In deadly combat, the smallest mistake often cost dearly.

The short man never suspected another person waited inside the room. Alex hugged the wall at right angles to the invader. Lunging, Alex grabbed hold of the Uzi and wrenched down hard.

The surprised gunman stumbled after his weapon. A knee to the groin caught him flush, loosening his grip on the gun. Sensing the slack, Alex whipped the barrel of the gun around in a short, devastating arc.

The heavy metal slashed the man in the cheek, tearing through bone and flesh. Blood spurted as the man staggered to the floor. Mercilessly, Alex slammed the Uzi down across the invader's skull, smashing it to pulp. The man slumped to the ground, dead.

The whole attack took less than 30 seconds. Adrenaline pumping through his body, Alex ripped off the attacker's black sweater. Blood stains wouldn't show in the snow and darkness. Quickly, he pulled on the man's garment. It fit poorly, but it served. There was little resemblance between him and his victim. The sweater would provide enough uncertainty. It was amateur night tonight. They always hesitated before acting. Those few seconds meant a lot to someone with combat experience like Alex.

Scooping up the Uzi, Alex glanced hastily around the room. Where the hell was that book? His gaze stopped on the refrigerator. In all of his visits to Rosenberg's shop, the old man had always placed the Sabbath candles on the counter in the front room. Tonight, they sat on the refrigerator. Never before had they required a platform, not unless that platform consisted of a thick hardcover book wrapped in brown paper. Alex rushed across the room and lifted the candles, beneath which Howie had concealed a parcel. Alex didn't have to open it to know he'd found what he was looking for. He quickly stashed the package inside his shirt.

For an instant, he paused and reviewed his next move. His enemies lacked the experience of hardened killers. Only novices made serious errors in timing. Such men worried too much about making mistakes. From his years in Vietnam, Alex had learned that in close situations his comrades always took care of themselves. It was the only way to survive.

Alex waited for a few more seconds. He wanted those outside to worry a little more about their companion. If they came looking for the dead man, Alex would be ready.

He drew in several deep breaths and oxygenated his system. Narrowing his eyes so as not to be blinded by the light, Alex sprayed the room with machine-gun fire. Still shooting, he backed swiftly out the door. To anyone outside, it would appear as if he were retreating.

As soon as he entered the alley, Alex jerked his head from side to side. He spotted two figures, one on either side of him, some 15 feet away.

The enemy at least knew where to position their backup men.

Both men raised their guns, but neither man fired. Alex knew that when they spotted the black sweater, they would mistake him for one of their own, and their attention would be switched to whatever menace lurked in the bookstore. In a few seconds, however, visual data would overwhelm instinct, and the men would realize their mistake. But those few seconds were all Alex would need.

He acted without delay. His gun growled, and an explosion of gunfire turned the face of the man on the left into a bloody ruin. The other gunman, realizing his mistake, braced his feet and sprayed the alley with machine-gun fire. Dodging the hail of bullets, Alex hugged the ground. Before the second gunman could get him in his sights, Alex fired and killed him with a well-placed burst to the chest.

Blood and guts soaked the snow as Alex rose to his feet. There was no time to search for identification. Blizzard or not, the police should be on the way. It was time for him to make a strategic withdrawal.

He considered returning to his car, parked at the far end of the alley, but old instincts warned him to stay away from the vehicle. Always avoid the obvious place for an ambush, his training told him. Turning, he jogged in the opposite direction.

His enemies—whoever they were—knew too

much about this meeting. The attack, even though it failed in its objectives, needed advance planning. The timed phone call to the shop made it quite clear the men in black knew about Dietrich Vril's original phone call. They must have arranged the ambush earlier in the day and been waiting patiently for Vril to arrive.

That implied a large and well-organized group. Only a tap on the phone lines could have gotten them the information about Vril. If that was the case, they must know about Alex's role in the affair as well. It was not a cheering thought.

He needed time to sort out a tangled web of intrigue. Five blocks from the bookstore was an el station. The trains ran erratically during storms, but they provided an alternate method of transportation uptown. He could retrieve his car tomorrow.

Decision made, Alex headed off in the direction of the elevated platform. Years of caution had him keeping close to walls. Every few steps, he turned and checked his surroundings, but in the heavy snow, it was hard to see much of anything.

In the distance, he could hear the sporadic sound of gunfire. The men in black still hunted Vril. Strangely enough, no sirens announced the imminent arrival of the police, and Alex found that vaguely disturbing.

Uneasily, he scanned what little he could see of the night sky. A primitive sixth sense, developed during years of jungle fighting, warned him that someone was watching his every movement, but there was no one in sight. The streets were empty of life. The night was too quiet. The wind howled and the snow pelted down, but otherwise nothing else stirred.

Once or twice, as he trudged on, Alex swore he heard the sound of huge wings flapping far over his head. And, during a momentary lull in the storm, he imagined a shadow darker than the darkness hovering silently in the night sky.

Chapter Two

Contrary to the opinions expressed by many critics of Chicago's transportation system, the elevated railroad functioned reasonably well during the blizzard. However, the trains moved extremely slowly due to the build-up of ice on the rails. Sharing his suffering with a half-dozen other unhappy souls, Alex sat silently as the el crawled its way uptown.

He eyed the other inhabitants of the car suspiciously. It seemed impossible that they had any connection with the attack on Rosenberg's store, but Alex had encountered stranger conspiracies during his years spent with Special Services. It never hurt to be careful. The incredible events of the past year had painfully reinforced that lesson.

Six months earlier, Alex Warner's world had been turned inside out by the murder of his closest friend, Jake Lancaster. The results of that killing were still echoing through his life.

Alex met Jake Lancaster years ago when the old man audited one of his courses on the history of witchcraft at the university. In his sixties and a widower, Jake attended classes for knowledge, not for credit. The only male in a class of strident feminists, he proved to be a fountain of esoteric knowledge on the supernatural. He and Alex had become fast friends. Often, after class ended for the evening, they adjourned for pizza and a glass of wine at Mama Mia's Italian Restaurant.

Mama Mia was in actuality Makoto Tsuiki, a close friend of Alex from his days in Vietnam. On slow nights, Mak would join them at their table, and they solved the world's problems in spirited discussions that lasted well into the night.

One such night, with only Alex present, Jake revealed that he was actually a practicing sorcerer. He did it in a dramatic and very convincing fashion by converting a pitcher of water into fine wine. Jake revealed to Alex that black magic worked only for a few gifted individuals who possessed the power. Anyone else trying to perform the rituals and spells as related in books of sorcery was doomed to failure. Throughout the ages, true witches and wizards had carefully kept their existence secret, while plying their trade among ordinary mortals.

After their discussion, Alex decided to experiment to see if he might also possess the incredible psychic gifts detailed by his friend. When all of his attempts failed, he concluded that he was no magician. It never occurred to him that Jake had revealed his secret for a reason.

Alex didn't learn the truth until much later. When Jake was killed, the sorcerer's estranged daughter, Valerie, returned from New York to hunt down his murderer. An ex-fashion model, Valerie Lancaster was the most beautiful woman Alex ever met. She was also one of the most ruthless. Positive the police would never apprehend Jake's killer, she swore to find the perpetrator herself. Alex found himself helping her, first out of loyalty, later out of love.

Psychic ability was inherited from generation to generation, and Valerie was a powerful though untrained sorceress. It turned out they needed all of her skills and more in the course of their investigation.

Jake was killed the night he received an invitation to the legendary Devil's Auction. Held once a generation, the fabled auction offered eternal life as a prize. Only those who held a letter from the mysterious host of the event, a powerful sorcerer named Ashmedai, could attend. Though Jake had been slaughtered for his invitation, he had managed to send it to Valerie before his death.

Reasoning the only way they could confront

Jake's killer was to attend the auction, Alex and Valerie found themselves entangled in a web of supernatural intrigue and sudden death. Faced with wizards and witches of enormous power, Valerie's own magic proved to be of little use. Only Alex's martial arts training and years of combat experience kept them safe. Before the close of the auction, Alex had fought a werewolf, come face to face with a golem, and discovered the dark secret of the man called Ashmedai.

Almost as astonishing to Alex was his discovery that he possessed the same power as Valerie and Jake and all those who attended the Devil's Auction. Unlike the others, he controlled the psychic force through his subconscious. Instead of enabling him to perform black magic, Alex's gift manifested itself as pure luck. By a fluke of the supernatural, he was one of the luckiest men alive.

A week after the Devil's Auction, Alex and Valerie were married. Makoto Tsuiki served as best man and caterer. It came as no great surprise to Alex when he learned that Mak was also a powerful magician and an old crony of Jake Lancaster. For several years, the two had schemed to introduce Alex to the old man's daughter; unfortunately it had taken Jake's death to make the match.

As he sat on the train, Alex wished his wife had been with him at Howie's bookstore. But Valerie had been in New York the past three weeks, closing out the final contracts of her modeling career. Until tonight, Alex had managed without much trouble. Now, another old friend was dead, and the supernatural was grabbing at him with gnarled claws.

Alex licked his lips. Before he had fought a werewolf at the Devil's Auction, he had assumed such creatures were the products of overactive imaginations. If werewolves existed, then perhaps Howie's story wasn't as far-fetched as it seemed. Alex shivered uncomfortably.

Finally, after nearly an hour, the el train reached his stop. Alex waited to the last possible instant before exiting. When no one else got off the train, he felt reasonably confident he had not been followed.

During the long ride Alex had forgotten the full fury of the storm. His every cell shrieked in protest as he stepped out of the el station and into the blizzard.

Snow and frozen ice pelted his exposed skin like tiny knives. The hair in his nose froze in seconds, and tears turned to ice on his cheeks. Alex pushed his way forward, cursing the wind, the snow and winter in general.

Twenty minutes later, he staggered up the steps to the three-story brick home that once belonged to his friend Jake Lancaster and was now his residence. Made cautious by the evening's events, Alex checked the snow outside the front door. No footprints other than his own marred the white carpet of flakes, nor did the snow show any signs of being brushed back to cover any such prints. Only then did Alex unlock the front door and slip inside.

A quick look at the old grandfather's clock in the hallway revealed that it was well over an hour since the fight at Rosenberg's store. Alex breathed a sigh of relief. He had evidently escaped unnoticed.

He hadn't left anything at the shop that tied him in with the murders. Even his fingerprints would be one set of many, customers coming and going all day.

The furnace hummed steadily as Alex removed his clothing. He gently rubbed his frozen toes, wincing as he touched them. Digging his feet deep into the old, worn carpet, he tried to absorb warmth from the floor. A small puddle formed where he stood, as bits of ice and snow melted off his hair and skin. Hands trembling, he pulled the package out from beneath his shirt.

Alex hated to admit it, but Howie Rosenberg's story about Vril and the Nosferatu had him spooked. He peered nervously into the dark recesses of the kitchen, ordinary shadows suddenly appearing much more sinister. Alex knew he was acting foolish, but he couldn't shake the feeling that possessing the book put him in deadly peril.

There was only one thing to do. He needed to examine the mysterious volume at once, but not here, unprotected from human or supernatural attack. Clutching the book tightly in one hand, Alex bounded quickly up the two flights of stairs leading to the attic.

A solitary door guarded the entrance of the

huge room that compromised the entire third floor of the house. Jake Lancaster had used magic spells to keep the steel-reinforced door from opening to anyone other than himself, but his enemies had managed to breach his defenses and kill him anyway. Alex depended on much more conventional methods of protection.

He had replaced the door with the best security systems available. Valerie knew the risks involved with the black arts and paid the bills without protest. Fortunately, her job as a model paid her more money than even Alex could spend.

Under a bank of bright lights, scanned by hidden cameras in the walls, Alex switched off the secret alarms only he and Valerie knew existed. At a small keyboard by the side of the door, he punched in the opening notes of the *Star Wars* theme. Each month they changed the song to another one of their favorites.

As the last notes died away, the steel door guarding the attic slid back. It disappeared on tracks leading directly into the right-hand wall.

As soon as Alex passed through the door, an electric eye sent a silent command to the sliding door which closed swiftly. All of the outer alarms reset, and the room was shut off from outside interference. The armored door could withstand anything up to a full-scale assault with artillery.

Jake Lancaster died because he depended entirely on his magic for protection, and Alex learned by the mistakes of others. He had survived years of combat in Asia through his ability to learn from his enemies, those same lessons applying equally well in the modern urban jungle.

Safely ensconced in the room, Alex breathed a sigh of relief. Ignoring the incredible clutter that surrounded him, he headed straight for the portable bar on the far wall. First he needed a drink to steady his nerves; then he would examine the book.

The third floor retreat originally had served as the attic. Under Jake's direction, contractors had boarded up the windows, reinforced the walls and ceiling with steel, and installed a special heating and air conditioning system. Deathly afraid of fire in a room filled with paper, Jake had cast a spell of non-combustion on the attic and all its contents.

The ceiling reached up ten feet in the center, but the roof gradually sloped down on both sides to a series of built-in bookshelves less than half that height. The first few times he had been in the room, Alex had smashed his head into the ceiling reaching for a book, but by now, he acted instinctively.

All around him were thousands of books, the combined collection of his library and Jake Lancaster's, filling every available nook and cranny. Other than the incredible selection of rarities assembled over the centuries by the arch-mage, Ashmedai, this assemblage represented the finest collection of works on black magic and demonology in the world.

A shot of brandy and Alex was ready. Gingerly, he removed the layers of brown paper that covered the book. A clear mylar wrap protected the ripped and torn dust jacket. Somewhat surprised, Alex stared at the cover illustration. A field of unusual yellow flowers glared up from a stippled black background.

Carefully, he turned the volume over, examining it closely from every angle. On the faded spine, a sinister figure, a repulsive mix of plant and human, stared back at him with unseeing eyes.

On the rear cover, the blurb touted the merits of the book's illustrator, Mahlon Blaine. The jacket did not mention anything about the contents of the novel. Nodding to himself, Alex noted that one line of the biographical sketch had been underlined in pencil. It was the only blemish on the jacket.

He rubbed his chin in an unconscious gesture of amazement. The mysterious doings of the past few hours took on a more sinister significance. No one killed for a ragged copy of *Alraune*.

The book hardly qualified as a rarity. Published in 1929 by the John Day Company of New York in an edition of 3,000 copies, the volume rarely sold for more than $40 in fine condition. A much nicer copy of the book resided in Alex's own collection. If he remembered correctly, the hardcover set him back $30 five years earlier. What made this copy worth its weight in blood?

Remembering talk of an inscription, Alex

opened the front cover of the book. Revealed on the front flyleaf was a long handwritten inscription. The dedication, written in German, covered the entire page. Fluent in most European languages, Alex read the words out loud.

> "To Karl Steiner—
> Who labors to make my wildest fancies his reality. May both our efforts work together to create a Reich that will last a thousand years. With all regards from the author.
> *Hanns Heinz Ewers*"

Ewers' signature, slashed out in thick black letters, dominated the bottom half of the page. Alex tried to remember what little he knew of the author. Not much, he decided ruefully after a few minutes. Ewers had been popular in the first quarter of the century. Since then, his works had faded into obscurity. The only thing Alex could recall reading about him was that late in life Ewers had joined the Nazi Party and that the circumstances of his death were shrouded in mystery.

Almost as an afterthought, Alex turned the volume over and read the line underscored on the back jacket. The passage described one of the major influences on Blaine's artwork.

"His master in black-and-white is Albrecht Durer."

The pencil markings beneath that line were so thick as to almost obliterate the text beneath that statement. Alex tried to puzzle out a hidden meaning to the words unsuccessfully. He suspected he possessed answers, but that without the right questions, the information meant nothing.

Outside the house, the wind howled. He rose to his feet and shivered, not only from the cold. Why did Dietrich Vril want this particular copy of the book?

His body craved sleep, but Alex found himself looking for an excuse to stay awake. He knew vampires would haunt his dreams.

Somberly, he poured himself another drink and raised the glass in an unspoken toast to his murdered friend. Life worked in strange coincidences. Vril had spared Rosenberg's life many years earlier and, through his intervention, saved the Jew from the Nazi death camp. Now, the favor came full circle as bullets meant for Vril killed the elderly storekeeper.

At least Rosenberg died swiftly and without much pain. He never knew what hit him. Alex drained the brandy in one gulp. The old man's death was terribly unfair, but death never played by the rules of good behavior.

The memories of other friends who died meaningless deaths filled Alex's thoughts. He grimaced, painfully remembering the war he had fought a lifetime ago. Years of grief buried deep within him struggled for release, but he refused to let it loose.

Without Valerie about to keep him cheerful, he grew depressed too easily. She labeled his mood swings as midlife blues. Alex despised the pop-psychology term, but otherwise agreed with her. After years of quiet, college life, his recent adventures in life-and-death situations had reopened wounds long healed.

Silently, Alex vowed vengeance against those who killed his friend. The guilty must pay for their crimes. All of the frustration from his war experiences now demanded action. "Justice," Alex whispered.

Struck with a flash of inspiration, Alex stepped over to the bookcases. He knew exactly where to look. Despite the helter-skelter appearance of the collection, a certain order prevailed. The books were arranged in roughly alphabetical order by title. Due to the odd size and shapes of many of the volumes, this method didn't always prevail, but more often than not, he found books where they belonged.

This time his luck held. His copy of *Alraune* in the John Day edition rested in proper sequence, and Alex pulled the book off the shelf, sending a small cloud of dust into the air. He couldn't remember the last time he actually had looked at it.

Placing the books side by side, he flipped through the pages of each. Except for the underlining on the dust jacket and some minor check marks on a few yellowed pages of Rosenberg's copy, the two volumes appeared identical.

Alex scowled. He had hoped a direct comparison would reveal why one volume was so much more valuable than the other. The only possible answer was the inscription.

With a heavy sigh, he dropped his edition of the novel onto the sofa. Time to reread this melodrama, he decided glumly. He remembered the story only vaguely, but he recalled it had stirred little enthusiasm within him the first time he forced himself through the pages. First, though, he decided to hide Rosenberg's copy.

Hiding the inscribed volume presented no problem. Alex wanted a place where the book remained accessible to him but hidden to anyone else. Rosenberg had relied on the same ploy with Vril. What better a place to hide a book than a library?

Ewers had authored a number of companion volumes to *Alraune,* most of them published by the John Day company with matching bindings and jackets. Thinking for an instant, Alex pulled *The Sorcerer's Apprentice* from its place on the shelf.

He paused, the title of the book striking a responsive note in his mind. Memories of Rosenberg's story caused him to shiver. Was Dietrich Vril the sorcerer's apprentice? Or possibly the sorcerer?

Carefully, Alex removed the Mahlon Blaine jacket from the hardcover and slipped it over the inscribed copy of *Alraune*. It fit perfectly. Looking at it, no one could tell that beneath the one jacket was a different book.

He placed the false volume back on the shelf.

Not taking any chances, Alex slipped the unjacketed copy of the other Ewers book behind a row of tall hardcovers that completely shielded it from view.

Satisfied with his precautions, he settled down in the black leather recliner with his own copy of *Alraune*. It was time for him to read through the book for some hint as to its value.

The Ewers book was originally published in Germany in 1911, a year after *The Sorcerer's Apprentice*. The sensational nature of the novels attracted considerable critical attention and for a brief time made Ewers famous. However, what was considered depraved and sexually shocking 75 years ago paled before the excesses of modern living. Alex yawned and fought hard to keep his eyes focused on the heavy black print.

The white house, in which Alraune ten Brinken originated, a long time before she was born, a long time before she was ever engendered . . .

Chapter Three

The shrill ring of the phone woke Alex from a deep sleep. Groggily, he pushed the book off his lap and stood up. Stretching, he raised his arms high over his head and gulped in huge lungfuls of the stale attic air. The phone continued to ring. Stepping quickly to his desk, Alex grabbed the receiver.

"Hello, Hello," he managed to repeat, sleep heavy in his voice.

"Hi, sweetie," Valerie said, laughing. "It never occurred to me you might be still asleep this late. You turning into a slug without me around to wake you up?"

"You bet," Alex said, rubbing his eyes with his arm. "See how much I depend on your cold feet for an alarm clock. I miss you lots. You coming home today?"

"You tell me. I'm calling from JFK. They put my flight on hold. Evidently, O'Hare is barely functioning. A clerk told me it could be hours before we ever take off. And the powers that be could still reroute our flight to Milwaukee once we're en route. What's the weather like there?"

Alex glanced at the digital clock on the desk, his eyes widening when he read 11:45 AM. No wonder Valerie thought him a slug.

"I'm up in the attic," he said, trying to put his thoughts in order. "I fell asleep in the sofa up here late last night. You want me to check with the airport and call you back?"

"No, don't bother." Valerie sounded disturbed. "Is something funny going on, Alex? You never slept in the attic before."

"I never spent most of the evening walking through a blizzard before, either," Alex said. "I'll tell you the whole story when you arrive back in town."

"Alex, don't act mysterious with me." The concern shifted to annoyance. "I want the facts, now."

"Not on the phone, my love. Too many ears could be listening."

"Ears? You mean somebody could be listening? This sounds an awful lot like a cheap spy novel." Valerie sounded suspicious now. "You haven't been partying with me out of town?"

"You remember my friend, Howie Rosenberg?"

"The old book dealer? Sure."

"Well, something bad happened to him last night. The worst."

Valerie said nothing for several seconds. Then, in a much more subdued voice, she asked, "No mistake about it?"

"Unfortunately not. I was there. I saw the whole thing. Enough talk for the moment. I need you back here the sooner the better. Pull a few strings with those important friends of yours in New York."

"You can count on me," Valerie said.

There now was a toughness in her voice that Alex remembered well. When he first met Valerie, she swore to find her father's murderer in those same cold tones.

"You stay out of trouble until I get back. Promise."

"I promise." Alex knew better than to argue with his wife when she was angry.

"Ha. I know you better," Valerie said. "At least try not to do anything too stupid. Or too dangerous."

"I love you lots," Alex said.

"I love you," Valerie said, her voice intense. "Let me hang up and make a few calls. Alex, take care of yourself. No funny stuff, okay? At least not until I'm there and can protect your back."

"Okay."

After hanging up the phone, Alex spent the next 15 minutes working the sleep out of his system. A hearty breakfast—then he corrected himself with a shrug—a hearty lunch would get him moving again. Before eating, he decided to make one quick call.

"Mama Mia's Italian Restaurant," someone answered on the first ring. There was no disguising the boredom in that voice. "Sorry, but we aren't delivering today. But, on the other hand, you don't need reservations for lunch, either."

"Rocky, it's Professor Warner. Is the big boss around?"

"Sure, Doc, hang on for a second. I'll go get him. He ain't doing nothing back in the kitchen."

Mama Mia's served the best Italian food on the south side of Chicago. The master chef and owner of the restaurant was Alex's best friend, Makoto Tsuiki. The two had first met in Vietnam. Both native Chicagoans, they shared a common homesickness that evolved into a deep friendship. That bond remained intact nearly 20 years after their initial chance encounter at a martial arts center in Saigon.

It wasn't until his adventures at the Devil's Auction that Alex discovered Mak was also a master sorcerer and had been plotting for some time to match Alex up with Valerie, the daughter of his teacher in the Black Arts.

Alex felt no animosity toward his friend for his attempt at matchmaking, because Valerie often seemed too good to be real. She made Alex's life complete, and he knew most men envied his luck. If anything, he owed Mak his thanks.

"Alex." Mak sounded unhappy. "Enjoying the snow?"

"Not as much as you, I gather. Business a tad slow today?"

"Slow?" Mak chuckled. "Fortunately, my father is a rich man. If he depended on the receipts of this place to pay his bills, my family would be on the first boat back to the Land of the Rising Sun."

Born and raised on Chicago's north side, the only time Mak ever visited Japan was on a brief R&R trip during his service days. Still, he liked to project an image of ethnic identity. "I'm baking a lasagna for the staff. No one else is here to eat it."

"Sorry to hear that, but I suspect the restaurant will survive until the weather clears. After all, the city does have a few snow plows.

"Listen, I didn't call to talk about lunch. How about coming over for dinner tonight? Valerie will be back in town, and it's been weeks since we saw you."

"Sounds great," Mak said, his voice picking up a bit. "Only you've got to let me bring the food. Neither of you characters can cook worth a damn. I'll make something special to celebrate Valerie's return. That way at least I know we can enjoy our food as well as the conversation."

"I won't argue with Mama Mia," Alex said. "Especially if you make canolli for dessert."

Alex hesitated for a second, then plunged on. "One last thing, Mak. Do you recall that time way back in 'Nam when we went to see that Christopher Lee movie?"

"Yeah, I remember. It was *Scars of Dracula*."

A note of apprehension crept into Mak's voice. "Why do you ask?"

"You remarked at the time that good old Chris acted much too civilized to be a vampire. I shrugged it off at the time. Lee seemed nasty enough to me in the film. I forgot all about it until last night. Now, I suspect I know what you meant."

"Last night? What happened last night?"

"I'll tell you at the dinner, Mak. You and Valerie should hear the story from the beginning and not over the phone. No reason for me to repeat it all twice. One thing I want you to tell me right now, though."

"What's that?"

"If we assume, just for an instant, that vampires actually exist, what do they look like? Are they sophisticated men in black looking like George Hamilton or Bela Lugosi? Or," and Alex's voice grew slow and serious, "are they inhuman monsters with hairless skulls and dead white skin and huge black wings—a hellish cross between man and bat?"

"The Very Old Folk," whispered Mak, as if in answer. "What the hell is going on, my friend?" he asked, his voice filled with dread. "What the hell is going on?"

"I wish I knew," Alex replied.

Chapter Four

A quick shower and a change of clothes improved Alex's outlook on the day immeasurably. As he pulled on his jeans, he considered whether or not to carry a gun. Several weapons, from a .22 automatic with silencer to a big and powerful .357 Police Special, resided in a hidden compartment in the linen closet.

He also owned a matched pair of Bowie knives and other assorted illegal weaponry. Alex believed in being prepared for any eventuality.

The events of the past 24 hours certainly justified taking precautions. Though he considered himself safe in his own home, it never hurt to be prepared. Alex settled on the .22. A small gun, without much punch, it was quite deadly in the hands of an expert marksman like Alex.

Carefully, he slipped it into a behind-the-back holster. If he went out today, he would take the .357 Magnum. The Police Special packed enough power to stop Dietrich Vril dead in his tracks. Feeling somewhat safer, Alex finished dressing and went downstairs.

Outside, blue skies and a bright winter sun beckoned. The sparkling coat of snow on the ground and the below freezing reading on the thermometer warned Alex that appearances were deceiving. The only footsteps marking the white blanket outside seemingly belonged to the mailman and the paper boy.

Pulling in the two newspapers from the steps convinced Alex that the wind chill factor was on the wrong side of the zero mark. He took the mail from the slot in the coat closet, then walked back through the front hall. The siren song of the kitchen pulled at his empty insides with unseen fingers.

Bacon and eggs, along with three slices of toast and a pot of hot coffee, satisfied his craving for food. It didn't seem too outlandish a meal for midday. At peace with the world, Alex opened the newspapers and started reading.

The lead article in both dailies told of a major fire on the South Side of the city the night before. The blizzard had hampered city efforts to extinguish the blaze which raged uncontrolled until the early morning.

Alex stared at the photo of the blaze in amazement, recognizing the scene immediately. The fire had centered on Howie Rosenberg's bookstore. The shop and all of the surrounding buildings were gutted shells. Only the perserverance of scores of firemen had kept the blaze from setting the rest of the neighborhood on fire.

An interview with the harried fire chief focused on suspected arson. The firefighter refused to state his reasons for that belief, other than a few words about the speed and ferocity of the blaze.

The next paragraph of the story hinted at dispatcher incompetence in reporting the seriousness of the fire. Too few engine companies had been sent to the scene originally. By the time someone on the scene had upgraded the number of alarms, the fire raged completely out of control.

Statements from nearby residents indicated a long gap between the initial calls to 911 and the arrival of the first firefighters. One or two of those interviewed even spoke of gunfire before the fire started. The newspaper story promised further revelations in later editions.

"Fortunately," the story concluded, "though a number of shops and small businesses were destroyed through what appears to be gross incompetence by the fire department's dispatching center, no lives were lost. So far, firefighters have not found any bodies in the wreckage of the gutted buildings. The toll could have been much worse."

Alex's hands shook with rage as he put down

the paper. He recognized the bitter truth about the fire.

After he had escaped from the store, powerful forces, working swiftly, had erased all evidence of the violent attack the one way possible. Fire left few clues for the unsuspecting. The unknown enemies had taken their dead and disappeared into the night.

Alex thought back to the lack of police response to the gunfire. It made a lot more sense when tied together to a conspiracy among dispatchers. Rerouted officers could spell the difference between life and death.

Powerful people wanted Dietrich Vril dead, and they obviously cared little about any other casualties resulting from his murder. That callous disregard for life told Alex all he wanted to know about the killers. He no longer felt the least regrets about killing the three men the night before.

While arson was mentioned prominently in both accounts of the fire, neither story offered any motives for the blaze. Both papers hinted at a possible insurance scam, which Alex dismissed as typical gossip. In Chicago, a city known for hidden absentee ownership of property, stories always circulated about insurance frauds.

Alex noted that both papers carefully avoided making any direct accusations. With Howie Rosenberg missing but presumed alive, the papers didn't want to leave themselves open to a possible libel suit.

Leafing through the *Post*, a story on page three caught his attention. A headline asked "Is a New KKK Rising in Chicago?"

Saul Royce, the leading muckracker columnist in the city, suggested in no uncertain terms that there were unspoken racial overtones in a spate of unsolved crimes taking place in Chicago during the past ten days. Though Royce's column had obviously been written well before the fire last night, it also dealt with a number of mysterious fires attributed to arson. In each case, no group claimed responsibility for the blaze, but, according to Royce, they were all set by the same group.

Some months ago, the Skinheads had made the news with their vandalism of Jewish stores on the North Side. Now, Royce suggested a new radical extremist group had emerged on the scene.

The columnist listed nine suspicious incidents, including four fires, that had taken place in the last ten days. One common thread tied all of the events together. In every case, from vandalism to a sniper attack, the police or fire department arrived long after the action occurred.

Following the same line as the page one report, Royce accused the city dispatching services of negligence or worse. The columnist ended his article with a pointed statement that not all the extremists roamed the streets and that it might be time for the police department to investigate the racists hiding on the force.

Leaning back in his chair, Alex mulled over Royce's column. Ten days ago, Howie Rosenberg's ad for *Alraune* appeared in *The Bookman*. That was also the beginning of these unexplained crimes.

Alex had met Royce years ago through mutual friends. Though the fiery commentator liked to stir up controversy, he never wrote anything without the facts to back him up.

The columnist despised bigotry in any form. His frequent campaigns against racial discrimination as practiced by the rich and powerful made him a target of both right and left-wing hate groups.

Acting on impulse, Alex went to the phone and dialed the *Post*. It took a few minutes to convince the switchboard operator to connect him with Royce's desk.

"We gotta screen all his calls," the girl told him by way of apology before transferring Alex's call. "So many nut cases dial poor Mr. Royce and want to curse him over the phone. It's a sick world out there, Professor, a sick world."

"Saul Royce's desk," a woman answered on the fifth ring. Deep, sexy and very feminine, the voice definitely did not belong to Saul Royce. "Sally Stevens speaking."

"Alex Warner here, Sally, from the university. We met a few years back. Is Saul available?"

"He's out on an interview, Mr. Warner. I'm not sure when I expect him back. Is there anything I can do for you?"

"A line like that will get you in trouble," Alex

said, laughing, "though I suspect you can take care of yourself without any help. We ran into each other at Jason Sutherland's party one time. You wore a red dress that matched your hair and that couldn't have been any tighter."

The woman laughed, a throaty sound that sent shivers up Alex's spine. "Saul likes women in tight clothes. He claims it's the result of a repressed childhood. I think he's just a dirty old man."

Her tone mellowed. "I remember you now. Tall and slender, dark eyes, very quiet. Single and unattached. Right? You teach history."

"Correct." Alex knew that Sally Stevens was not really Royce's flashy mistress though she acted the part to perfection. In reality, the redhead worked as the columnist's "right-hand man." She possessed a near photographic memory which she used to good purpose for her boss. "I'm still tall and dark, but no longer single."

"Congratulations." Sally said. She sounded as if she meant it, another necessary talent for a good investigative reporter.

A bit of excitement crept into her voice. "It all comes back to me now. Saul wanted to write a column about you."

Alex laughed. "Me?"

"That big ox, Krupowitz, one of Sutherland's so-called business associates, had too much to drink and started pawing a cute little cocktail waitress. The dumb jerk acted like a real asshole. Nobody wanted to cause a scene.

Then you casually walked over, tapped him on the shoulder and whispered something in his ear.

"Krupowitz took one look at your face and turned white as a sheet. He left the reception so fast he didn't say good-bye to his buddy, Sutherland. The party settled down after that.

"Saul loved it. He hated Krupowitz and dearly wanted to embarrass him in print. He dictated most of a column to me as we drove home. I never heard him laugh so hard. I thought he would bust a gut.

"Then, the next morning, the police caught those Puerto Rican terrorists and all of Saul's pieces for the next two weeks dealt with the PLF."

"So close to fame and so far away," Alex said, the details of the incident returning to him as Sally spoke. "All for the best, I think. I vaguely recall that a few months later Saul nailed Krupowitz anyway."

"Yeah, we discovered he bilked the city out of a couple of hundred thousand bucks putting up the new Civic Center. I think he's eligible for parole in a few years." She laughed, then said, "You didn't call to shoot the breeze with me. What can I do for you?"

"The article in the paper today. The one about this new hate group. Is Saul onto something or shooting his mouth off to make headlines. Fact or guessing?"

"Saul never guesses," Sally said, her tone anything but serious. "Well, not more than once a week at least. He's playing his cards close to the vest this time. I'm not sure exactly where he dug up his info. Why do you ask?"

"Howie Rosenberg was one of my oldest friends," Alex said. "I owed him a lot."

"Was?" Sally asked immediately. "The police merely list the old man as missing."

"I suspect otherwise," Alex said, growing cautious. "I noticed a few things the police overlooked. That's why I want to talk to Saul."

"Okay. I'll pass along the message. I'm not sure exactly when he'll check in with me. Better give me a number where he can reach you tonight."

Alex recited his phone number, then another thought occurred to him. "Last night, I heard the name of a certain group mentioned. It might not be connected with these incidents, but then again . . ."

"What name?"

"The Circumcellions," Alex said, trying to duplicate exactly the word Rosenberg mentioned right before Vril interrupted their conversation. "It mean anything to you?"

"Nope. Still, I recognize Latin when I hear it. I'll check into the name and see if I can find out anything. Royce will pass along whatever I discover."

Sally hesitated for a second, then continued, curiosity obvious in her voice.

"What did you say to that big goon at the party, Doc? Saul meant to call and ask, but he never did. Krupowitz looked ready to pass out after you whispered to him. I always wondered why."

"Sleazy types like Krupowitz can't cope with real violence," Alex said. "I learned that during my tour of duty overseas. Truly dangerous men keep their passions under tight control. I told him if he couldn't keep his fat fingers off the young lady, I'd cut his hands off and shove them down his throat. When he realized I meant exactly what I said, he panicked."

"And did you?"

"Did I what?"

"Mean what you said?"

"I'll leave that for you to decide," Alex said, coolly. "But never forget that an empty threat is no threat at all."

"Nice talking to you, Alex," Sally said slowly. "I guess."

Chapter Five

Alex brought down his copy of *Alraune* from the attic with a Benny Goodman tape he decided would work best as background music. Settling down on the sofa in the parlor, he opened the book to the beginning. He retained absolutely nothing of what he had read the night before. Prepared for a long read, he again delved into the bizarre tale of Frank Braun and Alraune ten Brinken.

Within a few minutes, he found himself caught up by the bizarre story. The novel featured a host of repugnant characters searching for the meaning of their unsavory lives. Each person struggled futilely to avoid their preordained end, as death claimed them one by one.

Hours passed as Alex carefully studied the book, trying to unearth something of importance in the sadistic melodrama. He grew to hate the unholy woman who brought dishonor and madness to all of her lovers, yet he felt no sympathy for those who died pursuing her. They all deserved to die.

He finished the novel late in the afternoon. Shadows darkened the room when he closed the volume with a thunk audible throughout the house. Numbly, he sat in the chair as if mesmerized by the story. One line, in the concluding chapter, reverberated in his mind.

That there are creatures in existence, neither man nor beast, but strange, unearthly creations born of the nefarious passions of distorted minds, you will not deny.

Ewers referred to Alraune, the product of a monstrous experiment in artificial insemination, but the passage bothered Alex for other reasons. He opened the book to the last page and read it again.

The epilogue grated on Alex's nerves. Several sections hinted at an evil left unsaid. Vague, nebulous thoughts swirled about in his mind, but nothing crystallized into hard fact.

Rising, Alex headed for the kitchen. He needed a beer to clear away the foul taste of the book. The entire novel reeked with a loving approval of sadistic practices. Vampirism burrowed through the story like some insidious worm, never openly discussed but hinted at again and again.

Blood tainted every kiss. The lovemaking between Frank Braun and Alraune was accented by their playfully nipping each other on the neck. Several times, Ewers mentioned how they drank the blood from each other's open wounds. In one section, the author declared, "Sin aroused bathes in pools of blood."

The doorbell rang shortly after Alex finished his second bottle of Coors. He hurried to the front hall, the Ewers book momentarily forgotten. He hoped it was Valerie, back at last. She had left all her keys at home, and the door was locked.

Still wary after last night, Alex peered out the spy hole in the door before opening it. His spirits dropped faster than the temperature when he saw a short, chubby priest, his cheeks red from the cold, standing on the stoop. Bald, with watery brown eyes, the man wore a look of perpetual suffering on his face.

A fierce wind whipped through the priest's thin coat and started him shivering violently. A twinge of pity ran through Alex, and the disappointment within him dissolved. The fat little man appeared lost and disoriented. Alex opened the door.

"What can I do for you, Father?"

"I am searching for Alex Warner, my son," the priest replied in a soft, hesitant voice. "Do you know where he resides?"

"You found me, Father."

"Praise the Lord, my son," the cleric said. "I have a message for you."

Reaching inside his thin coat, the priest pulled out a .45 automatic. He held the powerful gun with both hands, the muzzle aimed directly at Alex's chest. His voice lost all traces of piety.

"Never trust a helpless priest, my son. Now, if you will step back into your hall, I would like to come in out of the cold. No false moves, please, Mr. Warner. I am well aware of your reputation and your skills. Resign yourself to the fact that you are my prisoner."

Alex did as he was told. He knew better than to argue with a gun. The little priest held the pistol with the calm assurance of a man familiar with his weapon and how to use it.

"Put your hands on your head," the priest said, stepping back a few paces. "Spread your feet wide apart. Forget any tricks. I know them all. My organization wants you alive, if possible, Mr. Warner. However, if you insist on a different outcome, the death will rest on your head."

Knuckles rapped sharply on the door to the outside. Reinforcements for the little priest had arrived. "Enter in the living name of Christ, our savior," he called out.

Two more priests entered. They were big men with thick black beards, dressed in heavy fur coats. Once inside, both clerics pulled sawed-off shotguns from beneath their coats, and one said, "Good work, Brother Malachi," to the short priest. Three grim faces stared at Alex as they all leveled their weapons directly at his stomach.

"Please do not move while I search you," Malachi said.

The pink-cheeked priest did his job quickly and efficiently. He found the .22 automatic and tossed it to the side of the room.

"Keep close watch on him," he commanded. Sticking his pistol into his belt, he stepped into the other room. After a minute, he returned. Malachi nodded pleasantly to Alex.

"I admire your taste in furniture. A wise shopper buys nice sturdy chairs, built to withstand years of punishment."

He beckoned Alex forward. "Please sit down in the chair in the center of the room. Do not try anything foolish, Mr. Warner. My comrades are not inept fools like the men you dealt with last night. These two have served me for years and are trained fighters. If you make any attempt to resist, they will kill you. We fight for a great cause. All of us serve the Lord and would gladly lay down our lives in his name."

Mentally, Alex groaned. Fanatics meant that any sort of deal was out of the question. His undercover training covered hostage negotiations, but no amount of expertise worked with men anxious to prove their worth by dying for their cause.

He resigned himself to cooperate with the priests until the right moment arrived. He had escaped worse traps in the past; in fact, he specialized in surviving the impossible.

Alex counted on his luck to save him as it had done so many times in the past few months. Unfortunately, even his psychic gift had its limits. In situations not dictated by chance, his power remained dormant. At the moment, the priests controlled the scene.

Alex sat where he was told. Jake Lancaster had loved old furniture and filled the house with it. When Valerie took possession, she saw no reason to sell anything. Alex cursed that decision. The heavy wooden chair with high back, plush pillows, padded arms and sturdy mahogany frame served as a perfect straightjacket.

The chubby priest pulled a roll of nylon-reinforced packing tape from his pockets. "Grab hold of the arms of the chair, Mr. Warner," he commanded. "I strongly doubt if you can wrench the wood apart without any leverage. Standing up should prove equally impossible. Please abandon any hopes of breaking free. I know my business."

Malachi taped Alex's wrists and elbows to the arms of the chair. He used a dozen long strips of the flexible tape, wrapping each in several circles to insure a tight bond. Then he bound Alex's ankles to the legs of the chair.

When he finished, the two priests armed with shotguns lowered their weapons and relaxed. The chubby priest retired to the nearby sofa, his features serene.

Alex reviewed his position and concluded he had underestimated his enemy. The packing tape held his limbs tighter than any rope. Alex doubted that he could rip the nylon webbing. The chair's weight anchored him in place.

Meanwhile, the two priests stationed themselves at 45 degree angles from him, making sure no possibility of a crossfire existed. These men were nothing like the ones he had fought the night before. They were professionals—and that worried Alex.

The phone rang, shattering the silence of the moment. No one moved. It rang again. One of the shotgun bearers glanced over at the chubby priest. "Let it ring," Malachi said. "The caller will assume Mr. Warner stepped out for the afternoon. Answering it would be a mistake."

The phone rang six more times before the unknown caller gave up. Silence descended but not for long. The phone rang again. "The same person," the priest said smugly, "hoping they dialed wrong the first time."

Again, the caller stopped trying after a dozen rings. For a few minutes, the only noise in the room was the muffled sounds of their breathing.

With a jolt that shook the house, the front door crashed open. All three priests jumped up but relaxed when they spotted their visitor.

Alex tried swinging his head around, but the high back of the chair restricted his movement. It didn't matter. The newcomer came thumping into the parlor with all the grace of a wild elephant.

A huge giant of a man, he lumbered over to the little priest and hugged him emotionally. "A job well done," he said in a voice matching his size. "As usual, you justified my faith in your abilities. I only wish, Brother Malachi, I used your men last night instead of those incompetent fools."

Releasing the short priest, the giant swung around and peered at Alex. "He appears harmless enough. You are sure this fellow is the one who killed those three novices at the bookstore?"

"God aided me in my mission, Brother Ambrose," Malachi said. "A dangerous man strives to look ordinary. Before calling on Mr. Warner, I checked on his background. Locating his army records proved difficult for even our contacts in the police department.

"This seemingly harmless individual fought for several years in the jungles of Vietnam. He usually operated behind enemy lines and specialized in counter-terrorism and assassination. Because of the nature of Mr. Warner's work, no records detail his success. One estimate credited him with nearly fifty kills."

As the two priests discussed his war record, Alex carefully studied Brother Ambrose. The giant dwarfed the other men present. Using the door frames as a reference, Alex judged the man to be nearly seven feet tall. Solidly built, he had to weigh over 300 pounds. Huge muscles swelled in his chest and arms.

Ambrose moved slowly and ponderously, like some prehistoric dinosaur. Alex suspected the priest wanted others to think him slow and clumsy.

A full black beard covered Ambrose's face and was matched by equally thick hair and eyebrows. A big hook nose sat squarely between dark eyes that burned with fanatical zeal. In size and spirit, here stood a man who matched Dietrich Vril.

"Pull me over a chair," Ambrose said to one of the armed men. He spoke with the assurance of a man long accustomed to instant obedience. The guard quickly rested his shotgun on the floor and rushed to obey the order. Alex noted the frown that crossed Brother Malachi's face.

"I stationed the disciple there and told him to watch the prisoner," Malachi said petulantly. "I cannot guarantee your safety if you subvert my efforts."

"You perform your duties too well," Ambrose said, his voice booming slightly louder than before. He did not sound pleased with the criticism, and Alex sensed an unspoken conflict between the two priests.

"You worry too much about this sinner. I appreciate your concern, Malachi, but your mission is over. Now, let me get on with mine. Put those guns away and move out of my way. Let your men search the house. They know what to look for. Don't forget," Ambrose said, his tone growing harsh, "who leads and who follows."

Swallowing hard, Brother Malachi retreated to the sofa. He said nothing, but his face twisted in anger and defiance. With a wave of his hand, he dispatched the two other priests on their mission. Without a sound, the men disappeared upstairs.

"Finally, Mr. Warner," Ambrose said, turning his full attention to Alex, "we can speak man to man. I think you know what I want. Why not save my men all of this time and effort? Where is the book?"

"Book?" Alex said. "What book? Who are you guys? What gives you the right to break into my house?"

Ambrose laughed, a roaring that threatened to shatter the living room windows. "Come, come. No protestations of innocence to me, Mr. Warner. We traced all of Rosenberg's phone calls for days before our strike. We knew sooner or later Vril would come calling. Last night, the Jew contacted you for help. You were there during our attack. We even found your car not far from the shop."

The big man shook a huge finger at Alex in annoyance. "You murdered three of my most recent converts. And you used their own weapons to do it."

"I prefer the term self-defense over murder," Alex said. "I react violently when people try to kill me."

"A regrettable happening, but a necessary one," Brother Ambrose said, not a trace of remorse in his voice. "The old Jew had the book somewhere in his shop. It served our bait for Vril, but we dared not let him obtain it. Thus, we resorted to violence. We had no choice.

"Besides which," Ambrose said with a smile, "you still live and your attackers lie buried. I see no reason for you to complain."

"What about Howie Rosenberg?"

"A Hebrew?" The barest trace of fanaticism crept into Brother Ambrose's voice. "He lived and died without any possibility of salvation. I cannot worry about such rabble. As the world trembles on the brink of Armageddon, the death of one Jew means little."

Alex wondered what vampires, Dietrich Vril, fanatic priests and an eerie horror novel by a forgotten German author had to do with Armageddon. It made no sense.

"You shake your head in disbelief," Brother Ambrose said grimly. "Like most ordinary men, you doubt the word of our Lord. The apocalypse fast approaches, my naive friend. How can you doubt it after your encounter with the living Antichrist?"

"You mean Dietrich Vril?"

"Vril?" Brother Ambrose said with a snort of disgust. "He mocks us with that name. A man of absolute evil naming himself as a superman. Whatever title he chooses, nothing can mask the horror he represents. You saw the way he sweats. The fires of hell burn in his body. We know him as the Dark Child."

Alex laughed. He knew that it would upset the big priest. Mocking their most cherished beliefs always upset fanatics, and angry, annoyed men often made mistakes.

"Come now," Alex said, sarcastically, "perhaps a few hundred years ago, ignorant peasants believed such superstitious crap, but not any more. You can't scare people these days with hints of black magic and devil worship. This is the twentieth century. Where's your proof? People today want cold, hard facts—not the rumblings of some overweight Bible-thumper."

Brother Ambrose turned so red he looked ready to explode. His eyes burned in holy wrath. Angrily, he lifted both hands up in the air, curling his fingers into huge fists. His chest swelled like some gigantic bellows as he sucked in air through his nose.

"You fool," he shouted. "If Jesus Christ returned to Earth today, would you ask for proof as well? You make a mockery of faith."

"Nonsense," Alex said, staying calm. The more time he wasted, the better his chances of rescue. "If evil exists, and I won't debate you on that point, what stops it from masquerading as good? If Christ reappeared, I'd be first in line to question his legitimacy. What better form for the devil to assume than that of the savior returned?"

Brother Ambrose calmed down as quickly as he angered, leading Alex to suspect the righteous anger was merely a convenient facade.

"You make a good point, Mr. Warner. But in the case of Dietrich Vril, your logic fails. The man is the living embodiment of evil. He plots to establish Satan's kingdom on Earth."

"Proof, Brother Ambrose, proof?" Alex inquired. "Vril impressed me as a ruthless, determined man. These days the world is filled with such people. What makes Vril special?"

"He controls the forces of black magic," Brother Malachi interrupted, suddenly rising to his feet. His shrill voice rang with righteous indignation. "You met Vril. He has been a man of mystery for decades. Incredibly rich, incredibly powerful and totally evil. Everywhere he goes, death and destruction follow."

"Enough of this idle talk," Brother Ambrose said, spitting out each word like a curse. "Malachi, you talk too much. Sit down and keep silent."

The big priest scowled. "Mr. Warner, you argue possibilities when the truth stares you in the face. Forget Vril for a moment. Instead, look at the world around us.

"Moral decay infects our culture like a plague. Our youth thrive on narcotics while politicians debate legalizing drugs to save money. Permissive sex and licentious lifestyles have led to AIDS and uncontrollable venereal disease. Rebellion against authority flourishes.

"Businessmen steal millions and go unpunished. Best-selling books explain how to win by manipulating others. Your government wastes more money in a minute than many people earn in their entire lifetime. And America is considered the land of plenty."

"Doomsayers registered the same arguments a hundred years ago," Alex said. He fielded the same arguments every week in his History of Civilization class. "The world always teeters on the brink of destruction. Throughout history, frightened men proclaimed the end was near.

"A hundred times, a new Messiah heralded a new age. Each time, he proved to be a false prophet. Christians pointed to the Moslems, the Vikings and the Mongols all as proof positive the apocalypse approached. Every time, the invaders retreated and life continued."

Brother Malachi's two assistants reappeared as silently as they had left and whispered a few words to the chubby priest. Then, they resumed their posts, shotguns pointed straight at Alex.

"There is a locked door leading to the third floor," Malachi declared. "No doubt that is where the book resides."

"I suspect Mr. Warner hoped we might forget the reason for our visit if we argued long enough," Brother Ambrose said, chuckling. "Or perhaps he imagines some friend might come to his aid."

The big priest laughed louder now. "Two of my disciples, armed with rifles, watch your house from across the street, my foolish friend. Another man waits outside your door. We came prepared for action today. There will be no outsiders allowed entrance.

"Meanwhile, our friends in the police department monitor all calls to the station house. They will make sure any complaints from your neighbors go unreported. You are completely isolated. Forget any thoughts of rescue."

Brother Ambrose walked back to the couch, turning away from Alex. "Let us cease these futile discussions. Believe whatever you desire about Dietrich Vril. I want the book you took from Rosenberg's store last night."

"I didn't take any book," Alex said. "I know Vril came to buy one, but I have no idea which one. Your maniacal followers started shooting before Rosenberg produced the volume. He hid it somewhere in the shop. When you set the place on fire, you burned the book with it."

"How convincing," Brother Malachi said, back on his feet. His thin lips widened in a humorless grin. "You never learned what book Vril desired. Then, perhaps you can tell us," and the priest held out Alex's copy of *Alraune*, "why you picked this particular novel to read today. Why, Mr. Warner? Why?"

Chapter Six

Alex reacted the only way possible. He changed his story.

"I lied," he said, letting the right amount of annoyance color his tone. "Can you blame me for trying to make a quick buck?"

Neither priest said a word. Alex took a deep breath and continued. "Rosenberg suspected Vril would try a double cross. The old man asked me to guard the book until the money changed hands. After Rosenberg died, I figured the volume belonged to me as much as anyone else.

"I don't make a lot of money," Alex said, his voice bitter. "I thought I could make a little extra on the side. After all, I risked my life for the damned thing."

"So, confronted with the truth, you decided to atone for your sin and confess all," Brother Ambrose said, his eyebrows raised in mock astonishment. "How reasonable of you. I thought such bouts of remorse only occurred among grievous sinners on their death beds."

"You can keep the damned book," Alex shouted, trying desperately to make his lies sound convincing. "Just leave me alone. I gambled and lost. The game is over. You found what you came for."

Brother Ambrose casually thumbed through the pages of *Alraune*. He glanced down at the volume from time to time, ruefully shaking his head.

"Our order needs men like you, Mr. Warner. Religious fervor grips our recruits, but they sadly lack the basic training in espionage and treachery. They play at being soldiers. Only a few like Malachi and his disciples know anything about waging war. Too bad we work at cross purposes. No matter. Some things are not meant to be. God's will be done."

Ambrose gently closed the book and held it between his two huge hands. "You Americans make such poor liars. No wonder your CIA fails so miserably in its overseas operations.

"I'm afraid your explanation doesn't impress me, my friend. After all, we both know Dietrich Vril searched for a specific copy of *Alraune*—one inscribed by the author. Only that particular copy holds the secret of Leo's puzzle box. This volume," Brother Ambrose said, letting the book drop to the floor, "bears no such inscription."

Sighing heavily, the big priest turned to Brother Malachi. "Do what you must."

The shorter man grunted and motioned to one of his assistants. The guard rested his shotgun on the floor and then cautiously approached Alex. He was careful to stay out of his companion's line of fire. Not all of the disciples were anxious to prove themselves martyrs to their cause.

Though his captors treated him like a caged tiger, Alex was completely helpless. The tape bound him more securely than rope, and he could barely move. Unless he received outside assistance, he was a dead man.

The priest grabbed hold of the front of Alex's shirt and wrenched hard. Material ripped to shreds, exposing Alex's bare chest. Even in the cool room, he felt uncomfortably warm. Sweat trickled down the small of his back and collected under his arms.

He could guess what followed next. Horrifying memories of time spent in a North Vietnam prison camp flashed through his mind, and he dreaded the torture he expected to follow.

"You bring this sad situation upon yourself, Mr. Warner," Brother Ambrose said, a slight smile on his lips. "Oftentimes, the path of salvation forces us to resort to desperate measures. I detest violence. However, I also understand that the fulfillment of God's mission requires us to act harshly when necessary."

"For a humble priest, you seem to be on awfully good terms with the Lord," Alex said. He hoped to again anger his captors into revealing some useful bit of information. "I find it amazing how you anticipate his every wish."

Brother Ambrose refused to be baited. "I only serve as those before me served in their time. The Brotherhood of Circumcellions stretches back much further into the past that you can imagine. We trace our roots back to the earliest days of Christianity. I follow a path prescribed for me by my fellowship, my savior and my God."

Ambrose waved a hand in the direction of Brother Malachi. "Though I abhor physical methods to attain our objectives, Brother Malachi believes that the ends justify the means, no matter what those means might entail. He specializes in making people talk. You understand what I mean? Will you not reconsider and tell me where you hid the book? On the third floor, perhaps?"

Alex tried one last time. "What more do you want? Vril was looking for a copy of *Alraune*. Rosenberg found one for him. I don't know a thing about any inscription. Vril never saw the book. I told you that. Your gunfire interrupted the sale. Maybe Rosenberg left the real book somewhere else and used this one as a decoy. Why should I lie?"

Ambrose nodded solemnly to Brother Malachi. "Finish your preparations. I suspect Mr. Warner will prove to be a true challenge to your skill."

The big priest looked down at Alex. "You raise a good point, my foolish friend. Why *do* you lie? Perhaps you mistakenly think you owe the old Jew some loyalty. A commendable notion, but not a very wise one. The dead need nothing from the living.

"You are betrayed by the sarcasm in your voice. Misguided pride compels you to resist my offer. You refuse to recognize that a higher power guides my actions. I conduct the Lord's business, and thus I cannot fail."

"God wants you to torture me?" Alex asked incredulously. "Did you check with the Pope about that?"

"The Lord works in mysterious and terrible ways. God forgives the sins of those who fight his battles on the Earth. Violence is the only answer against the hosts of the Antichrist."

Again, Brother Ambrose's face grew red as he spoke. This time his anger sounded real, not merely for show. The priest's voice shook with emotion as he continued.

"As to the Pope, that impostor in Rome, his words mean nothing to me. Fifteen hundred years ago our order broke with him and his misguided rule. Only the Circumcellions follow the true words of our Lord, Jesus Christ. We alone know the path of everlasting salvation."

Alarm flared in Brother Malachi's eyes. He glared at Alex, then quickly stepped over to his companion. Resting a hand on Ambrose's arm, the smaller priest said in a gentle but persuasive voice, "You waste your time arguing with him, Ambrose. He struggles to gain an advantage through your anger. We must hurry before anyone discovers our presence. Our allies on the switchboards can only reroute calls for so long. Let me do my work. In a few minutes, we will learn all we wish."

Almost regretfully, Brother Ambrose nodded his head. Shrugging his huge shoulders, the giant priest walked to the front of the room and peered out the windows.

"Put him to the question. I tried my best to spare him from the torment." He turned his back on the proceedings, as if banishing them from his mind. "Whatever happens, it rests entirely on his soul."

Chapter Seven

A satisfied smile settled on Brother Malachi's face, giving the chubby priest an almost angelic look. Reaching deep inside his robe, he pulled out a thin oblong case, a few inches wide and six inches long. Stepping forward, he held the container close to Alex's face.

"I find it amazing the amount of pain one can inflict using the smallest things," Malachi said, with a sly chuckle. "For example, consider these . . . tools."

With a twist of the wrist, the priest flipped open the top of the black box. Alex caught a glimpse of a half-dozen slender silver metal rods nestled in a plush red lining. A sharp curved metal needle topped each instrument. He recognized the tools as ordinary dental probes. A shudder of fear rippled through Alex's back as he ground his teeth tightly together.

Brother Malachi pulled out a probe and closed the box. Smiling happily, the priest rubbed his thumb up and down the side of the lancet.

Alex tensed, realizing the truth about his tormentor. Sadists enjoyed making their victims wait, the long minutes before anything happened intensifying the torture when it occurred. Malachi knew exactly what he was doing. For all of his casual smiles and soft words, Brother Malachi was a madman.

Carefully, the chubby priest raised the lancet up in front of Alex's nose and slowly rotated the instrument in a small circle, the sharp point flickering in the light. The slender piece of steel seemed to possess a life of its own, as it swayed to and fro hypnotically.

"The intensity of feeling can often be measured in direct proportion to the expectation," Malachi said, his voice betraying the slightest hint of excitement. "This factor plays an important role in sexual relations, I have been told. Only a select few realize that the same link exists between anticipation and pain.

"Do you grasp what I am saying, Mr. Warner? The Chinese understood the underlying principles of my methods. You surely heard of the Death of a Thousand Cuts, a slow but steady method of execution that took weeks to administer. None of the wounds inflicted any serious damage, but the prisoner suffered incredible pain with each slice of the knife. Like this!"

Without warning, Malachi flicked the lancet forward. He caught Alex completely unawares. The metal point flashed directly at his left eye.

Instinctively, Alex jerked his head back. Cold steel ripped into his skin, tearing a painful gash in his cheek. A trickle of blood dripped down across his face. His eyelids flickered furiously in shock.

Malachi giggled as he flipped open the box and put the lancet back into the case. "As I expected, you react well for a man of your age. Unfortunately, Mr. Warner, your range of motion is extremely limited."

The priest laughed again, a frightening sound. "Normally, I concentrate first on my subject's chest. That is the reason for your open shirt. I find it quite amazing how sensitive a man's nipples are. However, your argument with Brother Ambrose threw off our schedule. Despite our safeguards, someone sooner or later will stumble upon us. So, excuse me if I hurry along with the interrogation."

Malachi reached into the box and pulled out a second instrument. It closely resembled the first except it had a tip a half-inch longer. "Shall we try our little experiment with reflexes for a second time?"

Alex's world narrowed to the sharp metal instrument Malachi held level with his face. From a great distance away, he heard the priest speaking.

"People say that the hand is quicker than the eye, Mr. Warner. We shall put that remark to the acid test."

Malachi sighed. "In the end, I always win. Oftentimes, my subjects scream for hours before they regain control. But once they can speak rationally, they tell me everything I want to know. Everything. The threat of losing *both* of their eyes to my toys provides all the incentive they need."

Alex concentrated on Malachi's arm and fingers. As the priest finished the sentence, the large vein in his scrawny wrist flared. The metal lancet flashed. Alex jerked his head back against the chair. The sharp tip of the instrument cut into his other cheek, again drawing blood—but it missed his eye.

"Normally, we could duel in such fashion until you grew tired," Malachi said, apologetically. "But time matters today."

He half-turned to one of his assistants. "Hold his head still, Bruno," he ordered.

The heavily built man circled around the chair. Reaching down with vice-like hands, he grabbed Alex by the ears. The priest's powerful grip effectively stopped him from moving an inch.

"Now," Malachi said, "comes the moment of truth."

Out of the black case emerged another lancet. It had a wide base that narrowed down to a needle-sharp point several inches long. "I save this one for special cases," Malachi said, his voice sunk to a whisper. "Squeezing your eyes shut will not save you, Mr. Warner. My favorite can rip through an eyelid without any trouble."

Smiling, the priest aimed the lancet directly at Alex's left eye. Bruno's hold tightened, making even the slightest motion impossible. Carefully, Brother Malachi gauged the distance to Alex's face. The vein in the priest's wrist throbbed.

"What the hell is going on?"

For an instant, everyone froze. The cavalry arrives just in the nick of time, thought Alex, immediately recognizing the voice. Hell hath no fury to match the anger of an enraged wife—especially *his* enraged wife.

Valerie stood in the entrance of the parlor, her hands on her hips, her blue eyes blazing. Blonde hair swirled around her face like a halo. Clad in a white mink jacket, jet black silk pants and long leather boots, she faced the four priests and for an instant held the men transfixed by the sheer force of her anger. Brother Malachi recovered first.

"Kill her," he said coldly, jabbing his lancet in Valerie's direction. "Kill her, you fools."

Bruno's shotgun rested against the sofa, but the other guard still held his gun. Malachi's command jerked him into action. Valerie stood so close he didn't bother to aim. Thunder crashed as the gun belched its deadly message.

Involuntarily, Alex's muscles tensed. His faith in Valerie's powers meant little at times like this.

Fear ate at his insides. Smoke and the smell of powder filled the air, as did the shrill cries of Brother Malachi.

"The bullets never touched her! They never came close. Damned woman is a witch. A witch!" he howled. "God save us all!"

Valerie stood unharmed, untouched by the gun blasts. A simple spell made her invulnerable to bullets. Every powerful sorcerer knew and used such magic. Alex suspected Dietrich Vril had escaped the night before using the same secret. However, the spell made no allowances for actual physical combat.

Brother Ambrose was made of sterner stuff than his assistant. Ignoring the shrill screams of Brother Malachi, the huge priest lumbered forward. Waving his arms, he bellowed loudly at his companions.

"Attack," he urged, his voice full of authority. "Forget your guns. Kill her with your bare hands. She is another one like Vril. Her magic only works on bullets. Get her before the whole neighborhood comes investigating."

Furiously, Alex wrenched at the tape holding him prisoner. Four madmen menaced his wife and he remained a helpless spectator. The strapping tape dug deep into his flesh as he struggled without hope.

Malachi, screaming curses, reached Valerie first. He lunged madly, wildly swinging his lancet like a tiny sword.

Stepping back and to the side, Valerie raised

her left hand, snapped her fingers, and said, "Sunfire."

The small priest's cry of rage suddenly dissolved into a howl of fear. A tiny white ball of flame, no more than an inch across, hovered a few inches over Valerie's hand. The miniature sun glowed with a fire so intense that it hurt Alex's eyes to stare directly at it. The other priests skidded to a stop, struck dumb by the burning sphere.

A thread of fire darted out from the globe and touched Malachi's lancet. With a hiss of steam that filled the room, the metal tool dissolved into a puddle of molten steel. The priest shrieked in pain and sank to his knees, clasping his burnt hand to his chest. "Mercy," he whimpered. "Mercy."

When Valerie hesitated for a second, it was all the time Malachi needed. Like a ferret, the little priest scrambled on hands and knees for the front door.

Angrily, Valerie jerked her hand down, her pointed finger aimed like a gun at the escaping priest. The ball of fire leapt forward a second too late. Malachi rounded the open door an instant before the sphere could reach him.

Glass crashed from the front of the parlor. Alex swiveled his head in time to see Bruno exit the room via a smashed window. Ambrose and the other Circumcellions were already gone. They recognized a power greater than brute strength.

"Looks like the party's over," Valerie said. She snapped her fingers and the miniature sun vanished as suddenly as it had appeared. "Who were those guys?"

"It's a long story," Alex said, wiggling in his chair. "You want to do me a favor?"

"I can guess," Valerie said and laughed deeply. She tugged at a strand of tape. "You do get tied up in your work. Damned stuff won't come loose. What a sticky situation."

"No time for jokes," Alex said, somewhat testily. "You better pull this stuff off me before the cops arrive. I hate to ponder what connections they might draw between shotgun blasts and a man Scotch-taped to a parlor chair."

"It would make all the gossip columns in town," Valerie said, grinning. "I bet all your friends at the university would love reading about your exploits."

Smiling, she bent down and kissed Alex on the forehead. Her lips felt cool against his sweaty skin. "Maybe nail polish remover will work. My mom used it when I got Scotch tape in my hair when I was a kid."

"This is grotesque," Alex said, trying to keep his temper. More than ever, he felt like an idiot letting himself be caught by Malachi and his companions.

"I'll say," Makoto Tsuiki said, closing the front door and walking into the parlor. Short and slender, Mak moved with the silent grace of a panther. His black eyes glinted with perpetual good humor. Little in the world troubled Mak.

He lived in peace with himself and his surroundings.

"Forget about the police," he continued. "I draped a curtain of silence over the house before Valerie entered. No one heard anything out of the ordinary. Nor did anyone seem to notice the unusual departures of your guests. What made them leave in such a hurry, anyway?"

"I experimented with Sunfire," Valerie said, proudly pointing to the droplets of steel on the carpet. "It made quite an impression."

"As it should," Mak said, kneeling down to examine the burn mark in the door. "That is the whole purpose of the spell."

"It caught our visitors completely by surprise." There was a trace of venom in Valerie's tone. "They planned an unspeakable fate for me and much the same for Alex. I gave them reason to change their minds."

Standing up, Mak nodded. His gaze shifted to Alex. "Your wife continues to amaze me. She is incredibly talented. I only taught her the secret of Sunfire a few weeks ago. You can't imagine the mental concentration to bring forth and direct a spark of pure energy. In truth, the magician controls a small part of the sun itself. Only a few magicians dare attempt the spell. Valerie handles it with ease. She truly possesses a wonderful gift."

Alex snorted in annoyance. "Terrific. Now, if you can contain your enthusiasm for a short while, would it be too much to ask you to remove this tape from me? I feel like the glue is starting to dissolve into my pores."

"Tape?" Mak said, shaking his head in astonishment. "What a novel way to bind captives. How very inventive. The way people use modern technology constantly astonishes me."

"Enough chatter, Mak," Alex said, wearily. "I'm losing all feeling in my fingers."

"Okay, okay. The thought of policemen carrying rolls of Scotch tape instead of handcuffs overwhelmed me for a minute."

Mak muttered a few words under his breath and waved a hand over Alex. "That should do it."

The tape began to darken, and in seconds it changed from a murky translucency to a light brown. A few seconds more and it started peeling back from Alex's skin. The glue flaked away, leaving the skin beneath it free and unharmed. The tape continued to darken, pieces crumbling into dust. After a minute, only a fine dark powder indicated where it once held Alex prisoner.

"Amazing what a few hundred years of aging does to stuff like that," Mak said, helping Alex to his feet.

"Very neat," Alex said. "When did you learn that particular trick?"

"The first time I got bubble gum in my hair," Mak said, his eyes twinkling. "My father used it on me."

Alex stretched, happy to be free—and alive. He wasn't the least bit misled by the bantering tones of Mak or Valerie. They were both very tough, dangerous people and extremely ruthless. Beneath all the humor was a dark undercurrent of anger. The Circumcellions had been lucky to escape alive.

"Your friends made a mess of my parlor," Valerie said, stepping over to the phone. "I'll call a glazier to come over tomorrow morning and repair the window. Meanwhile the two of you can find a wood plank in the basement to cover the hole for now."

"After that, we eat," Mak said. "Remember? I brought dinner with me tonight."

"Good," Valerie said. "I'm starving. But fix the window first. I'm freezing."

"I never argue with my wife," Alex said, moving around briskly to restore circulation in his arms and legs. "Food sounds great to me."

"Dinner comes first," Mak said. "Then afterwards," and his expression grew serious, "we get the whole story, Alex. All of it. Including the Very Old Folk."

"The whole story," Valerie repeated, sounding equally grim. "Told from the beginning with no omissions. When some maniac threatens my husband with a scalpel in my parlor, I want to know why."

"I'll start from the minute Howie Rosenberg called," Alex said, "right up to the moment you walked in and saved my neck. But don't look at me for any explanations, because I don't have any."

Chapter Eight

"Your phone call put me on edge," Valerie said between bites of lasagna. "So when my flight arrived at O'Hare, I decided to phone home to check up on things. When you didn't answer after two calls, I panicked."

"And so she called me at the restaurant," Mak continued with a overdrawn dramatic sigh. "During the busiest time of the day, of course. But friendship means sacrifice, I guess.

"Whatever the reason, Valerie took a cab from the airport, and I left the restaurant in the hands of an untrustworthy assistant. We met at Kaplan's Deli down the block.

"A little bit of scouting revealed several suspicious characters watching your house. Once we determined their exact location, we attacked. I handled the outside forces, leaving your captors for Val. She insisted, and I knew better than to argue with a woman with blood in her eye."

"Dangerous little character, isn't she," Alex said affectionately. "What happened to the men outside?"

Mak leaned back in his chair and tried to look very solemn. In a drawn-out mumble that only he thought sounded like Marlon Brando, he said, "We Italian restaurant owners have a saying about sleeping with the fishes."

"I get the message," Alex said, shaking his head in amusement. "Though you sound more like Charlie Chan than the Godfather. And Brando wasn't the one who said that line in the movie, anyway."

"Details, details," Mak said. His voice turned cold and deadly serious. "They wanted to play rough, so I played rougher."

Alex dropped the subject since Mak disliked speaking about violence. He said it disturbed his karma, his state of being. The actual physical acts never bothered him. Mak never let philosophy stand in the way of necessity. He merely hated being reminded about it.

"It's time for a council of war," Valerie said, gathering up the dishes. "Let's clean off the table and then get down to business. I want an explanation of this whole mess."

"Remember my warning," Alex said. "I only possess the facts, not the answers. Wait till you hear everything and you'll understand the problem."

Alex spent the next 45 minutes relating his adventures of the past two days. Valerie and Mak sat silently during the entire recital, interrupting a few times with questions to clarify a particular incident. When Alex finished, it was Valerie who spoke first.

"What makes this book so valuable?" she asked, sounding puzzled. "I thought you said it's pretty common."

"It is," Alex said. "Though I never ran across an inscribed copy before. I suspect it's only importance is as a clue to the location of an incredible treasure. According to Brother Ambrose, this particular volume pinpoints the location of Pope Leo's puzzle box."

"What's that?" Valerie asked patiently. She knew how Alex liked to draw out his explanations dramatically.

"Leo was one of the greatest Popes," Alex said. "He ruled the Church from 440 to 461 A.D. History credits him with firmly establishing the universal scope of the Bishop of Rome. According to his orations, while every other bishop took charge of his specific flock, Peter cared for the church as a whole. And what stood true for Peter remained true for those who succeeded him. In other words, he centralized the rule of the Church, with all of its powers vested in the person of the Pope."

"I know you teach history, my dear," Valerie

said, drumming her fingers on the dining-room table, "but I don't need a lesson. Skip all the unimportant details. You haven't said a word about any box."

"Patience is a virtue," Alex said. "You sound like one of my students. They all want to skip the boring stuff. You can't treat history like a video tape and fast-forward the dull parts. But I won't bore you with any more of Leo's accomplishments. Instead, let us consider Attila the Hun.

"The Scourge of God, as he was known to all of his friends, invaded Italy in 452 A.D. His barbarian horde seemed unstoppable. Rome trembled as the invaders drew closer and closer. Attila planned to loot the city and then burn it to the ground. The Vatican and all of its treasures appeared lost.

"It was then that Leo and two civil authorities went out to bargain with Attila. According to the historian, Prosper, the Pope arrived in the Mongol camp surrounded by a golden glow and accompanied by the spirits of Peter and Paul. In his hands, he carried a jewel-encrusted puzzle box that burned with holy fire. This vision of unearthly strength so frightened Attila that he withdrew his troops and left Rome alone."

"Sure," Mak said sarcastically. "You believe that stuff, Alex?"

"Jordanius listed other reasons for Attila's retreat. He claimed plague and famine ravaged the Huns' camp and forced the departure. However, the Roman offered no explanation why the plague struck only the invaders. He also credited Leo with saving the Eternal City. In his account, Jordanius mentioned the same mysterious puzzle box as the source of Leo's miraculous powers."

"So the Pope used this box to save the city. What happened to it after that?"

"That's a good question. I wish I had a good answer. The puzzle box vanished into history. The story came to an abrupt end. In all of my studies of the occult, I never once came across another mention of Leo's mysterious box. I assumed, like most other scholars, that it disappeared in the sands of time or ended up in the treasure vaults of the Vatican."

"These priests evidently think otherwise," Valerie said.

"You're concerned with the unimportant things," Mak said. "The history of the puzzle box isn't important. What matters is why this sect wants it. And, for that matter, how Dietrich Vril fits into the whole picture."

"Money," Valerie said. "A church relic that old, with such a history, must be worth millions."

"I don't think Vril cares about cash," Alex said. "He wasn't the—"

The shrill ring of the telephone cut him off. He frowned, suspecting he knew the identity of the caller.

"Raise the devil by speaking his name," Mak said softly, reflecting the same fear.

Taking a deep breath, Alex picked up the receiver. "Alex Warner here."

"Mr. Warner." Vril's voice was loud and grating over the telephone. "I'm pleased that you escaped from last night's inferno. Those damned Circumcellions haunt my footsteps. A group of them follow me still. Soon, they will cease to annoy me—permanently."

The tone of Vril's voice left no doubt to his meaning. Alex felt a cold chill travel down his back. He had dealt with dangerous men in the past, but no one like Dietrich Vril.

"What do you want, Vril?" Alex asked, knowing the answer before he stated the question. "Howie Rosenberg died because of you."

"Not so," Vril said, not sounding the least bit disturbed. "Those religious fanatics killed him. They also tried to kill me and you. In fact, if my sources are not mistaken," Vril said and hesitated, as if emphasizing the fact, "Brother Ambrose and his followers tried murdering you again this afternoon. Blame the Circumcellions, not me, Mr. Warner."

Vril paused again, but only for a second. "As to what I want? I merely desire that which rightfully belongs to me. Once I deal with my pursuers, I want the book, Mr. Warner. I want the signed copy of *Alraune*."

"What makes you think I have it?" Alex asked. "I already told Brother Ambrose the book went up in flames."

"Don't waste your time lying." Vril's voice

was harsh and filled with menace. "My friends tell me you rescued the volume from the fire."

"You rely a great deal on secondhand information," Alex said.

"My sources are never wrong."

"They didn't warn you about the attack on Rosenberg's store."

"Even the powers of the night are not infallible," Vril said, sounding annoyed. "You talk too much, Mr. Warner. I want that book. There is no room for discussion. When I come for the volume, have it ready. Or suffer the consequences."

"*Alraune* is hidden where you'll never find it, Vril. Try something and I'll burn the damned thing. If you want to discuss the matter further, come see me. In the daytime."

Vril laughed, a loud, crackling sound more frightening than anything he ever said. "Do not confuse me with my allies, Mr. Warner. I function quite well in the sunlight."

"Come whenever you want, Vril," Alex said, "but—"

"No buts or maybes," Vril interrupted, his voice deep with menace. "The book belongs to me, and I intend on getting it, Mr. Warner. No matter how many die, in the end it will be mine."

Then, almost as an afterthought, he added, "In the meantime, take care of yourself. The Circumcellions following me are mere annoyances. Brothers Ambrose and Malachi are not so easily managed. I can personally attest to that fact. I do not want you killed and *Alraune* lost again."

"I'm touched by your concern," Alex said.

"Your premature death would upset years of careful planning." Vril hung up without another word.

Chapter Nine

Alex stared at the receiver for a few seconds before replacing it on the phone.

"I gather that was the mysterious Mr. Vril?" Valerie asked.

"In the flesh," Alex said. He summarized the telephone conversation for the others. "Sooner or later, I'll have to deal with that monster."

"You don't plan to give him the book, do you?" Mak asked. "He doesn't sound like the type of guy you can trust to keep a bargain."

"If Vril gains possession of *Alraune,*" Alex said, grimly, "he'll try murdering us all. Dead men tell no tales."

"Vril isn't the only one we have to worry about," Valerie said. "Brother Ambrose and his bunch don't sound like good losers, either."

"They've never dealt with people like us before," Mak said, snapping his fingers in the air. A puff of black smoke materialized for a second, then vanished. "We can handle any threat they can muster. It's the Very Old Folk who bother me."

Valerie groaned. "Oh, no, don't tell me you believe all that bogeyman stuff."

Mak nodded. "Yes, I do. And you should, too. After all, I recall a werewolf in your not so distant past."

"That was different," Valerie said, using logic only she understood. "I can accept people using the power to change into beasts. But the dead returning to life to feed on the blood of the living? That's stretching my credibility too far. Come on, Mak. Nazis and vampires and the Antichrist, all rolled up in one package? Frankly, I find the whole story pretty difficult to swallow."

She turned to Alex. "I understand your feelings, sweetie, but I think Howie Rosenberg fed you a line and you fell for it. He knew all about your fascination with the occult. Everyone does. He made up a crazy adventure and tied it to the present through the odd appearance of his latest client. Obviously, the old man realized the danger of dealing with contraband and wanted protection. He needed a free bodyguard, and you fit the bill."

"No way," Alex said, sinking down into a chair. The three of them often worked this way, playing devil's advocate to each other, in order to solve some problem. Mostly the questions involved Alex's research or Mak's business investments. Together, they managed to analyze and conquer the most complex enigmas.

"Rosenberg had no reason to make up a crazy story. I owed him plenty. He did me plenty of favors over the past twenty years. And he was close with Jake. Howie knew I would never refuse a request for help. He told me the story for one reason. He wanted me to know the truth. You didn't hear him; I did. When he spoke to me about those vampires at the concentration camp, he wasn't lying."

"He spoke the truth," Mak said, somberly. "I can assure you of that, Valerie. I know."

Grimly, he looked at both of them. "Vampires exist. They are nightmarish creatures lurking in the dark shadows of our world. And they match Howie Rosenberg's description."

Mak leaned forward, elbows on the table, his folded hands resting beneath his chin. "Forget everything you ever heard about Dracula and Transylvania. Pretend you never saw movies with Bela Lugosi or Christopher Lee or Frank Langella. Instead, listen to the truth about the Very Old Folk.

"As a young boy, I foolishly accompanied my brother to a screening of the Hammer film, *Horror of Dracula*. The British film makers of the 1950's believed in realistic vampire movies. This picture featured a number of gory scenes that sent me scurrying home with a bad case of the shakes. After I woke up screaming the next few nights, my father resorted to dramatic measures. He sat me down and told me everything he knew about actual vampires. He then suggested I do some reading in his library about the creatures. Only through knowledge, he told me, could I conquer my fears.

"Dad knew me like a book. Once I realized that vampires existed but were completely different from the monsters of the movies, my fear of them evaporated. Instead, I devoured every volume of esoteric lore I could find dealing with the monsters. I became an expert on the creatures."

Mak ran his tongue over his upper lip as if considering how to continue. He spoke softly as if awed by the facts he was about to reveal.

"Augustian Calmet's *History of Apparitions* contained an entire chapter about weird creatures known only as the Very Old Folk. The French grimoire, *The Secret of Secrets,* devoted nearly twenty pages to veiled references to similar beings. And Aleister Crowley filled an entire issue of his magazine, *The Equinox,* with their secrets."

"Get to the point, Mak," Alex said.

"All three sources agreed on the basic facts, though Crowley provided the most detail. He understood certain modern concepts that the authors of the other two, earlier books barely grasped. Let me tell you what he wrote."

Dark shadows invaded the corners of the room as Mak paused. Only the quiet throb of the furnace broke the silence. Outside, the winter wind howled, as Mak told his friends the history of the Very Old Folk.

Omarth, high priest of Atlantis, raised his arms high over his head. In his hands he clutched the sacred stones of power, gems of darkest obsidian carved from the rock that-fell-from-the-sky thousands of years before. "Join together now," he commanded the half-dozen acolytes who surrounded him on the central platform of the great temple. "The time draws near."

Immediately, his fellow priests linked hands, forming an unbroken circle around their leader. Clad in black robes, beardless and with shaven heads, they resembled a flock of hungry vultures. Or so thought Allus Cale, vice-commander of the city guard, who watched the ceremony from the shadows.

Tonight Omarth planned to break the barrier between the real world and the Land of Shadows. For months, the high priest, the greatest magician of the time, greatest magician of all time, had been in mental communication with Semjaza, Lord of the Dark World. Together, the two schemed to open a dimensional gate so that the inhabitants of the Shadow Land could enter the real world. After much planning, the time was now.

The high priest had made an impassioned plea to the high council for permission to perform the necessary rites. The Shadow World was dying, and only a few of its inhabitants still lived. Masters of magic, they needed help to escape their doom. In return for their rescue, the beings promised to transform Atlantis into the most powerful kingdom in all the world.

Reluctantly, the council had approved Omarth's request, but several cautious members had insisted that Cale and a squad of his finest men be on hand during the ceremony. The high priest trusted Semjaza's word without question. More practical politicians wondered in secret about the Shadow Lord's true motives. Cale and his soldiers were officially only observers to the rite, but the grizzled warrior operated under secret orders to protect Atlantis at all costs—even if it meant killing Omarth and all of his disciples.

The oil lamps scattered throughout the huge central hall of the temple flickered and sputtered as Omarth began to chant. The high priest, taller by a foot than most of his followers and thin as a spear, droned on in an ancient language known before the rise of civilization. The other magicians remained quiet. Omarth was the central player in this ritual. The rest were there only to provide extra psychic energy if his own powers did not prove adequate for the task.

Cale grimaced, his eyes burning from the dark smoke. It was difficult enough to see at night in the huge domed temple. The swirling clouds of dust made it near impossible. Unfortunately, the high priest insisted that the summoning would only work at night. Cale, always suspicious, wondered if the condition truly came from Omarth or from his ally in the Shadow World.

The high priest's voice rose in volume and intensity. With a shrug of anticipation, Cale rested one hand on the hilt of his sword. Following his signal, 50 handpicked men, the best of his troops, scattered in strategic positions throughout the hall, drew their blades. Whatever happened next, the warriors of Atlantis were ready.

"Gart! Boroda! Nictal!" Each word echoed under the temple dome louder than the last. Omarth, his hands clenched so tight that blood dripped from his fingers, lifted his head, his eyes fixed on a point above him in the air. Cale, following the priest's line of sight, gasped in amazement. The dark air rippled as if alive. A small patch of space a dozen feet across crackled with unseen energy.

"Nictal!" repeated the priest even louder, his breath coming in great, ragged gasps. Around him, one by one, the black-clad acolytes dropped to their knees, white-faced, as the high priest drained the psychic energy from their bodies. The gateway flickered and grew darker.

"Nictal!" shrieked Omarth in a voice that seemed to shake the foundation of the temple. For an instant, the seething darkness forming the doorway turned murky and glowed with an unnatural green glow not of this world. The incredible sounds of giant wings filled the temple. Two score of huge black shapes swarmed through the gateway, swirling up in the air to the roof.

"Nictal!" screamed Omarth one last time before collapsing to the floor. Dark streams of blood dribbled from his ears, eyes and nose. The spell had proven too much for even the greatest sorcerer of Atlantis. Omarth was dead.

And with his passing, the gateway to the Shadow World dissolved. One second it was there, eerie light filling the temple, and then the next instant, it was gone, the link between dimensions broken.

Stunned by the sudden change, Cale hardly noticed the manlike shape that glided down to the altar, landing close to the body of the high priest. In the dim light, it was difficult to make out the creature's features, but what registered frightened the normally unflappable soldier.

The Shadow Lord stood taller than the tallest man, with vast shoulders and barrel chest. Its body was covered with a dense matting of black fur. Unnaturally long arms ended in huge hands that touched the ground. Vast wings, half-folded against its body, draped the thing like some gigantic cloak. Eyes the color of fire glared out from a stark travesty of a human face. A mouthful of yellow teeth reflected the dim light of the oil lamps. The beast was a nightmarish mix of man and bat, a combination unlike anything before on Earth.

Seemingly without effort, the monster reached down, grabbed one of the recumbent priests by the shoulder and raised the man into the air. It spoke in a coarse whisper that revibrated in Cale's mind. He remembered Omarth saying that the Very Old Folk communicated by telepathy. Despite the distance separating him from the creature, he could hear its every word clearly.

"I am Semjaza, Lord of Death. Reopen the portal," the creature demanded. "Only a few of us passed through."

"Impossible," answered the acolyte, squirming like a hooked fish in the creature's grasp. "Only Omarth possessed the necessary psychic powers."

For an instant, the man-bat stood frozen, as if paralyzed by the answer. Then, with a savage lunge almost quicker than the eye could follow, the creature sank its huge teeth into the acolyte's neck. With an inarticulate howl of blood lust, Semjaza clenched its powerful jaws shut, ripping out a huge chunk of neck and shoulder.

As if that act was a signal, the other monsters dropped to the ground. Jaws clacking horribly, they tore into the helpless priests, sending blood and guts spurting across the abandoned altar.

"Stop, stop!" screamed one of the acolytes as clawlike hands tore deep into his flesh. "We are allies!"

"Allies?" retorted Semjaza. Inhuman laughter flooded Cale's mind. "We make no compacts with the beasts of the field. You are food."

Cale shuddered. What incredible horror had Omarth released upon the world? Though his men outnumbered the monsters two to one, he dreaded sending them into battle, but he had no choice.

"Attack!" he cried and rushed forward, waving his bronze sword like a banner.

Cale swung his weapon in a glittering arc at the nearest creature. The monster, intent on the remains of one of the acolytes, never even saw the blow coming. Metal met unearthly flesh and glanced off, as if striking stone. Cale cursed, as the man-bat swiveled about, blood and gore dripping from its lips. Grisly claws grabbed wildly for the soldier. Dancing to the side, Cale shifted tactics and stabbed.

The point of his sword caught the creature in the left eye. Shoving with all his strength, Cale slammed the blade up to the hilt. The monster hardly seemed to notice. One huge hand swatted Cale across the chest, smashing bones and sending him flying.

He crashed to the floor a dozen feet back, away from the one-sided battle that raged between his soldiers and the creatures from another dimension. The man-bats had the strength of ten men and seemed virtually indestructible. As he watched in shocked amazement, the thing he had run through with his sword ripped the blade out of its eyesocket and went back to its feeding. Already, half his troops were dead, and the rest were desperately trying to escape.

Coughing blood, the veteran commander dashed for the temple entrance. His chest burned with an inner fire, and it felt like several of his ribs were broken. Ignoring the pain, he forced himself forward. Nothing mattered other than escape. The people of Atlantis had to be warned.

Miraculously, Cale made it through the giant bronze doors and onto the wide stairs leading down to the city proper. Behind him, the death cries of his men rang horribly in the night. Bleeding from a score of cuts, Cale hesitated, the screams of his troops bringing tears to his eyes.

Drawn by the noise, a squad of guards came running up the steps to the wounded officer. Raising his torch, the leader of the group stared closely at Cale.

"Vice-commander?" It was Talos, one of his lieutenants. "What—"

With a crash loud enough to wake the dead, the huge doors of the temple slammed open. A horde of monstrous figures hurtled into the night sky, wings blotting out the moon.

"Devils!" Talos swore, overwhelmed by the sight of the inhuman shapes.

"Worse," Cale answered. He looped one arm around Talos' neck. "Take me to the council chambers. We must alert the people of Atlantis of their peril."

But it was much too late for warnings. Hundreds died that night as terror reigned in Atlantis. The man-bats swooped down on unsuspecting homes, ripping sleeping citizens from their beds and gorging themselves on human flesh. There was no defense from the monsters, no place to hide. The moon turned red with blood.

And then the sun rose.

Nearly half of the monsters died witnessing their first sunrise. Creatures from a world of eternal twilight, they knew nothing of the sun. They learned a fatal lesson that morning. Direct sunlight burned their flesh to ashes. Only in darkness could they survive.

The brief respite enabled the magician-priests of Atlantis to regroup and organize. Omarth had died opening the portal, but many other sorcerers possessed near equal powers. While none of the individual Atlanteans could match the magic of the monsters from the Shadow World, there were thousands of them against only a handful of the vampires. The man-bats fled before the wrath of mankind. Only their power of flight saved them. Possessing enormous strength and tremendous recuperative powers, they scattered and vanished throughout the ancient world.

"How many got away?" Valerie asked, as Mak paused to take a drink of water. He had been talking for nearly an hour straight. "And what happened to them?"

"Only a handful escaped Atlantis," Mak answered, "but those few never died. The creatures aged at a different rate than us. The same ones who crossed the dimension bridge to Atlantis survived in dark caverns in the great mountain ranges of the world for thousands of years. Thus came about their title, the Very Old Folk.

"They managed to stay alive by feeding on unwary travelers who wandered into their domain. In times of great hunger, they made desperate raids in the night, using tremendous mental powers to cloak their attacks.

"Gradually, they became part of our mythologies. Roman legends spoke of malevolent ghosts called Lemures, who existed on human blood. These creatures as described by the ancient historians only faintly resembled men. Instead they were described as a cross between man and bat, combining the features of both. The Lemures not only drank the blood but also ate the flesh and drained the marrow of those unfortunate to cross their pass. The Romans feared these monsters so much that they dedicated May Thirteenth as the day sacred to them.

"The Greeks of that same period feared the Night Riders, cannibalistic ghosts who lived on human flesh. Hecate, Queen of Darkness, commanded those spirits. Witches worshiped Hecate and changed into birds or bats to fly to their meetings. Once there, they feasted on the blood of still-living victims.

"Arcane writings from Northern China of nearly two thousand years ago described similar horrors known only as Mountain Ghosts. They too lived on the flesh and blood of men. Little else was known about them since no one survived an encounter with the fiends. However, the inhabitants of the region until recently designed their kites to resemble giant owls, the reason being that owls were the natural enemies of bats.

"In hieroglyphic inscriptions found on ancient tombs, the Egyptians wrote of the Devourers of the Flesh. They were hideous, unnatural things who roamed the pyramids, guarding the tombs of the pharaohs. Archaeologists routinely dismissed the stories as fabrications to discourage grave robbers. They never understood the sinister implications of the portraits of the Devourers, white-skinned men with heads of bats."

"Then all those stories about undead humans preying on the living are mere fabrications," Valerie said. "Which leads me to believe that their bite doesn't . . ."

". . . create new vampires," Mak said, finishing the sentence. "As you said, it is just a peasant superstition that crept into the legends. The Very Old Folk devour life. Their bite is fatal."

"They don't sound the least like the arrogant fiends from the movies," Valerie said with just a trace of bewilderment in her voice.

"The Very Old Folk fear mankind's numerical superiority. For all of their great strength and powers of magic, the vampires cannot defeat a hundred determined men, properly armed and protected. They survive only by staying hidden.

"According to *The Secret of Secrets,* death comes to them in one of two ways. Sunlight kills them instantly, the heat and light burning them to a crisp.

"The other method is the notorious stake through the heart. Evidently, the creatures possess tremendous recuperative powers. Wound them anywhere else and the injuries heal within seconds. Destroy the vampire's heart and the creature dies."

"Well, Dietrich Vril isn't covered with black fur. And sunlight doesn't worry him either," Alex said.

"Nor is he one of their descendents," Mak said. "The only vampires are those who crossed over from their home world. Fate played one last joke on the creatures. The crossing from their world to Earth rendered them all sterile. All of the horror stories of the Very Old Folk trying to breed with human women are unfortunately true. But no children ever resulted from the union of the species.

"Nor could the monsters create another bridge between dimension. Omarth of Atlantis was the most powerful sorcerer ever to walk the Earth, and he was only able to hold the gate open for a few seconds. The path between worlds remained closed."

Mak stared directly at Alex. "Now you know why I never doubted Rosenberg's story. Only true magicians possess the truth about the Very Old Folk, and we don't broadcast our secrets. Howie obviously discovered his facts firsthand."

Valerie, her face white and drawn, asked the

question that had to be asked. "Then how did Crowley learn so much?"

"No one knows," Mak said, "but many suspect he made an unholy bargain with the vampires. During his days at Trinity College, Crowley gained a reputation as an expert mountain climber. Yet, on an attempt on Kangchenjunga Peak, he lost his partner in what he described as a freak accident. No one ever found the poor unfortunate's body. You can fill in the blanks."

"Human sacrifice," Valerie murmured, with a shudder. "Surely not that."

"Perhaps worse," Mak replied. "You see, the Very Old Folk prefer their victims still alive."

Chapter Ten

They sat quietly for a few moments, as if stunned by that final revelation. It was Alex who spoke first.

"Forget Crowley and his sins. For all of his posturing, he accomplished little during his lifetime and affects virtually no one today. According to Brother Ambrose, Dietrich Vril threatens us all, and I suspect the priest might be right."

"He possesses the will," Mak said. "Remember Rosenberg's story. Forty years ago, a very young Vril commanded two of the Very Old Folk that night in Dachau. He actually directed their attack.

"I barely touched upon the unbelievable mental powers of the creatures. Only a handful of fabled magicians matched their strength. All legends agreed on one thing. The vampires were creatures of absolute evil. If Vril bound them to his will, he was the most powerful sorcerer in the world as a child."

"Imagine his powers now," Valerie said softly.

"Ambrose yelled something about their bullets not hitting Vril," Alex said.

"What about him sweating through the blizzard?" Valerie asked. "That surely doesn't sound natural."

Mak shook his head. "I'm not sure. Sometimes, when great sorcery is involved, it affects the user in strange ways. Major disturbances on the psychic plane rebounds as heat energy. Many magicians, including myself, have experienced a sudden rise in body temperature when performing a particularly difficult ritual, but I never heard of anyone sweating continually. I know of no spell that operates for such an extended period of time. The amount of mystic energy necessary to cause such a reaction is incredible."

"Everything about Dietrich Vril seems to fit that one word—incredible," Alex said, folding his hands together. He twisted his fingers about nervously.

Drawing in a deep breath, he rose from his chair. "Forget Vril for now. We'll deal with him when he comes to call. Maybe we can attack this problem from a different angle."

"The Pope's treasure box," Valerie said.

"Everything revolves around the inscription in *Alraune* to Karl Steiner," Mak declared. "Otherwise, any copy of the book would work." He turned to Alex. "What do you know about the author?"

"Hanns Heinz Ewers? A little, but not very much. I tried looking him up in some of my reference books today, but the information is pretty sketchy. The only link to the quotation was a mention that Ewers was a member of the Nazi party late in his life."

"Karl Steiner?" Mak asked. "His name rings a bell in my subconscious, but I can't put my finger on it. Valerie, what about you?"

"Steiner . . ." she hesitated for a minute, her eyes tightly closed in concentration, ". . . and the Thule Society. I vaguely recall the name. My father must have mentioned him at the dinner table once upon a time."

Valerie opened her eyes but remained lost in her thoughts. "Jake liked discussing unusual topics at dinner. Conversation normally centered on whatever esoteric book he was reading at the time. I remember Karl Steiner's name came up one night. He must be discussed in a book in Jake's collection."

"Terrific," Alex said, with a short laugh. "That narrows it down to only ten thousand or so volumes."

"A lot less," Valerie said. "The dedication makes it clear that Steiner was a Nazi—from the sounds of it, an important and influential one, too."

"And I suspect one who was deeply involved in black magic," Mak said. "I feel certain of that."

"The Thule Society," Alex said, letting the phrase roll off his tongue. "And Vril . . ."

Alex snapped his fingers. "No wonder his name sounded familiar. I couldn't place it earlier, but now I remember. Our buddy, Dietrich, was playing mind games with the Nazis when he assumed that name. In Bulwer-Lytton's 19th century novel *The Coming Race,* Vril represented the enormous reservoir of universal psychic power. A few gifted men could tap into that energy source, transforming themselves into superhuman beings."

Growing excited, Alex rushed on. "A number of scholars claimed *The Coming Race* foreshadowed the theory of Aryan supremacy embraced by the Nazis. In any case, a secret Vril Society flourished in Germany between the two wars. Several of Hitler's closest advisors and confidants belonged to it. The group maintained close links with the Thule Society, another underground occult fraternity.

"Somehow, that organization forms a common bound between our three names—Vril, Ewers and Steiner—and I think I know exactly how to discover the link."

"Fly to Germany and investigate?" Valerie asked, her tone only half-mocking.

"You read too many Robert Ludlum novels, my dear," Alex replied. "Only in spy novels does the hero take a transatlantic flight to check out a theory. I prefer a little more concrete evidence before we go dashing off on a wild goose chase.

"And I doubt if such action would do much good. Try finding a German willing to discuss the events leading up to the Second World War. They suddenly experience a total memory loss. Most of them want to bury the past—and with good reason."

"So? What's your alternative?"

"History, my love, history. After all, I do belong to the history department of one of the finest universities in the United States. The library is open tomorrow, and I am a trained researcher. Give me a few hours, and I'll be able to tell you the name of the toothpaste Steiner used and where he bought it."

"Sounds good to me," Valerie said. She wrinkled her nose at Alex. "You're cute when you start bragging, even if you are a little vain."

"Huh?" Alex stared at his wife with startled eyes. "I'm not vain."

Mak coughed discreetly and stood up. "Enough debating for me tonight. I've got to get home through all this snow. How about if we continue the discussion tomorrow?"

"Good idea," Valerie said.

Mak departed a few minutes later, leaving Alex and Valerie alone for the first time all evening.

"I am not vain," Alex repeated. "Perhaps a little smug, but definitely not vain."

"We can talk about it upstairs," Valerie said with a smile. "In the bedroom."

"Oh no," Alex said, grinning. "I know you.

You never want to talk in the bedroom."

"You got it," Valerie said, starting to unbutton her blouse. "We can talk tomorrow."

Watching his wife casually remove her clothes and stack them neatly on top of the dining room table, Alex had to agree. Talking could wait till the morning.

Alex woke to the sound of Valerie banging around downstairs with the pots and pans. Shaking his head, he rolled out of bed and headed for the stairs. "Hey, keep it down," he cried. "I had a rough time yesterday, remember?"

"Tut, tut," Valerie said, looking up the staircase and laughing. "Poor, poor Alex. My heart bleeds for you. How about some breakfast?"

"Sounds fine. After last night, I could eat a cow."

"You'll have to settle for bacon and eggs. We're clean out of cows."

The doorbell rang just as Alex finished the last few crumbs of his meal.

"Mailman," Valerie called from the front room, as he rose from the table. "There's a box for you. Want me to open it?"

"Sure," he replied.

He frowned. Packages arrived all the time from used and rare bookstores. Still, he couldn't remember ordering anything from his usual sources recently. Vril's warning flashed through his mind.

"Val, don't open it!" he yelled, sprinting for the parlor.

An ear-splitting screech answered him. When Alex barreled into the front room, his wife stood frozen in the middle of the floor, her face twisted in horror. Sprawled at her feet was a small, brown cardboard box. Several plastic bags had tumbled out from the container and littered the floor.

Ignoring the packages, Alex rushed over to Valerie and hugged her close. "Those dirty bastards," Valerie muttered, her tone a combination of fear and anger. "Those dirty bastards."

Alex inhaled deeply, still holding his wife tight. Despite Valerie's feelings, it could have been worse, much worse. If this had been all-out war, the Circumcellions could have sent a letter bomb or a spring-action poisoned needle. Instead, they opted for horror and shock to make their point.

Releasing Valerie, Alex bent over and examined the three plastic bags. They were ordinary zip-lock plastic freezer bags, but their contents were anything but ordinary.

There had been no attempt to be neat. The cutting job had been crude but effective. Bits of flesh and bone still clung to the organs, but they were pretty much intact.

In one bag was a pair of human eyes. The second contained a man's tongue. The third held a pair of ears. Trying to visually match the organs to a human being was impossible, but Alex suspected he was staring at the last remains of his friend, Howie Rosenberg.

"There's a note in the bottom of the box,"

Valerie said, her voice still shaky.

Calmly, Alex pulled out the single sheet of paper and read its contents. The message was short and to the point.

The book will be ours. One way or another.

Grimacing, Alex crumpled the paper up into a ball and shoved it back into the box. The three plastic bags followed.

"This stuff goes into the furnace," he said, his voice steady. "I wouldn't put it past Brother Ambrose to have the police come visiting on a tip that I murdered Howie Rosenberg. Combine these grisly souvenirs with a neighbor seeing me enter the bookstore that night and you have a pretty strong case. My record in Vietnam would serve as nails in my coffin."

"These guys play rough, Alex," Valerie said, her face still a pale shade of green.

"Not as rough as your husband," Alex said harshly. "Not nearly as rough."

Chapter Eleven

Alex sighed and leaned back in his chair. "That's it," he declared. "I can't eat another bite. That was terrific. As good as anything I've ever eaten at your restaurant, Mak."

"It should be," Mak said, "considering I slaved for hours preparing everything from scratch. Nothing's too good for my buddy, Alex."

"I saved your life in 'Nam," Alex said, mock-serious.

"And I've been feeding you ever since for it," Mak replied. "That one rescue has cost me a small fortune."

Alex grinned. "Think of your culinary skill in a historical sense. Many men aspire to greatness. Only a few achieve it. Talent such as yours ranks you with the immortals."

"I've never thought of it that way before. I guess in my own way, my cooking puts me on the level of Charlemagne and Napoleon."

"More likely Lucrezia Borgia," Valerie said, with a laugh. She rose from her seat. "Let's clear off the dishes and get down to brass tacks. We can leave dessert for later. Alex, do you want a cup of coffee?"

"Thanks, honey, not now." His face clouded over. He was not happy with what he had discovered that afternoon at the university.

The shrill ring of the telephone greeted them as they made their way into the parlor.

"I'll get it," Valerie said, scrambling to the hallway.

"Not Vril again?" Mak asked.

"I doubt it," Alex said. "I suspect Mr. Vril won't bother making any more calls. He'll just come by when he's ready."

Valerie came back. "It's for you, Alex," she announced icily. "A woman."

"For me? A woman?"

"Most definitely." Valerie was a wonderful, understanding wife. She was also extremely jealous and overly suspicious.

Alex knew when to retreat. "Probably one of my graduate students needing advice," he offered lamely and hurried into the hall.

"Alex Warner here."

"I didn't mean to upset your wife, Doc." The deep, sultry laughter of Sally Stevens echoed on the phone. "Tell her not to worry. I can't compete with her looks."

"You've been checking up on me," Alex said, slightly annoyed.

"Comes with the territory. My compliments, Doc. Not many college professors meet top fashion models, much less marry one."

"Her father and I were close friends. Did you hear from Royce?"

"You bet, chief. He wants to know if you can go for a little ride with him tonight."

"A ride? Where, when, why?"

Sally laughed again, and the sound sent shivers running up and down Alex's back. She had the sexiest voice Alex had ever heard. "You sound like one of my old journalism teachers. Sorry, but I can't tell you a thing. Sometimes Saul plays it close to the vest. He keeps a few secrets even from me. I'm just relaying his message. When can you be ready?"

Alex hesitated for an instant. He had no desire to go out into the bitter cold, but he was anxious to talk with Royce. "I'm in the middle of something right now. How about in an hour?"

"Sounds fine. There'll be a car in front of your place in sixty minutes."

"Well?" Valerie asked, a nasty glint in her eye. "Was that a graduate student in distress?"

"Actually, it was Saul Royce's secretary. I'm going out to meet him in an hour. I should be able to tell you everything important by then. The last thing I feel like doing right now is talking about Nazis, but I'll feel better if the two of you know the whole story—or at least as much as I've been able to find out."

"Forewarned is forearmed," Mak said.

"Exactly. While I'm gone, maybe you can puzzle out the truth behind this whole charade. In the meantime, let me tell you what I learned about the Thule Society and its leading spokesman, Karl Steiner.

"I was lucky. Last year the department sponsored a project where the graduate assistants keypunched all of the indices of the major reference volumes on World War One and Two into a computer data base. It placed the wisdom of a thousand scholars at my fingertips. All I had to do when I arrived at the library today was punch Karl Steiner's name into my keyboard, and in a few seconds the computer unearthed more than forty citations on him. I spent the rest of the afternoon reading and taking notes. I think I've tied it all together, but you be the judge."

Alex leaned forward, his hands clasped together tightly, his muscles taut with an inner tension. From time to time, he paused for a few seconds for dramatic effect. For all of his self-proclaimed modesty, Alex was a topnotch historian and he knew how to tell a story.

"Modern history books gloss over the importance of occult societies and their teachings in the rise of the Third Reich," he began. "Materialism rules our world today, and that philosophy colors our thinking. Fundamentalists argue that history books ignore the importance of religion throughout the millennia, and I agree with them wholeheartedly. Man has always been a creature of passions, both real and imagined. To give credence to one and ignore the other is foolish.

"In our cynical, liberal age, we too often forget the importance irrational belief played in past events. So, fewer and fewer textbooks dealing with the events in Germany after the First World War mention the Thule Society and Karl Steiner. They omit any mention of Adolf Lanz and his Order of New Templars in the formation of the Reich.

"Every year, in my History of Magic class I force my new students to investigate the origin of the Swastika. It takes them quite a while usually to find any reference to Dr. Friedrich Krohn, a member of the Germanen Order, who designed the symbol for the Nazi Party. None of the reference volumes discuss the importance of that twisted cross in ancient Tibetan black magic rituals. Did you know, for instance, that the word 'Swastika' comes from the Sanskrit word 'svastika,' meaning good fortune?

"Our generation tends to believe that we discovered everything of interest since the beginning of time. This recent wave of mysticism that swept the country demonstrates what I mean. For the past few years we have been bombarded with channeling, pyramid power and New Age Harmonics. None of the people involved in any of these great new revelations seems to have ever cracked open a history book. History tends to repeat itself.

"If you think Shirley MacLaine is insufferable, then rejoice that we live in modern America. A hundred years ago, crackpot philosophers whose ramblings make her ideas sound like the soul of rationality dotted the landscape of Europe like weeds.

"Many of the wildest characters lived in the Germanic States and Austria. Fortunately, they faded into oblivion as fast as they rose from obscurity, except for one notable exception—a starving writer named Guido von List. A charismatic figure with a flowing, white beard, he claimed to possess great psychic powers that enabled him to see the ancient past.

"These mystic visions revealed to List the existence of a forgotten Germanic race of supermen he dubbed the Armanen. These superior beings controlled all sorts of occult powers and possessed the great secrets of the universe. Not surprisingly, List claimed he was the last surviving descendant of the Armanen.

"A number of young, impressionable Austrian men fell under the spell of List's incredible pronouncements. His theories of racial purity and superhuman beings, tossed together with a strong dose of rabid nationalism, appealed to these teenagers unhappy with the state of the world."

"Sounds all too familiar," Valerie commented.

Alex nodded. "The most depressing fact of history is the recurrence of insane behavior among the young. Witness the Skinheads and the Neo-Nazis of today.

"These young men banded together in a secret society of Armanen Initiates, but they soon grew dissatisfied with List's runic occultism. Several important members broke rank and formed new secret organizations furthering List's original ideas with their own variations.

"One of these rebels, Adolf Lanz, founded the Order of New Templars. An Austrian, born in 1874, Lanz originally planned to become a monk. However, after spending six years in a Cistercian monastery, he was expelled for carnal sins. A notorious eccentric, he was obsessed with the notion of racial purity. Among his many ideas, he promoted the concept of sterilizing inferior races and the use of forced labor camps to exterminate lesser breeds.

"Adolf Hitler first met Lanz in Austria in 1909. Twenty-three years later, the founder of the New Templars wrote in a letter, 'Hitler is one of our pupils. Through him, we will one day develop a movement that makes the world tremble.'

"So far, I've just been giving you the background necessary to understand where Karl Steiner fits into the history of the Reich. Steiner's early days closely paralleled Lanz. The son of wealthy Austrian parents, Steiner joined the Armanen Initiates in their early days but soon grew dissatisfied and left. He became a member of the Thule Society, another mystic society of the period.

"A dynamic, forceful individual, Steiner quickly rose in the order until he became grand master of the German Lodge. Within a few years, he transformed the relatively esoteric occult organization, based on the theosophic teachings of Madame Blavatsky, into a powerful underground organization dedicated to German nationalism.

"The Thule Society emerged then as the most powerful secret society in Europe. Steiner openly practiced black magic ceremonies at his meetings and often mocked Christian beliefs in public. He advocated a return to pagan worship of the Germanic Gods.

"According to theosophist belief, humanity evolved on the primal continent of Thule. These godlike beings controlled all manner of psychic forces and built the globe-spanning kingdoms of Atlantis and Lemuria. Slowly, though, over millions of years, this fourth race degenerated due to inbreeding and mating with beasts.

"Only a small number of these supermen remained free from sin and thus retained the necessary racial purity to comprehend the secrets of the cosmos. A few of these golden super beings escaped the destruction of Atlantis and Lemuria that resulted from vast geographic disasters. The rest of mankind sank back into savagery and then slowly evolved upward.

"I've summarized in a few minutes an incredible scenario that combined occult lore, pseudoscience and racist nationalism. Such nonsense, ranging across vast spans of space and time, appealed to the romanticism so prevalent in Germany at that time. Members of the Thule Society traced their ancestry back to the last survivors of the fourth race. Fanatics, they considered it their destiny to rule the world, wresting control away from the degenerate descendants of men and beasts.

"A young Rudolph Hess belonged to the group and considered himself one of Steiner's disciples. Another pupil was Dietrich Eckart, a drunken poet and philosopher. Eckart served on the main committee of the German Workers Party.

"In 1919, Adolf Hitler, acting on secret orders from the German Army Political Department, attended a meeting of that fledging political group. The High Command thought that the Workers Party was a Communist front because of its name.

"According to *Mein Kampf*, Hitler wanted nothing to do with the Workers Party. He planned to start his own political movement. However, after two days of agonizing, he changed his mind and joined the organization. Within a year, the group changed its name to the National Socialist German Worker's Party with Hitler as its absolute leader.

"During the next three years, Dietrich Eckart served as Hitler's closest advisor, and through him, the ambitions of the Thule Society gained a voice. A lifelong alcoholic, Eckart died from too much drink early in 1923. However, before he died he told his friends, 'Follow Hitler. He will dance, but it is I who called the tune.'"

"Fascinating," Valerie said. "I never realized Hitler was so closely tied to the occult."

"Dietrich Eckart and Dietrich Vril," Mak added. "Coincidence?"

"I doubt it," Alex said. "Especially if you consider Vril as his last name. Anyhow, let me continue. It really becomes interesting now.

"Brought together by Dietrich Eckart, Hitler and Steiner became close friends. In the Nazi leader, Steiner found a champion for his belief in the Armanen superman. Like a multitude of others, he succumbed to the Fuhrer's incredible personal magnetism. He soon joined the National Socialist Workers Party. After Eckart's death, Steiner served as Hitler's unofficial expert on matters of the occult as well as his spiritual counselor.

"Then, in 1927, Steiner cut all his ties with the Thule Society and vanished for two years. During that time, Hitler continued to consolidate his power. Steiner returned in 1929, offering no explanation for his disappearance. He made no effort to rejoin the theosophists and instead served as a special diplomatic envoy for the Nazi Party. As far as I could learn, Steiner never spoke of those missing years.

"My one clue to his mission came from a totally unexpected source. Rudolph Hess belonged to the Thule Society and served as one of Steiner's closest confidants for many years. During extensive questioning during the Nuremberg trials, Hess mentioned in passing that

Steiner traveled to the East to study black magic in the hopes of furthering the Nazi cause."

"Did Hess say where Steiner actually went?" Valerie asked, a quiver of concern in her voice. Alex suspected she already knew the answer.

"Can't you guess?" he answered. "According to Hess, Steiner journeyed to Tibet where, according to theosophist philosophy, certain great masters of the occult lived in perpetual darkness. They are referred to in the texts as the Very Old Folk."

Valerie sucked in her breath sharply, then exhaled. "I should have expected that."

Alex nodded, then continued with his story. "Karl Steiner served as a top advisor to Hitler for the next four years. During that time, he made numerous trips to Switzerland for an inner circle of Nazi leaders. He acted as a liaison between top Germans and certain Swiss banks, arranging a number of secret, numbered accounts for Hitler and his closest cronies. Steiner spoke six languages fluently and possessed great personal charm. He made a perfect emissary for the fledgling Reich. At the same time, with the cooperation of his Fuhrer, Steiner worked to eliminate all those who might challenge his authority.

"In 1934, soon after Hitler's ascension to supreme authority in Germany, the police banned all types of fortunetelling. Shortly afterwards, a nationwide confiscation program of occult books and literature took place throughout the country. The Fuhrer personally issued orders forbidding Nazi office to any former members of the Germanen Order and the Freemasons.

"When the Nazis overran Austria in 1938, they issued strict directives forbidding Adolf Lanz from writing for publication. It was a major setback for the man who only a few years earlier had bragged about his influence on Hitler.

"On orders from the High Command, the German Army crushed the Order of New Templars. Members were imprisoned or killed. Only the Thule Society remained.

"Organized religion fared little better. Karl Steiner hated the Christian Church and preached a return to pagan worship. He proposed a National Reich Temple. On its altar would be a copy of *Mein Kampf*, and standing beside it, a drawn sword.

"Steiner personally issued the order outlawing the Catholic Youth League and banning all Catholic publications. During the next few years, thousands of priests, nuns and lay leaders vanished without a trace. Protestants, even though they formed the bulk of the Reich's religious population, also suffered. Many hundreds of pastors disappeared during the mass arrests of the late 1930's.

"In a little over four years, Karl Steiner, working through Adolf Hitler, effectively eliminated any rivals to his claim as the master sorcerer of the Third Reich.

"Ironically, during most of the time that this unprecedented attack on organized religion took place, Steiner served as the Reich's emissary to the Vatican. No doubt it amused the Fuhrer to delegate his most notorious anti-Catholic as liaison to the Pope.

"Very amusing," Mak said grimly. "How long did Steiner hold that position?"

"He left Rome early in 1937 and returned to Germany. He settled down on a huge country estate given him by the Fuhrer. Except for occasional short trips to Switzerland on behalf of the High Command, he rarely left this retreat for the rest of his life."

Alex paused for a second, as if directing his remarks to the jury at a murder trial. "No one ever discovered what experiments Steiner conducted at that secret laboratory in the Black Forest. The master magician never kept any records, and he employed no assistants. His only helper was his daughter, Magda, born of a short, loveless marriage twenty years earlier."

"A daughter?" Valerie asked. "What happened to her?"

"Dead. Reports gathered by British Intelligence from the period claimed that she entered a passionate affair with a high-ranking official of the Nazi Party and bore him a child in 1937. She died giving birth. Rudolf Hess was often mentioned as the likely father as he visited the Steiners quite often.

"In an odd turn of events, Magda's father ended up raising the child. Not much was known about the boy. According to those same reports, he disappeared during the final stages of the war, but no one really knows for sure what happened to him."

"I have a bad feeling about that," Mak said, but allowed Alex to keep going.

"Even without the aid of his daughter, Steiner continued working on his mysterious project. Hitler visited him from time to time, and Hess continued to call. Then, overnight, Steiner's fortunes shattered.

"On May 9, 1941, Rudolf Hess traveled to Karl Steiner's estate for his monthly briefing on the magician's project. What he saw there, no one ever learned. All we know was that the next day, May 10th, Hess secretly commandeered a plane at Augsburg and flew alone to Scotland.

"For some unstated reason, he desperately wanted to make peace with England. What he told his captors in secret was never revealed. After the war, Hess refused to discuss the matter. In all of his years of imprisonment, Hess never once hinted at what inspired his mad action.

"Hitler must have known, though. He reacted in a most unexpected manner. Within a month, the Gestapo arrested all occultists in the Reich. They spared no one, including the highest-ranking members of the Thule Society. The purge included faith healers, gypsy fortunetellers and astrologers. Karl Steiner was placed under house arrest and treated as a non-person.

"Unable to work, a prisoner in his own home, Steiner turned to drink. Surprisingly, Hitler allowed him to live, unlike most of the other victims of the June raids. Perhaps the Fuhrer still feared the most notorious black magician of the twentieth century.

"Steiner died nearly two years later, on June 12, 1943, the victim of an Allied air raid. According to reports, the bombs literally blew his body to pieces."

"Brr," Valerie shuddered. "Now I see why you wanted us to hear this story. Things are starting to tie together. One thing, though. This secret project that Karl Steiner worked on those last few years—the one that prompted Hess' flight to Scotland—did it have a name?"

Alex nodded. "Can't you guess? For some unexplained reason, Steiner called it 'Project Mandrake.' Or, in the original German, *Alraune.*"

"Score one for our team," Mak said. He rose to his feet. "Your ride is due in a few minutes. How about a cannoli before you go?"

"Sounds good to me. Maybe we can figure out what to do next."

"We could just burn the damned book," Valerie said, as they munched on the Italian pastry. "That would put an end to all this insanity."

"No," Alex said firmly. "Howie Rosenberg deserves better. If I destroy the book, his death means nothing."

"You going macho on me?"

"Don't be silly. It's a matter of responsibility. Too many of these right wing characters bluster about honor and revenge. They never understand what really matters is a moral obligation to principle. It's obvious that Rosenberg's murder is one link in a chain of events stretching from before World War Two right up to the present. Something very evil lurks in the pages of that book and I mean to learn its secret."

"I wish we knew what really happened to Steiner's grandson," Mak said. "He might provide the answers to a lot of our questions."

"It hit me right between the eyes this afternoon," Alex said. "Like all those with the power to perform real magic, Steiner passed on his gifts to his daughter. And she, in turn, passed it along to her son."

"The grandson of the most powerful sorcerer in the past hundred years," said Mak. "Is it possible he's alive today and using the name Dietrich Vril?"

"But the age factor?" Valerie said, puzzled. "According to what you told us, Vril would have only been a young boy when he visited Dachau in the company of the Very Old Folk."

"I wondered about that, too," Alex said. "Remember what Rosenberg said about the vampire's master having the features and mannerisms of a young child though the body of an adult?"

"There are certain spells," Mak said slowly, almost as if reluctant to speak, "that accelerate aging. Forbidden, dangerous spells which require a great deal of human blood."

He paused for a moment. "I don't know much

about such rituals. But, a possible side effect . . ."

". . . might manifest itself in Vril's incredible body temperature," said Alex, finishing the thought.

Valerie shuddered. "What a tangled network of horrors."

Outside the house, a car horn honked loudly.

Alex grabbed his coat from the closet. "Mak, do me a favor and stick around till I return home. Vril's heritage worries me. He wants that book badly. And who knows what Brother Ambrose plans next."

"Valerie will be safe with me, my friend," Mak said. "You armed?"

"I'm ready for war," Alex said, grimly. He carried a .357 Magnum in a shoulder holster as well as a razor-sharp stiletto in a sheath strapped to one leg.

The horn outside sounded again.

"Better hurry," Valerie said, the barest trace of anxiety in her voice. "It sounds like Saul Royce is the impatient type. Stay safe, and keep away from sexy secretaries."

"My heart belong to only you, my love," Alex said and dashed out the front door.

Chapter Twelve

A tall, rugged man with a face carved out of old ivory stood waiting for him at the side of a black stretch limo. A powerfully built individual of indeterminate age, the driver wore a heavy black overcoat that swathed him from head to toe. A dark chauffeur's cap hid most of his features. As Alex approached, the man swung open the rear door and motioned him inside, never once saying a word.

The stench of cheap cigar smoke greeted Alex as he slid onto the plush seat. He had long forgotten Saul Royce's fondness for stogies, the fouler the better.

"Make yourself comfortable, Professor," the columnist said, from a seat facing the rear.

"We've got a long drive ahead of us."

The chauffeur entered the limo and started the engine. In seconds, they were on the way.

"Care for a drink?" Royce asked, holding out a metal flask. "It takes the sting out of the cold."

Saul Royce looked like a character out of a Damon Runyon story, and he worked hard at maintaining that image. As an editor once remarked, the only thing louder than Royce was his clothes.

Tonight, he wore a thick white overcoat that made him look like a jovial polar bear. Bright blue eyes twinkled in the midst of a wrinkled, beet-red face right out of the Sunday comic section. A matched white fur hat covered the few strands of hair left on the columnist's head.

He waved a huge cigar in the general direction of Alex. "Maybe you want a good smoke? It puts hair on your chest."

Coughing hard to clear his lungs, Alex shook his head. "No thanks. I value my life too much. Those things are gigantic cancer sticks."

Royce laughed loudly, a cackling sound like the squawking of a chicken. "They keep me going. I'm sixty-two and healthy as a horse. You're looking good yourself, Warner. My secretary tells me you married well."

"Good news travels fast," Alex said. "What's this all about, Royce? I don't understand the secrecy. Where are we going and why?"

"Relax. I can't tell you much 'cause I don't know a real lot myself. A certain important person wants to talk to you. He flew in special from Rome a few days ago. My understanding is that he has lots of enemies. All of these precautions are designed to keep him safe."

"This interview involves the Circumcellions?"

"I guess so," Royce said, shrugging. "He's been feeding me information for my column about this new hate group. In return, I've passed along any feedback that comes across my desk. Yours was the first bit of news that interested him."

Unexpectedly, their car swerved right, cutting a corner sharply. Immediately after, the driver stepped hard on the accelerator. Their auto barreled down the deserted street at 60 miles an hour. The burst of speed sent Alex sprawling across the seat into Royce's lap.

"Better wear your seatbelt," the reporter said, grinning. "Seems to me that we picked up a tail."

As if to confirm Royce's words, the driver interrupted their conversation. "I believe, gentlemen, that we are being followed. Two cars, in tandem, latched onto us soon after we left Mr. Warner's domicile. They tried staying out of sight, but I forced their hand in the past few minutes. They dared not risk falling too far back. Sorry for any discomfort you suffered."

"What are you planning to do?" Alex asked.

"I hope to lose them once we get on the highway. The city streets are too treacherous with snow to do much maneuvering."

"Speaks well for a chauffeur, doesn't he?" Royce said, chuckling. "A smart man might suspect he does something else for a living."

"Like what?" Alex asked, barely listening to Royce's chatter. Hands gripping the edge of the seat, he leaned forward, anxious to check the driver's claims. Peering out of the smoked glass windows in the rear, he immediately spotted the two cars in question. On city streets edged with snow, they couldn't stay too far back without running the risk of losing contact.

Wordlessly, Alex drew his gun from his shoulder holster and laid it on the seat next to him. If push came to shove, he wanted to be ready to deliver the first punch. He disliked being in a position where his safety depended on someone else's skills, as was the case right now.

"You think we'll need that?" Royce asked, his eyes widening slightly. Otherwise, he seemed completely unconcerned by the turn of events.

"If they're only trying to follow us—no. If they plan something more, I prefer to be prepared for the worst."

They eased onto the Kennedy Expressway doing 40. Slowly and subtly, their driver increased their cruising speed. Within a few minutes, they were doing 60, weaving in and out of three lanes of traffic.

"Both cars are still behind us," the driver announced, sounding quite pleased. "Traffic is pretty steady tonight. I'll let them stay within striking distance until we reach the airport. Then I'll take a swing around the terminals. It's down to one lane in arrivals. The merge will do them in. By the time they untangle themselves from that mess, we'll be long gone. O'Hare is a wonderful place for losing tails."

"You spot anyone up front?" Alex asked.

"No one," the driver replied. "They drive pretty well, but they're still amateurs."

Alex settled back in his seat, feeling a little more relaxed. Professionals used a third car in tailing maneuvers, usually patrolling in front of the pack. The agents in the lead car used a car-phone to keep the trailers abreast of any sudden reversals by their prey. In effect, the stalkers maintained a moving box around their quarry. It was a difficult technique to master, especially in dense highway traffic.

"A certain important person?" Alex said, his thoughts returning to what Royce said. He turned the phrase over in his mind. "Who, Royce?"

"His name is Francesco Cova. He calls himself a simple Italian priest, but he wields a lot more power than any priest I ever met. As far as I can tell, he reports directly to you-know-who."

"What's he want with me?"

Royce shrugged. "Beats the hell out of me. According to my sources, Cova heads some sort of in-house investigative task force for the Church. You know what I mean. He checks up on the conduct of priests and stuff like that."

"You make him sound like a hatchet man for the Pope."

"Yeah," Royce said, waving his cigar. "I guess so. And the description fits. Cova's as tough a character as you'd care to meet. I ran into him a few years ago while investigating a story linking certain church figures with the international crime syndicate. There were rumors of financial hocus-pocus taking place at the Vatican Bank. A smart man, backed by the wealth of the church, could make millions manipulating the currency market, especially if he was working closely with the Mafia."

"I seem to remember reading about a certain Bishop, originally from Chicago." Alex said.

"Tell me about him," Royce said, sarcastically. "Damned fool took advantage of his friendship with the Pope at the time to line his own pockets. Anyway, that's when I ran into Cova. Working our separate ways, we both came up with the same name around the same time. Somehow, Cova found out about my research. He visited me at my apartment in Rome the night I started writing up my story. He didn't waste any time with idle threats. Three days was all he wanted. Then, the story was mine. An exclusive, no less, with the full cooperation of the Church."

"And if you didn't agree?" Alex asked, sensing more.

Royce laughed. "If I refused to cooperate, as soon as he left my apartment, he would pass my name along to a powerful Mafia boss. Father Cova assured me that the local syndicate would be very put out by my investigation."

"You delayed the story?"

"You bet," Royce said with a snort. "A good reporter knows the difference between courage and stupidity. I never let my principles stand in the way of my life. The series broke three days later, just like Father Cova wanted, with me safely back in the U.S. of A. In the meantime, the bishop in question quietly vanished, as did most of the scandal involving the Church. Italian police blamed his disappearance on his disgruntled partners. I suspected otherwise."

Alex nodded. During the Vietnam War, he had met several Special Forces Agents engaged on missions similar to Father Cova's. They maintained surveillance on their own forces, watching for signs of corruption or treason. In all cases, the men left nothing to chance. They dispensed justice ruthlessly and without mercy.

"No further signs of pursuit," their driver announced, sounding very satisfied with himself. "If we encounter no further problems, we should be at our destination in twenty minutes."

"Easy enough," Royce said, taking another drag on his cigar.

"Almost too easy," Alex said, holstering his gun.

He wondered if the whole episode hadn't been set up merely to get their attention. But for what reason? And, more important, by whom? Alex suspected that he would know the answers to both those questions before the night was over.

Chapter Thirteen

A half hour later, the limo pulled up to the gates of a secluded estate in the far western suburbs. Located in the center of three forest preserves, the house was totally isolated from the outside world.

Without a word, their driver rolled down his window. The beam of a powerful flashlight swept the interior of the car, stopping on Alex's features for an instant, then disappearing. "Any trouble?" asked an unseen watchman.

"Some jokers tailed us for a while, but I lost them at the airport."

"Circumcellions?"

"Probably. Stay on your guard, though. The whole incident could have been staged to lull our suspicions. If they already know the location of this base, an attack could come at any time."

"I'm ready for them," the watchman replied. His tone of voice implied he welcomed the possibility. "Drive on. I'll signal the house."

A short private drive led to a large mansion. The huge stone and brick house backed right up to the forest. In front, two large searchlights illuminated the grounds. Several men, all wearing black, lounged about close to the lights. They all carried automatic weapons and appeared ready to use them.

"Welcome to the war zone," Royce said, as their driver steered their limo up to the front door of the mansion.

Another man, carved from granite and equally silent, escorted them to a large, empty parlor. Without a word, he took their coats and departed.

"Sure are a talkative bunch, ain't they?" Royce said, cackling. Then he spotted a bottle of brandy and several glasses on a nearby table. "Hospitable, though. They even got the right brand. Have a snort?"

"No thanks," Alex said. "Don't let me stop you."

The columnist needed no encouragement. He downed a hefty slug, then poured himself a refill. "Keeps the blood flowing."

Alex grinned. Royce explained every vice with a homily.

"You pick up any clues to what's going on here, Warner?" Royce asked, sounding a bit nervous. "I'm in over my head now.

"That was no ordinary chauffeur who drove us here, and those guys outside weren't choirboys. I've seen their type before. They eat nails for breakfast and like it."

Alex had his suspicions but kept them to himself. He disliked speculating without any hard evidence to back up his opinions.

"Who do you think tried following us? Some sort of gang of urban terrorists?"

"Not terrorists, Mr. Royce—fanatics," answered a voice from the far side of the room.

A short, muscular man came striding across the room. Iron-gray patches dotted his jet black hair, and his beard was flecked with white. But the harsh lines of his face betrayed no signs of age. Dressed in the simple garb of a priest, he walked like a soldier.

"Gentlemen, I am pleased you could join me tonight. Mr. Royce I have met before. Professor Warner, I am honored to make your acquaintance. I am, as you probably already know, Francesco Cova."

They shook hands. Cova had a grip like a steel vise. His calloused, gnarled hands and sun-darkened skin made it quite clear he did not spend much of his time behind the pulpit.

"I am here in your country visiting relatives," Cova said. "Or so the story goes. This mansion belongs to a friend of a friend."

"I gather you associate with people in high places," Alex said, dryly.

"I expect Mr. Royce told you of my work,"

Cova said, betraying the bare traces of a smile. "Actually, several of my cousins live in the Chicago area. The best falsehoods always contain a shred of truth at their center. If possible, I will even stop in and see them once my real mission is completed."

"Now you're talking," Royce said, perking up. "Let's cut out this chatter and get down to business. What's goin' on here, Cova? Why did you drag me and Warner up here to see you? And who are those goons outside?"

Cova shook his head slowly, sorrowfully. "No one ever would accuse you of civility, my dear Mr. Royce. However, I accept you with all your faults. We are all God's children."

The priest swung around and faced Alex. "Perhaps you might care for a drink, Professor? A light snack?"

"I'm fine. All I need are some straight answers. And maybe a beer."

Chuckling, the priest waved a hand. As if by magic, a burly man appeared in the door carrying a tray with several frosted bottles of beer and a bowl of pretzels.

"Your usual brand, I trust," Cova said. "Mr. Royce's assistant provided the information."

"A remarkable woman," Alex said.

"Remarkable," Royce repeated, grumbling. "Now that you've finished playing the considerate host, Cova, can we get down to hard facts?"

"Certainly," Cova said, no longer smiling. "Shall we be seated?"

They settled in a circle of plush chairs. Leaning forward so that his elbows rested on his knees, Cova did most of the talking. He spoke with the barest trace of an accent. Though he laughed easily, his eyes remained hard and wary.

"Like any multinational organization, the Catholic Church needs a few dedicated men to act as troubleshooters, dealing with emergencies that cannot be handled on the local level. I normally work alone or in conjunction with the local church hierarchy. Only rarely will I call upon the resources of the Vatican for assistance."

"The men outside and the chauffeur?" Alex asked slowly, with dawning comprehension. "Jesuits?"

"Does their identity really matter? They traveled here from all over the Midwest at the request of my mentor. Dozens of them scour the city as we speak. They all search for the whereabouts of one man, a man who threatens the entire structure of the church. A man I think you've met, Mr. Warner."

"Brother Ambrose," Alex said.

Cova's eyes narrowed. "Correct. Do you know the location of the renegade and his followers?"

"Sorry, Father, but we parted on bad terms. He never mentioned any secret hideaway during our brief conversation."

Cova grimaced. "I had hoped for more. Exactly what occurred at this meeting?"

Seeing no reason to lie, Alex gave a brief account of the events of the past few days. He edited out any mention of black magic and transformed Dietrich Vril from a sinister figure of mystery to a wealthy rare book collector who happened to be hated by Ambrose for some unknown reason. Otherwise, he let the facts speak for themselves.

"A book?" Cova said thoughtfully when Alex finished speaking. "But if he was aware where the volume was all along, why did Brother Ambrose have his men commit those other, earlier crimes? They were completely unnecessary."

"I can guess the answer to that one," Royce said. "Protective coloration. Ambrose organized the first attacks as a ploy to divert attention from the one that mattered—the last. The priest used random violence as a smoke screen. He reasoned that a series of raids would imply the crimes were racially motivated, which is exactly what he wanted people to think. If it hadn't been for Warner, you would have never realized that only the burning of Rosenberg's store mattered."

"But why didn't he just buy the book?" Cova asked.

"He tried," Alex said. "But he was dealing with a man of honor. Rosenberg had already promised the volume to another customer. To Howie, a bargain made was a bargain kept."

"He sounds like a man worth knowing," Cova said.

"He was," Alex said. "The Circumcellions killed him."

"Hey," Royce said, interrupting in a loud voice, "the police reports never mentioned any murder."

"Ambrose Haxley is a master schemer," Cova said. "He is guilty of a thousand crimes but has yet to be prosecuted for any of them."

Royce shoved an unlit cigar into his mouth and started chewing on it unmercifully. "This stuff is getting too complicated for me. I need a story that makes sense. How about if we start at the beginning? That okay with you?"

Cova grimaced. "The roots of this conflict are buried fifteen hundred years in the past. Most of it is of interest only to Church historians and a few men like myself who battle the enemies of the Church in secret. How much do you want to know?"

"All of it," Alex said. "Saul probably couldn't care less, but I want to know the truth—the whole truth. I must know." He hesitated for a second, then went on. "An innocent man died, and I still don't understand why."

A dark shadow passed across Cova's face. He frowned, deepening the lines on his forehead. Reaching out, he gripped Alex by the wrist. "The fate of the Church depends on my mission. Are you willing to share that responsibility?"

"Hell's bells," Royce said, angrily. "Will you two old women stop beating around the bush and lay your cards on the table. After all, we're all on the same side. Right?"

"Correct," Cova said, as if making an important decision. "I sense that each of us in our own way struggles against the darkness."

The priest rose to his feet. "Excuse me for one moment. I cannot deal with this problem without a glass of brandy."

Cova drained a snifter with one gulp, then poured another. "My one vice," he said, not sounding particularly contrite. "I am forbidden good women, so I find solace in good brandy."

Then the priest's voice grew serious. "Listen carefully to the greatest threat ever to face the Catholic Church. This threat must be quashed before it makes the religious conflicts of the past thousand years seem like children's conflicts."

Cova tossed off the second drink as quickly as the first. The powerful liquor seemed to have no effect on him. "It all began in the fourth century. A major split occurred between the Church of Rome and that of North Africa. This schism, which lasted nearly three hundred years, was known as Donatism, after its leader, Donatus of Numidia.

"Two pillars of faith supported the African branch of the Catholic Church. One was the ideal of purity among priests, and the second was that a zeal for martyrdom took precedence over all other acts. Following that belief, congregations felt strongly that they could not follow any priest who was also a sinner.

"The original rift started when the clergy and congregations of Carthage refused to accept the election of the archdeacon Caecilian as Bishop of Carthage. Many there felt that Caecilian had maltreated prisoners in jail and thus was a sinner. By their beliefs, he therefore could not administer a valid sacrament."

"I'm bored already," Royce said. "When does the action start?"

"After long legal arguments, the petition of the Donatists was rejected by both the Pope and the Emperor. Persecution followed, but the movement thrived. The Donatists reigned supreme in North Africa for a hundred years.

"However, early in the fifth century, Augustine wrote a series of famous tracts that showed there was no justification in the schism. He further stated that their rejection of universality as the standard of Catholicism as well as their erroneous teachings on the sacraments made the Donatists heretics. The edict of 412 A.D. banned Donatism, confiscated their property and sent the leaders of the movement into exile. It was the end of the threat.

"However, not all of the Donatists accepted the judgment of the Church. As early as 340 A.D., a band of extremists formed a secret order known as the Circumcellions. A secret band, they met *circum cellas,* or 'around the tombs' of martyrs. A revolutionary group, they regarded the Church of Rome as too lax. To them, martyrdom was the greatest reward possible for a good Catholic, thus no sacrifice was seen as too extreme."

"Sounds like the same type of dogma spouted by the SLA, PLF and all those other seventies revolutionary groups," Royce said.

"Not to mention a thousand other band of

zealots since the dawn of time," Alex said. "I take it the Circumcellions did not comply with the edict."

"From that time on, they held the Pope personally responsible for their persecution. They regarded him as their enemy and did all they could to undermine his rule. According to many historians, they played a major role in the invasion of Roman Africa in 429 A.D. by the Vandals. Shortly after that event, they disappeared without a trace.

"Church historians assumed the heretics perished during the hundred-year Vandal occupation. Evidently, they went underground to escape persecution. The order developed into a small, fanatical band of extremists, dedicated to the destruction of the Papacy. New members were recruited from the ranks of priests sympathetic with their ideas. While never numbering more than a few hundred, the Circumcellions continued to plot against the Pope over the centuries."

"I never heard of them," Royce said, sounding unconvinced.

"They engineered the death of two Popes and unsuccessfully tried to murder a dozen others," Cova replied, his face a mask of harsh lines and angles.

"Faced with an unseen enemy, the Church put into effect a series of strict measures designed to wipe out the heretics once and for all. Until recently, all signs indicated that the counterstroke had effectively ended the Donatist threat."

Thoughtfully, Alex rubbed his chin with thumb and index finger. He knew a little about the Donatist movement, but the story of the Circumcellions was new to him. Still, none of the facts he possessed jelled together to make any sort of sense. He still had no idea what was going on. He hoped that Francesco Cova would provide the necessary pieces to solve this elaborate mental jigsaw puzzle.

"As you probably know, many conservative Catholics feel that recent changes in the Church are much too liberal. They feel such moves to the left border on heresy. Prime targets of their wrath are the activist priests in Central and South America and the outspoken clergy in your country.

"These conservative elements constantly push for a return to the dogma and ritual of the old days. Bound by their faith, they cannot question the teachings of Christ's vicar on Earth, the Pope. However, in secret many of them wish for a day when the Holy Father no longer ruled the Church.

"It is to those elements that this latest incarnation of the Circumcellions aims its messages. No longer a secret society, the order represents itself as an alternative to liberal Catholicism. Under the brilliant leadership of Ambrose Haxley, the Circumcellions have recruited thousands of dissatisfied churchgoers to their cause.

They preach a brand of religious and racial intolerance similar to the credo embraced by many of the ultra-right-wing groups flourishing in your country today. Forging strong ties with conservative religious orders throughout the world, they continually hammer away at one steady theme. The Pope and the Church of Rome no longer represent the beliefs of a majority of Catholics. Only the Donatists offer a path to true salvation.

"The Circumcellions continue to work quietly, recruiting many of their members from the body of the Church itself. Not all of them work in the open. Instead, they bore from within. I suspect many high-ranking Vatican officials are aiding them. Haxley is a determined, relentless fighter. He knows that most Catholics are faithful to the Pope. Instead, he plots to overthrow the Holy Father with treachery and deceit."

"Can't the Church do something about these guys?" Royce asked. "You banned them once before."

"These are different times, and the Church has different powers," Cova said, sounding frustrated and annoyed. "The Vatican can do nothing against the Circumcellions. They no longer call themselves a branch of the Catholic Church. Laws bind us like any other organization or government. The heretics break no legal rules by preaching against the Pope; many outside the Church do the same. Haxley and his followers laugh at us as they plot our downfall."

Cova smiled. "In their arrogance, the

Circumcellions forget one thing. We both come from the same roots. The Church has survived nearly two thousand years not through piety or luck, but by plot and counterplot. Desperate threats call for equally desperate measures. Drawn into this struggle by sheer coincidence, I have sworn a vow to destroy this threat to the Church—forever. And that is what I will do, no matter what means are necessary."

Cova did not expand on what he meant by that last sentence. Not that it was necessary. The determined look on his rough features spoke louder than any words. As Alex watched he wondered if the priest weren't a fanatic equally as dangerous as any of the Circumcellions.

Suddenly, a muffled thump caught Alex's attention. Then, without any other warning, the floor shook beneath his feet. Cova staggered, nearly falling. The glass of brandy in his hand went flying, spraying his shirt with liquor. Outside, guns barked with the dull chatter of automatic fire.

Chapter Fourteen

"We're under attack!" bellowed a big, ruddy-faced man, stumbling into the room. "By the looks of things, they outnumber us two to one."

The big man cursed. "Haxley outmanuevered us. While my men hunted him in Chicago, he gathered his forces and attacked us at our base. Only a skeleton force of Jesuits remained on patrol tonight. That half-hearted attempt to follow our car put us off guard. The Circumcellions caught us by surprise."

"The men at the gatehouse?" Cova asked. "What happened to them?"

"Gone." There was no mistaking the finality of that pronouncement. "And the same fate faces you if you don't flee immediately. We can only hold them back for a few minutes."

"I don't run from fights," Cova said, angrily.

"If you die, then they win," the other man said just as passionately. "You are the only one who knows the full extent of Ambrose's schemes. That is why he staged this wild attack. Without you to thwart their plans, the Circumcellions triumph."

"Enough," Cova said curtly, obviously not liking what he was hearing. "We will do as you say."

"Stay here," the big man said. "I will return in a moment."

"What the hell?" Royce fumed, once they were alone again. "It sounds like a war is taking place out front. Where are the police?"

"The same place they were when Rosenberg's store was attacked," Alex said. "In any case, our attackers probably took out the phone lines when they struck. We're trapped."

"Not true," Cova said. "This mansion backs up onto forest preserve land. A path behind the house leads through the woods to a small picnic area a few miles away. Beyond that lies Oakwood Park. Most of my men are stationed there incognito. Once in town, we will be safe."

Just as Cova finished speaking, the lights went out. Total darkness enveloped them. Cova muttered a few phrases in Italian that Alex felt sure were not prayers for their safety.

"They cut the power lines," Alex said. "They must be getting ready for their final push."

The big man hurried back into the room. In

one hand, he held a flashlight, and across his shoulders, he carried their overcoats. "You must depart immediately. My men are not sure how much longer they can defend this haven."

They quickly donned their coats. Alex shoved his automatic into one of the pockets, where he could retrieve it in an instant. Royce nodded briefly, indicating that he too was armed.

The man aiding them passed along a pistol and flashlight to Father Cova. "You know the path. Go now. We will hold them off as long as possible."

"Do not sacrifice yourselves," Cova said, shaking hands with the other man. "Hide in the woods once the mansion falls. I want no martyrs in my name."

"Let's go," Royce said, chomping hard on his unlit cigar. "I just remembered I forgot to pay the last installment on my insurance policy. I wanna get home and put it in the mail!"

With Cova in the lead, they made their way to the rear of the mansion. Cautiously, they exited through a sliding door onto a huge wooden deck that extended many feet back into the dense forest.

A blanket of deep snow covered the deck to within a few feet of the tempered glass doors. The wind howled mournfully as they forced their way through the drifts.

Sporadic gunfire echoed from the front of the house. "Make haste, make haste," Cova said, anxiously. "My men cannot hold out very long against such overwhelming odds. We must be well into the woods by the time the Circumcellions overrun this place."

Without another word, they pushed their way into the underbrush. Cova took the lead, with Royce second and Alex bringing up the rear.

The priest followed a narrow path cut through the heart of the forest. The trail wove back and forth among the giant trees. According to Cova, the picnic area was three miles away. A brisk half-hour walk in the summer—an eternity on a winter night.

For the first five minutes, they made good time. The sound of gunfire faded into the night, and soon the dense foliage swallowed up all traces of the mansion. They trudged their way through the silent forest, each man lost in his own thoughts.

The wind whistled about them, blowing snow up and around with each gust. Soon, all three men glistened white with a thin coating of frost. The heavy snow clung to their boots like anchors. Every step took an effort, and their pace slowed.

The intense cold drained them of strength. "Just call me Frosty the Snowman," Royce said, trying to brush his overcoat clean. "Damn, I hate this stuff."

"Keep your voice down," Alex said, softly. "Sounds carry in this weather."

"You think they're following us?" Royce asked.

"Not yet," Alex said. "And we have too much

of a head start in this cold to worry about anyone catching up with us from behind."

"You suspect an ambush?" Father Cova asked, glancing back at Alex.

"Of course. You understand why."

His face drawn and forlorn, the priest nodded. "One of my men must have betrayed us. How else did Ambrose learn the location of my headquarters and the best time to attack? I realized the truth as soon as the fighting started. Nonetheless, this path offered the only chance of escape."

"If he told them about the mansion, then the traitor probably mentioned the escape route as well," Royce said, sounding grim. "Talk about rats caught in a trap."

"Armed rats," Alex said, pulling the gun from his pocket. "I've escaped from worse. Remember, these fanatics lack experience in this type of fighting. I lived and breathed covert actions for years. If anything happens, follow my lead."

He saw no reason to mention that all of his experience in outdoor fighting came from jungle warfare in Asia, not in the snowbound woods of northern Illinois. Royce's confidence needed a boost. "Trust me."

They pressed deeper into the silent woods. Royce peered suspiciously behind every tree and every snowbank. The shuffling of their feet through the heavy snow was the only sound breaking the quiet of the night.

Father Cova maintained a steady pace, carrying the flashlight in one hand and the automatic in the other. His wary eyes surveyed the surrounding forest.

Alex let the feel of the woods flow into his consciousness. He learned the trick long ago in Vietnam. Taking long shallow breathes, he imagined his mind merging with the forest that encircled them. Relaxing his mind, he let his thoughts become one with the peace and tranquility of the wilds. In doing so, he heightened his awareness of the surroundings, thus letting his subconscious mind sort out any inconsistencies in the solitude.

His mind functioned on two levels. Externally, he kept a close watch on the trail behind them. At the same time, his inner eye probed the night, searching for danger ahead.

They navigated their way through the woods in the dim moonlight. Father Cova used the flashlight only when clouds hid the moon. Nothing stirred. Nothing moved as they trekked on. The woods seemed frozen in time.

"How much further?" Royce asked. "I think my toes turned to ice cubes five minutes ago."

"Stay cool," Alex said, chuckling. "I estimate we've walked nearly two miles. Another fifteen or twenty minutes—"

The barest hint of sound stopped him in mid-sentence. It rippled through the night air, battering his senses like a tangible wave. Alex stopped, clenched his hands into fists and tried to pinpoint the exact location of the sound. It seemed to come from above where they stood, high above the treetops. Before he could be absolutely sure, the sound vanished, not to be repeated.

A coldness unrelated to the chill of the night air swept through his body, and he shivered with unknown dread as he remembered that same whisper from a dozen trips to the zoo. Bats made that strange noise, gliding through the air in flight. Magnify their eerie whistle a thousandfold . . . His mind reeled with the thought. Suddenly, he knew something monstrous and inhuman haunted the woods tonight.

His mood immediately communicated itself to his companions. Both men raised their guns and looked around nervously. Trees seemed to reach in at them menacingly. Royce's well-chewed cigar dropped from his lips to the earth, but he made no move to pick it up.

"What is it, my son?" Francesco Cova asked, so softly he could barely be heard. The priest gripped his flashlight like a club, his gun momentarily forgotten. "Are we at risk?"

"I don't know, Father," Alex answered, drawing in a breath. "In any case, better let me take the lead. I sense something is wrong up ahead—something very, very wrong."

Chapter Fifteen

They proceeded cautiously, trying to make as little noise as possible. Their heavy breathing vibrated like drumbeats in the dead quiet of the night. The total absence of any other sounds worried Alex. Even during the coldest winter nights, predators prowled the forest. This absolute hush was unnatural.

Peering ahead, Alex saw the line of trees came to an abrupt end 100 feet ahead. Motioning the others to remain, he slipped off the trail and crept forward. The snow muffled the sound of his passage, as he darted from tree to tree, doing his best to blend in with his surroundings.

A small clearing some 50 feet across stood before him, and he realized it was the picnic grove mentioned by Father Cova. Several old wooden tables and benches dotted the expanse, along with a solitary black garbage drum. A narrow road, not much wider than a car, disappeared into the forest on the far side of the expanse. A lone metal sign, perched on a rusted pole, proclaimed: "James Donne Forest Preserve—For Picnics Only."

Nothing stirred. The area appeared devoid of life. His inner eye indicated nothing amiss. Cautiously, Alex rose to his feet. Only then did he notice the bodies in the snow.

Time stopped for an instant. Howie Rosenberg's tale of horror 50 years ago flashed through his mind. It, too, took place on a bitter cold night. According to Makoto Tsuiki, the Very Old Folk thrived in temperatures below zero. The frightful whisper of giant wings haunted his memory. He knew, without any question, that horror awaited him in the clearing.

With the wave of an arm, he beckoned his companions forward. Not waiting to see if they followed, he walked out onto the field. He stopped a few feet away from the nearest body. Five dead men sprawled face down on a small rise of land in the center of the clearing.

The hard-packed snow blended in with the white pants and ski jackets they all wore. Dropped in apparent disregard near each body was a high-powered rifle. Alex glanced at the guns. One look told him all he wanted to know. Hunters rarely used sniper-scopes, unless they hunted human prey.

"You notice any footprints?" Royce asked, coming up behind Alex. "Other than our own, that is? The ground right here is too chewed up to record any markings, but that ain't the case for the rest of the park. Check out the snow surrounding these guys. There's not a mark other than their own prints. See what I mean? Even snowshoes or skis leave a trail."

"Here's proof positive of a traitor in your midst, Father Cova," Alex said, stepping closer to the nearest body. "See these rifles. They planned to wait for us here and pick us off when we came out of the woods. They probably parked their car a little way back up that road to hide the sound of their arrival. Their footprints circle back that way."

"Maybe they left another man with their vehicle?"

"Possible, though I doubt it. Or, if they did, I'm willing to bet he's dead, too. Whoever killed them was pretty thorough."

"The question remains," Royce said, "who killed them—and how—and why?"

"I don't know," Alex said. "There's only one way to find out."

Reaching down, he grabbed a corpse by the shoulder. "The body still feels warm. They died only a little while ago."

With a tug, he turned the man face up—and recoiled in horror.

Behind him, Father Cova choked down an oath. Prepared for the worst, Alex still felt faint. He recognized the victim immediately. It was the sadistic priest, Brother Malachi. Or what was left of him.

Powerful jaws had ripped the man's throat and chest to shreds. The head rested on an impossible angle against one shoulder. There was too little left of his neck to hold it upright. Strands of flesh and cartilage hung down like strings across crushed white bone.

Alex forced himself to look at the carnage. He could see where incredibly strong teeth had bit right through the muscles of the neck, ripping them apart. The man's chest had been torn open, exposing his heart and lungs. Broken bones were everywhere. But, except for a few red marks, there was no blood.

"Even Malachi Ganzer deserved a better fate than this," Cova whispered, fear thick in his throat. He made the sign of the cross. "God grant peace to his troubled soul."

Royce bent down for a closer inspection. Without the least hesitation, he stared intently at the terrible wounds.

"I worked for ten years as a police reporter," he said without the least trace of emotion in his voice. "You grow hardened to murder after a while, though I can't recall seeing anything this brutal before. Whoever bumped him off made it look easy. Spooky as hell, the way there's no blood around. The other four die the same way?"

"I'll check," Alex said, not relishing the thought.

Father Cova assisted him in turning over the

other corpses. Each one revealed the same terrible mutilations. With one body, so much of the neck was gone that the head remained stationary when they started shifting the torso. That cadaver they left alone.

"Whoever killed them all believed in uniformity," Alex said, shaken. He had no doubt he knew the identity of the killers, but he didn't think the other men were ready yet to accept his explanation. "They all died the same way, their throats slashed to ribbons, their chests ripped apart."

"All the bodies still warm?" Royce asked.

"You guessed it," Alex said.

Father Cova walked up and down the rows of bodies. Each man he identified as one of Brother Ambrose's followers. Two of them were the men who had accompanied Malachi on his mission to Alex's home. According to the priest, the victims were the most notorious killers and assassins belonging to the Circumcellions.

"Ambrose sent the best men he had to finish the job," Cova said. "The attack on the house was merely a ploy to herd us in the right direction. We were meant to die in this grove. In a way, we should feel flattered. He sent five ruthless killers to finish the three of us."

Cova chuckled, sounding a bit ghoulish. "Wait until he discovers how these men died. The condition of their bodies should make him pause and wonder."

"Let him worry," Royce said. "He's not the only one. Who wasted these bozos?"

"I have no explanation," Father Cova said. "Divine providence works in mysterious ways."

"Let's find their car," Alex said, refusing to be drawn into the discussion. "No sense walking to town if we can ride. They sure aren't going to need it."

As they backtracked the footprints, Royce continued to chatter away nervously. "They dropped their rifles and collapsed. There was no sign of a struggle from any of them. That indicates to me that none of them reacted to the plight of their comrades. They all succumbed at the same time. Maybe a powerful sleeping gas put them out. Lots of nerve toxins work by merely touching the skin."

"Nonsense," Father Cova said, his voice none too steady. "Even if we assumed the existence of such an element and an agency to use it, those men passed out in the middle of a clearing. No gas cloud could hold together long enough in tonight's wind to drift through an area that large. And what about the killing wounds? No gas cloud did that."

"A wolf . . . or a wild dog," Royce said uneasily, "driven mad by rabies. Or I got another idea. It's possible that this region of the forest preserve once housed an experimental base used by the army for dangerous chemical warfare experiments. That would explain the gas. Maybe government workers buried canisters of the stuff in the clearing. You know, the way they handled radioactive waste. Pretended it didn't exist and left it here to be forgotten.

"One of the Circumcellions accidentally stumbled on a trigger mechanism, releasing the stuff. Rising from the ground, the fumes killed them before anyone realized what was happening. Then, the wind blew the gas away before we arrived on the scene."

"And what of the wounds? Are you suggesting that the same lab also housed an experimental lab animal that came along and ripped out their throats? A creature that left no footprints and vanished into the night without a trace? Or perhaps some flying monster landed where they stood and killed them. At least, that explanation would account for the lack of tracks. I think your ideas extend beyond the limits of credibility, my friend."

"Then you figure it out," Royce said angrily. His face was flushed with fear. "At least my theory fits the facts. Not very well, but at least they offer some explanation for the killings."

"And not a bad one at that," Cova said, a bit more subdued, "but you ignored one important detail. One fact that we all noticed immediately but never once stated aloud. A thing we feared so deeply we dared not ask. What happened to all the blood?"

Royce inhaled deeply. "Not a trace of it on their clothing," he said, his voice shaking. "And their wounds showed clean. Not a drop visible anywhere."

"Gashes like those spurt blood like a fountain," Cova said. "The ground should have been soaked with it, and yet the snow around them was perfectly white. Not a trace of red anywhere. I repeat," and there was a quiet note of desperation in the priest's voice, "what happened to all the blood?"

Chapter Sixteen

They found the car a few hundred feet up the road. Alex, least shaky of the three, drove. Oakwood Park was only a short drive down the road, and it would only take a few minutes to get there.

The first few minutes, all three men remained silent, muted by the killings in the woods. Then Royce, no longer quite so loud or so bold, spoke. "How did you get involved tracking down Ambrose Haxley, Father?"

Cova licked his lips, as if contemplating his answer.

"I stumbled on the Circumcellions' plot against the Pope entirely by accident. Others in the Church monitored their activities. My work never put me in contact with the heretics until recently.

"As Mr. Royce already knows, I act as an internal policeman for the Catholic Church. It is my duty to correct situations that might embarrass the Holy Father or the Church itself. In this area, I reign supreme, answering only to the Pope. My word is law. It is a position of great power, and I try never to abuse it.

"In most cases, I deal with scandalous behavior by brethren who have succumbed to temptation. It is not a pleasant job, but one that must be done. I flatter myself in thinking I do a good job. I do know for a fact I perform the task as best it can be done.

"From time to time, my investigations take an odd turn. Recently, the curator of the Vatican vaults began a detailed survey of the treasures of the Church. It was the first comprehensive study done in nearly a century. Only a few older priests had any idea of the full scope of rarities preserved from the public eye. It was a long, laborious task that should have been done years before.

"A few weeks after beginning the project, the curator came to me with disturbing news. He had discovered one of the rarest pieces in the collection was missing.

"At first, he assumed that the item had merely been misplaced. However, the further he checked, the more he became convinced that the treasure had been taken from the vaults—and not recently. According to what inventory lists existed, the piece had not been cataloged in over a half-century, meaning that it vanished during the late 1930's."

"Who took it?" Alex asked, sensing something very important in what Cova was saying.

"No one knows for sure. There are several theories, most of them centering around the curator of the vaults at that time. An elderly priest named Bruno Scaretti, he was notorious for his extremely conservative beliefs. The few friends of his still alive remember that he openly expressed his admiration for the Nazis and Adolf Hitler.

"Scaretti belonged to a group of high-ranking church officials who believed that the Vatican should work closely with the fascists. They felt that cooperation was the only way to protect Catholics in Germany from Nazi repression. There was even talk of a possible bribe. Fortunately, those ideas were rejected by the Pope, but I suspect Scaretti plotted on his own.

"During that period, the Nazi envoy to the Vatican was a close friend of Hitler with a reputation for delving into forbidden mysteries. I suspect that Scaretti smuggled the relic out of the Vatican and presented it to that diplomat sometime in 1937. The envoy left for Germany soon after. Scaretti died under suspicious circumstances the following month.

"Why the priest betrayed his trust we shall never know. Possibly the diplomat promised him a high position in the new order the Germans were constantly proclaiming. Or perhaps

Scaretti actually thought by giving up the relic he was saving the lives of thousands of innocents.

"It matters little. My concern is with the present and finding the missing relic before Brother Ambrose can obtain it."

"Why?" Royce asked, sounding very much the reporter. "I don't see what the fuss is all about."

"Under normal circumstances, it would not have been a cause of great concern, merely another lost artifact stolen from the Church. Then I learned that Ambrose Haxley and his followers were searching for the relic. They had obtained a clue to its location. Puzzled by their interest, I instructed my spies to learn more.

"Their report brought me to your country. I am engaged in a desperate race with Ambrose Haxley to locate the treasure. I cannot allow him to find it. The Circumcellions plan to use the relic to discredit and ultimately destroy the Papacy."

Features tight with emotion, Father Cova harshly explained.

"The Catholic Church often finds itself accused of anti-Semitism. No one denies the excesses of the past, but demonstrating that such a policy no longer influences the Church today often proves difficult. The Holy Father has not made matters any easier with several questionable meetings and statements over the past few years.

"More to the point, a great many people still believe that Pope Pius made a deal with the

Nazis before World War Two. He agreed not to speak out against their atrocities against the Jews as long as they left German Catholics undisturbed."

"Pure hokum," Royce said, flourishing a new cigar that appeared from some inner pocket of his coat. "That theory lost all credibility years ago. Lots of priests helped the Jews at the risk of their own lives. Plenty of books offered conclusive evidence that such a deal never existed."

"You know that, as do I, but most people remain unaware of those facts. Remember, there are those who refuse to believe the Holocaust even took place. Forget the truth, my friend. Only the public perception of the truth matters. If Ambrose Haxley presents physical evidence that the Pope collaborated with the Third Reich in their extermination of the Jews, the entire structure of the Church would suffer irreparable damage.

"At the same time, it would strengthen the Circumcellions' claim that the Church is willing to compromise faith for material gain. Remember, his order believes that martyrdom is one of the basic tenants of belief. Bargaining with the Nazis for the lives of priests would amount to heresy to Ambrose and his followers.

"Such arguments would unite conservative Catholics throughout the world with the Circumcellions. Could priests who escaped persecution by cooperating with the Reich administer the sacraments in good faith? It would be a rebirth of the whole Donatist debate. In these liberal times, such a schism could split the Church into two warring camps."

"You lost me again," Royce said. "What evidence does Haxley have that Pope Pius cut a deal with the Nazis?"

"The relic," Father Cova said. "Take into consideration the circumstantial evidence. You begin with the persistent rumors of a bargain made between the Vatican and the Nazis. Weigh the silence of the Pope against the momentary freedom of Catholic priests in Nazi Germany, then produce a priceless church treasure given to the Nazis as a good faith offering, and you have an argument that would convince many people that the Pope actively cooperated with the hated Nazis."

"Maybe throw in some old photos," Alex said, recalling his own espionage experiences, "directly linking high Vatican officials with Nazi generals."

"Such meetings often took place," Cova said, shuddering. "A number of times Pope Pius personally pleaded with the German ambassador for religious tolerance and restraint."

"Add pictures of those meetings to the physical evidence of the missing relic, and Brother Ambrose's arguments suddenly sound awfully believable," Royce said. "It adds up to one of the most audacious con jobs in all history."

"The success of the whole story depends on the heretic obtaining the lost relic," Cova said. "The future of the Church rests on me finding it first. I must locate it and return it to the Vatican

—or destroy it before it destroys us."

"What is this thing already?" Royce asked. "You never once mentioned that."

"A jewel encrusted box," Cova said, "that once belonged to Pope Leo. Legends describe it as having mystical powers. I know nothing about that. All I know is that it has the power to cripple, perhaps destroy, the Catholic Church."

"The Armageddon Box," Alex whispered, wondering what dark secrets, unsuspected by the others, the Pope's legacy contained.

Chapter Seventeen

Six of them sat in the Lancaster house parlor the next afternoon. Saul Royce rested on the sofa. He was dressed comparatively conservatively. In honor of the Christmas season, he wore a green pin-striped shirt with a red bow tie. Next to him sat Sally Stevens, pen poised over a steno pad. Dressed in a tight green sheath the same color as Royce's shirt, she was even more dazzling than Alex remembered. Even his wife seemed plain when compared to Royce's flashy companion.

On the columnist's other side sat Father Cova, his hands folded neatly in his lap. Stationed outside the house were a half-dozen Jesuits spoiling for a fight.

Makoto Tsuiki lounged in the rear of the room. Alex knew his friend never felt entirely at ease unless he was able to keep a watchful eye on everyone else in the room. There was a worried look on Mak's face. The account of the vampire attack had shaken him badly. For the first time Alex could remember, his friend looked frightened.

Valerie sat in one of the overstuffed lounge chairs facing her guests. She was dressed in a simple black and white jumpsuit that accentuated her blonde hair and trim figure. Alex stood behind her. Like Mak, he was never comfortable sitting when there were several people in a room, especially when Dietrich Vril was somewhere in the city.

The night before, they had abandoned the Circumcellions' car in a deserted section of town. A quick phone call from Cova had brought immediate aid. Two cars, filled with Jesuits armed to the teeth and ready for battle, picked them up in minutes. They were overjoyed to learn that Cova had escaped the trap.

"We returned from our trip downtown to find the mansion in ruins," declared an unnamed priest whose thick, bushy eyebrows gave his face a perpetual scowl. "All of the others were dead. Yours was the only body not found, so we assumed that you were Haxley's prisoner."

"Why would he want me alive?" Cova asked. "I escaped the attack through the sacrifices of our brethren. Professor Warner guided us through the forest. Without him, I would have been lost."

Cova said not a word about the intended ambush or the fate of the assassins. Alex followed his lead. There was still a traitor among the Jesuits.

They agreed to meet again the next afternoon. Alex anxiously wanted to question the priest about the missing treasure box. Cova's story added a few more pieces to the puzzle. Gradually, a web of intrigue stretching across half a century of history was taking shape. One thing was certain. Both Vril and Brother Ambrose wanted Pope Leo's legacy. And the only clue to its location was buried somewhere in the pages of the inscribed copy of *Alraune*.

"The time has come," Alex said, grimly, "to speak of many things."

"Like crazy religious fanatics who died with their throats ripped out," Saul Royce said, equally solemn. "You gonna give us the straight dope now, Warner?"

"Enough subterfuge," Father Cova said. "The mysterious killings we stumbled upon last night announced in particularly convincing fashion that a third party sought the Pope's puzzle box. Last night you revealed very little about your own motivations in these affairs. I understood your reluctance to trust a stranger to stay silent, but after finding those bodies . . ."

"Yeah," Royce said. "I never walked away from a fight, Warner. I don't plan to now. No one ever accused me of being a coward. Still, I like to know what I'm up against." The columnist shivered and shook his shoulders. "We trusted you. You gotta trust us."

"That sounds fair to me," Alex said. "Believe me, though, you might find this story hard to swallow."

Earlier that morning, after consulting with both Valerie and Mak, he had decided to divulge everything to the two men. He realized that anything he told Royce would filter down to Sally Stevens, so he had invited her to this council of war as well.

"It all started," he began, "in Dachau."

Nearly an hour later, he finished telling the tale. He left nothing out, from the vampires at the concentration camp to Brother Ambrose's assertion that Vril was the Antichrist.

Father Cova never said a word during the entire recitation. From time to time, Royce interrupted with a question to clarify a point, while Sally Stevens took copious notes.

"You spin a good yarn, Warner," Royce said, sipping from a cup of coffee provided by Valerie. "Now I understand why the three of you look so spooked. That Vril character has you pretty worried. Unfortunately, I suspect he's just a lunatic with a glandular problem. Vampires only exist in horror movies, and the only people capable of performing magic work in circuses."

Alex turned to Francesco Cova. "What about you, Father? Do you think I'm crazy?"

"I accept your story with minor reservations," the priest said solemnly. His face was grim. "Remember, the Church stands firmly against witchcraft in any form. However, I also am a very practical man. Sometimes the only way to defeat the devil is to use his own tools against him."

Alex nodded, wondering again why Cova was so intent on the puzzle box. The priest seemed willing to bend any belief in his pursuit of the treasure. He was dedicated to locating the box.

"Besides," Cova continued, with a slight smile, "I find it much easier to believe in vampires than hidden containers of nerve gas and wolves that stalk their victims without leaving tracks."

Royce grimaced, then laughed. "Okay, so my theories wins no prizes either. The Church accepts miracles. I don't. If there's so much black magic in the world, why haven't I ever encountered any of it?"

Slowly, carefully, Sally rose to her feet. Tucking her notebook under one arm, she looked down at her boss, a twinkle in her eye. "Saul—shut up."

Royce opened his mouth and then, after a moment's hesitation, closed it without saying a word.

"You always brag about being open-minded, but when faced with an impossible situation, you instantly reject the only explanation that fits all the facts. You wanted the truth, and Alex told you. Accept his story."

Royce shook his head. "Sorry, doll, but you

know me better than that. I can't work on faith alone."

A sly smile on her face, Valerie walked over to Royce. "We expected a line like that from you," she said, "so Sally and I prepared a little demonstration for your illumination."

Valerie's words caught Alex completely by surprise, but not half as much as they did Royce. "Sally and you?"

The redhead shook her head and sighed. "So much for the vaunted male ego. Did you really think we never were injured investigating all of those fringe groups because of our good looks? Or that they respected you as an important journalist? Your reputation might have helped a little, but my talents saved us more than once. Don't you remember that night at Steel Sam's bar?"

Royce groaned. "I always thought it pretty odd that the roof collapsed right when those punks started acting mean. Then there was the time we confronted those racists at the armory." He paused for a moment, thinking. "Hey, what about the fight at the KKK rally last year? You again?"

"Nope. You weaseled out of that mess on your own. Even my powers can only do so much."

"Show me," Royce said, sounding unconvinced. "I'm willing to admit that there were some incidents in the past that gave me pause more than once, but I always found some explanation if I searched hard enough. I love you, kid, but the stubborn streak in me demands hard evidence. I need solid proof, not a string of coincidences. There ain't no such thing as black magic."

"No sweat," Sally said. "I know you like a book, Saul. I'd be shocked if you asked for anything less."

She turned to Valerie. "All set?"

"Sure. You remember the spell?"

Sally nodded. The two women faced each other. Twisting their arms, they each grasped the other by the wrists—left hand to right wrist, right hand to left wrist. Eyes closed in concentration, they started chanting in a language unknown to Alex.

Royce watched intently, his eyes fixed on the two women only a few feet from him. He remained quiet, but the knowing, sarcastic smile on his face seemed to say, "Show me."

Nothing happened for nearly a minute. Then an odd look passed over Royce's face. He rose to his feet, looking bewildered. Shaking his head, he dropped his hands to the sides of his trousers. His eyes widened in amazement. He grabbed his hips with both hands and squeezed. Astonishingly, his face turned bright red with embarrassment.

"Wh-wh-what did you do with them?" he gasped, almost tongue-tied.

"Upstairs, first door to the left," Valerie said, starting to giggle.

Royce rushed out of the room, heading for the

stairs. The two women exploded into laughter. After a few seconds, they collapsed onto the sofa, still roaring.

"What the hell did you do?" Alex asked, grinning but not knowing the reason why.

"A trick we learned years ago," Valerie said, trying to maintain a straight face. Tears of laughter trickled down her cheeks as she continued.

"As teenagers, Sally and I both studied black magic with Simon DuBois on the South Side. Following the protocols of magic, no one used their real name so we never knew the other's true identity. I moved from Chicago to New York a few years later, so we never ran into each other again. The other night, when she called, I recognized her voice immediately. While you were running all over the countryside, we girls had a nice long chat.

"Today, after you decided to tell Saul and Father Cova everything, I gave her a call. Sally swore her boss would never believe the story without a demonstration. I remembered a trick we learned way back when, and we decided to try it. Needless to say, it worked."

"What worked?"

"Telekenesis," Sally said, breaking into the conversation. "Neither Valerie nor I possess the necessary strength on our own, but working together, we can do it. Saul is a real sweetie, but he only understands things he can touch, taste, feel or smell. It's one of those qualities that makes him a good reporter. So we teleported his underwear to the upstairs bathroom."

"You did *what?*" Alex asked, flabbergasted.

"We teleported his jockey shorts," Sally repeated, grinning from ear to ear. "I think it convinced him."

Even Father Cova, who had watched and listened with a stone face, chuckled. "Perhaps not all witchcraft is inspired by Satan."

"It sure as hell would make me a believer in the supernatural," Alex said. "Here comes our doubting Thomas now. It's time for some serious talk."

"Yeah," Royce said, his face a bright shade of crimson. "No more arguments from me."

He dropped back to his place on the sofa. "Chalk up one for the forces of magic."

Chapter Eighteen

Makoto Tsuiki walked casually over to the windows at the front of the parlor. He peered outside, as if reassuring himself that no enemy approached.

"We possess a great deal of raw data," he said. "I suspect we have all the information necessary to find Pope Leo's treasure box. What we have to do is take the clues and fit them together into a cohesive whole."

"I agree," Father Cova said. "I think we would all agree that it was Karl Steiner who acquired the treasure from Scaretti in 1937, though I am puzzled why he wanted it."

"I can answer that," Valerie said. "Any magician would kill for a relic of such incredible age and power. Alex and I recently fought several powerful mages over an object similar to the treasure box. A powerful charm magnifies the strength of the user, enabling him to perform incredible feats of sorcery. The older the talisman, the greater the power it contains. According to what we've been told, the box bestowed on Pope Leo superhuman abilities over fifteen hundred years ago. It has been aging and thus gaining power for centuries. Who knows how powerful it would make a magician now?"

"Which raises a very interesting point," Mak said quietly. "Steiner had the box in his possession for years. During that time he worked on the enigmatic Project Alraune. What was he doing with it?"

"I suspect the secrets of that experiment are the key to this whole mystery," Alex said.

"Hold on," Royce said, his raspy voice commanding attention. "You skipped the sixty-four-thousand-dollar question. Steiner called his undertaking *Alraune,* the same name as the book with the clue to the treasure. What's the connection between the two?"

"How about this character Dietrich Vril who claims the book belongs to him?" Sally asked. "What part does he play in this whole affair? From what you implied—"

With a crash that echoed throughout the house, the front door slammed open. Steel glistened where the lock had been ripped out from the wood. The door rocked back and forth, held to the wall by only one hinge. Cold air blasted through the room as a giant of a man, dripping sweat, entered. Vril's gaze swept the room, searching for Alex.

"I've come for my book, Warner!" Vril bellowed, raising a clenched fist. "No more excuses. I want it now."

Alex stepped back, away from Valerie. He was very conscious of the automatic shoved in the waistband of his pants. His mouth felt very dry. He was afraid not only for himself but for his wife and friends.

Vril looked ready and willing to kill for the book. Cova had stationed six men outside the house, yet there was no sign of any of them. As if reading his mind, Vril laughed.

"You are all alone. Give me the book or die. I'll wipe the walls with your blood."

"Then how will you find the volume, Mr. Vril?" Valerie asked, her voice calm. She rose to her feet and stood next to Alex. "The only one who knows its location is Alex. He hasn't told anyone else. Killing him would insure you'd never get your hands on the book."

Vril's face reddened with anger. Snarling, he reached with surprising quickness to grab Valerie, but, almost quicker than the eye could follow, Mak was there. His hands flashed, and Vril barked in pain. The giant wrenched his arm back, flexing his digits in shocked surprise. By then Alex had his gun out, aimed straight at the giant's head.

Saul Royce and Sally Stevens were on their feet. Each of them pointed a gun at Vril. Off somewhat to the side was Father Cova. In both arms, he cradled a small but very deadly looking Skorpion pistol.

"I bet you use a spell to deflect bullets, Vril," he said, his voice flat and very cold. "But I happen to know that spell doesn't function properly in the presence of other practitioners of the black arts. You're in the wrong place, at the wrong time, with the wrong people."

The giant drew in a deep breath, as if suddenly realizing the precariousness of his position. After a second, he spread his arms wide, as if signaling his mistake. He even attempted a smile.

Alex kept his gun steady. Dietrich Vril was not a man to be trusted.

"My temper sometimes overwhelms my good judgment, Warner," the giant declared, his voice perfectly calm. He made no mention of his earlier threats. "I am perfectly willing to pay for the book. Name your price."

"Why do you want this book so badly?" Sally asked.

"The volume holds certain attachments for me," the big man answered without hesitation. "It once belonged to my grandfather."

"Oh," Sally continued, "you mean, Karl Steiner?"

A startled expression crossed Vril's face. For an instant, he seemed less confident than before.

"Yes, you guessed correctly," he answered, the faint smile no longer in evidence on his face.

His eyes blazed white hot. Droplets of sweat stained his shirt. "The book contains an inscription to Karl from my godfather, Hanns Heinz Ewers."

"A notorious heritage," Francesco Cova said. The priest stepped around so that he looked directly at Vril. "Of course, you were only a child when your grandfather died in a bombing raid."

"My mother perished giving me life," Vril said without any trace of emotion. "Steiner raised me. The old man taught me a great deal."

"I bet he even introduced you to some of his friends," Mak said from the corner. "The Very Old Folk."

Vril sneered. "My grandfather dealt with beings greater than himself. Friendship never entered in their bargaining. Did you consider a pet dog your equal? So it was with them. They taught him the dark secrets he desired—for a price. When they sought to impose their will on me, I resisted. Instead, I forced them to do my bidding. They learned to obey my wishes."

"Was that before or after you killed Steiner?" Royce asked. Silence dropped over the room like a shroud. "Why didn't you take the book then?"

"I could not find it," Vril answered, his face a demonic mask of hate. "The old man hid it and refused to tell me where. I tried ripping the information out of him, but he was weaker than I realized. The old fool died much too quickly, as did my godfather, Hanns Heinz Ewers. Neither man revealed a thing. The bombs didn't rip them to shreds. I did."

Even Saul Royce was shocked to silence by Vril's cold-blooded admission of murder.

"Steiner was paranoid with good reason." Vril spoke like a man possessed, reliving events 50 years in the past. "An extremely suspicious man, he dared not keep Pope Leo's treasure at his estate. Too many others desired the box and were willing to do anything to find it. He kept the relic safely hidden at another location. Only the book contained a clue to that spot.

"Grandfather enjoyed threatening me with the secrets of the box. It contained power beyond belief. Even the Very Old Folk feared the energy only Steiner controlled. Then, one morning, the Nazis placed the old man under house arrest. The Gestapo refused to let him leave the estate and allowed no visitors. Those orders isolated him from the treasure."

Vril chuckled. "Steiner aged ten years the first week. Hitler blamed grandfather for Hess's flight to England. The Fuhrer ordered all traces of Project Alraune wiped out. Like most despots, what he did not understand, he feared. Realizing the danger of my position and no longer bound by Steiner's bluster, I escaped the compound and fled to the hills."

The giant paused, as if waking from a vivid dream. "I talk too much at times. The past is dead. All that matters is the present. I will pay you one million dollars for the book. Take it and give me *Alraune*."

"I will pay double that amount," Francesco Cova said.

"Do not meddle in my business, priest," Vril said, his voice rising slightly. "Very well. Two million."

"Pope Leo's treasure belongs to the Church," Cova replied, undaunted. "Again, I double the offer."

"Priest," Vril said, clenching his hands into fists, "you try my patience."

"I represent the Holy Father in this quest," Cova said, his voice quivering with emotion. "No price—"

"Enough!" shouted Dietrich Vril. His nostrils flared as he gulped in huge lungfuls of air. His cheeks glowed the color of blood. An inhuman growl rose from the man's chest.

"I will have the book," he said, emphasizing each word with a shake of the fist.

"I think not," Father Cova said, his gaze shifting to the door. Unnoticed by anyone, four Jesuits had entered the parlor. Each of them held a Skorpion, aimed at Vril's midsection.

Reaching into one pocket, Father Cova pulled out a simple crucifix. "Get thee behind me, Satan."

"You fools," Vril said, with a mad laugh. "You think your ancient superstitions bother me? You blind yourselves to the truth. So be it."

Ignoring the guns, he turned and walked to the front hall. No one moved as he stepped through the doorway into the late afternoon sunlight. "I am not an unreasonable man. My offer of one million still stands. Think it over."

"Never," Father Cova said.

"Never," Alex repeated.

"Consider the fate of those you found last night," Vril said, "before you make your final decision. I rule the night. And death is my emissary."

Chapter Nineteen

No one moved for a minute after Vril's departure. Then slowly, Mak lowered his hands. Worry lines creased his face, and his expression was grim. Alex suspected he looked no better. His friend walked cautiously to the front door and peered out into the gathering twilight.

"He's gone," Mak announced to no one in particular.

He made his way back to Alex. "Don't count on your luck helping you in a fight with that character. Vril's psychic powers are as powerful as yours. The two energies would cancel each other out. Any battle would be on purely physical terms. He outweighs you by a hundred pounds and looks awfully mean."

Next, he turned to Valerie. "No question in my mind that he's a warlock. His aura burns incredibly bright. He's even stronger than I expected. Strange, though, he was not using the Repel spell. Bullets would have worked. It makes you wonder how he escaped the Circumcellions." Mak paused and shook his head in bewilderment. "I sensed no reason for his continual sweating. Whatever caused it was a mystery to me."

Finally, he faced Francesco Cova. "A crucifix, Father? Do you actually think Vril is the true Antichrist?"

"As described by the Holy Book?" Cova said, his features equally grim. "No. He is no mystical being out of Scriptures sent by the devil, but if ever a man existed who defined evil, Dietrich Vril is that person. To me, he is the living, walking, breathing embodiment of the Antichrist."

Then, as if to break the mood of despair, the priest smiled. "I was taught that threat in seminary. I never expected to use it, but I couldn't think of anything else to do."

"According to folklore, crosses only work on vampires, not sorcerers," Sally said.

"Remind me of that the next time I face such a monster," Cova replied. "None of my previous assignments prepared me for Dietrich Vril. Professor Warner's description never conveyed the man's incredible force. He is truly frightening."

"Let's dispense with the small talk," Royce said. "You heard Vril's threat. I think he meant what he said. What are we gonna do about it?"

"Wait a minute," Alex said, quietly. "It's time to set things straight. This is my fight, not yours. I owe a debt to Howie Rosenberg, and I don't like being pushed around by anyone, neither Dietrich Vril nor Brother Ambrose. Still, I can't ask you to risk your lives for me. I appreciate your concern, but I feel responsible for involving all of you in this mess."

"Forget your heroic speeches," Father Cova said. "This fight concerns us all. Vril wants the book. So do I. Saul wants his story. You cannot put us off so easily."

"You tell him, Father," Royce said. "The big lug ain't gonna let any of us off the hook. His type never forgives and forgets. Even if you handed him over the book, he would still keep after us. With him, it's kill or be killed. And I'm not ready to cash in my chips just yet.

Royce bit down hard on the end of a new cigar. "Besides, I never quit a story in the middle. And where I go, Sally follows."

"To protect his ass," she added, sarcastically.

"The same as your sweet wife," Valerie said with an emphatic nod and wrinkle of her nose at Alex. "Don't forget who saved you from the Circumcellions."

"I made a vow to find Pope Leo's treasure," Father Cova said, a little louder than necessary. "I mean to keep it."

"Royce is right about Vril," Mak said. "Men like him obey only their own rules. Powerful sorcerers dislike being thwarted. He will not rest until he owns the book and we are all dead. Despite your concerns, there can be no hesitation. There is no turning back now."

"I withdraw my objections," Alex said. "A wise man knows better to argue with fate—or his wife."

"Good thinking, Warner," Royce said. "Now that the emotional stuff is over, let's talk about food. It's pretty late in the day. How about if Sally and I run over to the local deli and pick up roast beef sandwiches? No reason to starve while we prepare for the worst."

"Let me translate that into simpler terms," Sally said patiently. "Saul needs a cigar, and he knows Alex doesn't approve of smoking. We'll be gone twenty or thirty minutes."

"Mind if I tag along?" Mak asked. "I can use the air."

"Fine with me if the boss doesn't mind," Sally said. "He's the one with his name in the paper."

"Sure. Come on along," Royce said. "You can be navigator. I don't know anything about this neighborhood. Too many yuppies live here for my tastes."

Grinning, Royce pushed his assistant and Mak out the door.

"He's incredible," Valerie said, shaking her head in dismay. "Absolutely incredible."

"I will take advantage of the lull to check with my men and find out how Vril got past them," Father Cova said. "And to warn them that he might return. I, too, shall return in a few minutes."

The priest departed, closing what was left of the front door tightly behind him. Alex sighed. Between Vril and the Circumcellions, his home was taking a beating. Shaking his head in disgust, he glanced over at his wife.

"Paper plates and plastic silverware?" Valerie asked, heading for the dining room. "No dishes to wash tonight."

"Sounds great to me."

"How about a hug?"

"Sounds even better."

Valerie snuggled up close, burrowing her head into Alex's chest. He wrapped his arms tightly around her.

They stood silently for a few moments, enjoying the feeling of their bodies pressing together intimately. The past few days had provided little chance for much affection. Alex loved his wife dearly, and her closeness renewed him. In the harsh, dangerous world, she added meaning to his life.

"You okay?" he asked softly, as his fingers curled strands of her golden hair.

"Not bad," she replied, "considering the circumstances. I've turned down modeling assignments so that I could spend more of my time with you. Maybe, I acted a bit hastily."

"I had no choice," Alex said, defensively.

"Nope," Valerie said in agreement. "I love you for what you are, Alex Warner. You helped Howie Rosenberg for the same reasons I find you so irresistible—honor, loyalty, courage. Once you stepped into Rosenberg's bookstore it set off a chain of events that is still going on. Call it destiny if you want. I only wish that the fates allotted us a little more time for each other."

"Time to break," Alex said. "The others will be back any minute. We don't want to shock them."

"They probably suspect the worst anyway," Valerie said, giggling. "From what I remember of Sally Stevens, she was a real hot number as a teenager. She doesn't act like she's changed a whit."

"I'll say."

"Watch it, buster." Valerie ran her hands down across her dress, straightening out the wrinkles. "I know what you college professors are like."

Suddenly her mood shifted.

"By the way, your friend, Brick, stopped by this afternoon. He dropped off a package."

"Good. I called him earlier. Where did you put it?"

"Up in the attic, by your desk. Alex, that man spooks the hell out of me."

"Brick? He's as harmless as a fly."

"He reminds me of an undertaker. And you know what I think of his profession. He sells death."

Brick owed Alex his life from their days together in Vietnam. These days, the ex-Special Services operative ran the largest illegal weapons depot in the Midwest. He never questioned any requests from his old buddy. Alex placed a call and within hours Brick provided the necessary hardware.

Valerie felt Brick belonged in prison, but Alex disagreed. As long as people wanted weapons, they would get them, legally or illegally. Brick satisfied that need.

Alex relied on Brick's resources in dangerous situations. The best policy, he had discovered, was to let Valerie express her disapproval and deal with Brick only when absolutely necessary, as was the case now. The bag upstairs contained an insurance policy against the powers of darkness.

Chapter Twenty

After a quick dinner, they all made their way up to the attic. Alex wanted to bring the book down to be examined, but both Father Cova and Saul Royce expressed a strong interest in seeing Jake Lancaster's huge occult library. Alex voiced no objections. Secretly, he enjoyed showing off the immense book collection.

"Who you expecting, Warner?" Royce asked as Alex disengaged the alarms permitting access into the room. "Zombie headhunters looking for a good read."

"Actually, the volumes in this room are worth several million dollars," Alex said. "Many of the scarcer grimoires are one of a kind."

Alex did not mention that Jake Lancaster had

been killed by a werewolf in the attic. No reason to worry Royce more than necessary.

The columnist was properly impressed by the display. He spent his first five minutes in the attic darting from one section of the library to another, muttering under his breath the entire time. Mak stood next to him, pointing out special volumes of note.

On a love seat in one corner, Valerie and Sally spent the time catching up on past history. Alex sighed with relief. His wife could be extremely jealous at times, so it was a pleasure having a beautiful woman visit without Valerie treating her like a foreign spy.

"Let me see this million dollar book," Father Cova said impatiently. "I have a theory."

Alex retrieved *Alraune* from its hiding place and handed it to the priest. "If you can find a clue in the text, you're a better detective than I am."

"After you left last night, I requested a copy of the novel be sent to me immediately. It arrived early this morning. I skimmed the contents before coming here. Let me examine this volume to see if it differs any from the one I read."

Alex left the priest alone with the book. The man's plain appearance gave no hint of the money and power at his fingertips. Cova commanded an army of the faithful. He made a strong ally and a dangerous enemy.

A large brown paper bag awaited Alex at the side of his desk. Surreptitiously he checked it contents. As usual, Brick had delivered the goods.

He made no mention of the package to any of the others in the room. He trusted them all but saw no reason to say anything. No one knew for sure the powers of the Very Old Folk. Crowley's story of Atlantis had mentioned telepathy. If they could read thoughts, the fewer who knew about his surprise, the better.

Feeling restless, Alex walked over to the sliding metal doors that sealed off the room from the rest of the house. Silently, he counted off a dozen paces into the room. Picking his spot, he pushed over his heavy black leather armchair so that it faced the doorway.

Next, he carefully set the package from Brick next to the chair. Finally, he carried over a gooseneck floor lamp behind the seat. Tilting the light exactly right, he positioned the light so that it glared directly at the entrance. Hurrying over to the door, he squinted into the brightness. After raising the rim of the lamp another few inches, he shut it off. His arrangements were finished.

"You expect Vril to come back tonight?" Royce asked, wandering over to watch what Alex was doing.

"Either him or one of his allies. He might attack or may be thinking the better of it, but I believe in always preparing for the worst. If we're threatened, I'll be ready. That's why it made sense to examine the book up here. That steel door offers quite a bit of protection."

"Yeah? Then why rearrange the furniture?"

"Call it a second line of defense. If Vril sends one of the Very Old Folk after the book, I hope the thing will reach the door, try to open it and fail. Being the pessimist that I am, I suspect it won't be quite that easy."

"Tell me," Royce said, dragging out a cigar from his pocket and chewing on it nervously. "The bad guys never take no for an answer."

"If it makes it into the room, we'll kill it," Alex said. "The odds are in our favor."

"Sure, sure," Royce said. "I bet the natives said the same thing right before King Kong attacked."

Chuckling, Alex walked over to Father Cova while Royce anxiously inspected the steel panels. The priest closed the book as Alex approached.

"A bizarre story," Cova said, his face crinkling up into a look of disgust. "On long trips, I read your American cowboy adventures. They pass the time pleasantly enough, but these weird novels disgust me."

"Did you find any clues to the treasure box?" Alex asked. "If we discover the secret the book holds, I think we'd all rest a little easier. And we'd be one step closer to defeating Dietrich Vril. By his own admission, the box contained powers much greater than his or his ghoulish allies'."

"I agree. The sooner we settle this matter the better."

The priest rose to his feet, still holding the book. "I reviewed the novel for other reasons than merely reinforcing my views on its contents. I guessed the importance of the volume when you first described its condition."

"Care to elaborate on that, Father," Royce said, waving his cigar like a pointer.

The priest took the copy of *Alraune* and removed the jacket. Turning the book upside down, he held it by the pages, letting the boards point to the floor. A nearly naked woman and ugly sorcerer stared at them from the exposed endpapers.

"Examine the binding closely," Cova said. "Notice how it hugs the paper. Sewn signatures hang free. Some person tampered with this book. He glued the cloth to the pages."

Alex slapped his head in annoyance. He had been so caught up in the contents of the book that he never once thought to examine it for purely physical evidence. He felt like an idiot.

Cova turned the book over so that the spine faced up. Gently, he rubbed a finger of the bright red flowers on the spine. "That same individual slipped a thin piece of lightly gummed cardboard into the opening. Heat and pressure finished the job for him."

"Easy enough for us to undo the damage," Alex said.

He walked over to his desk and found a letter opener. Trembling slightly with excitement, he passed it over to Father Cova.

The priest pushed the thin metal blade firmly

beneath the cloth. Carefully, he rotated the opener across the spine, cutting away the dried glue. Removing the knife, he reinserted it so that the blade pressed up against the sewn signatures. Again he rotated the opener so that it cut away the dried mucilage.

Cova handed Alex the knife and delicately grasped a thin slip of cardboard revealed by his exertions. Pulling it loose from the binding, he held it out for all to see.

"Karl Steiner's last secret," he said, softly.

"Of course," said Mak, who had come over and joined them along with the two women. "Why didn't we think of that before?"

In Cova's hand rested a narrow chunk of cardboard. Wedged in its center was a two inch metal key. Cova ripped it free from the paper and held it up for closer inspection.

"I suspected as much," he said after a brief examination. "According to what you told me, Steiner spent a great deal of time in Switzerland dealing with bankers. What better place for him to hide Pope Leo's treasure box?"

"Great," Royce said with a shrug of disgust. "How do you propose finding the right bank and the right safe deposit box? The Swiss enforce their privacy laws quite strictly. Their banking industry depends on that confidentiality."

The priest smiled and shook his head, as if dealing with an ignorant child. "You forget, my friend, that I am an expert on financial matters. Remember the subject of our first meeting. I know the Swiss banking industry better than most, and my contacts are excellent."

Father Cova held up the copy of *Alraune*. "As to finding the proper safe deposit box, you ignore our most vital source of information, the book. It contains all the information we need."

"That's right," Alex said, recalling his earlier examination of the volume. "Steiner circled certain page numbers."

"Correct," said Cova. "He also underlined a specific passage on the rear dust jacket. 'His master is Albercht Durer.' So the box was probably registered under the name of that famous artist."

"All we need then is the number," Sally said, sounding excited.

Alex grabbed a pen and paper from his desk. Taking them, Father Cova carefully leafed through the book. Each time he came across a page with its heading circled, he wrote the figure on his list. It took less than ten minutes to complete the examination.

"An eleven digit code," the priest said. "If I remember correctly, the amount of numbers used for box identification by most banks in Zurich."

"Vril's never actually seen this book," Mak said, a smile forming on his lips. "If we resealed the binding exactly the way we found it . . ."

"He'd never know about the key," Alex said, finishing the thought. "I could pass the volume on to him tomorrow without him being any the wiser."

"And if the Circumcellions somehow learned

it was in his hands . . ." Mak continued, grinning broadly now.

"They could fight it out while we flew off to find the treasure," Alex concluded. "It sounds like a perfect plan to me."

"Agreed," Father Cova said. "But before patting ourselves on the back, there is one other point of importance we must discuss. In our rush to discover the location of the Pope's treasure by using the book, we never once considered the importance of the contents of the story itself."

"I read it," Alex said. "It dealt with vampirism, but not the type Howie Rosenberg encountered."

"Those passages meant nothing," the priest said. "You reacted too strongly to your friend's story and missed the underlying theme of the novel. The real topic of the book was whether God actually exists. Frank Braun no doubt spoke with Ewers' voice when he stated, 'If your God is alive, then he must answer your arrogant question.' "

"What question?" Alex asked.

"Can man duplicate God's work? Braun challenged his uncle, Jacob ten Brinken, to duplicate the legend of the mandrake root through modern technology. According to the original medieval belief, when a male criminal died by hanging at a crossroad, he ejaculated the instant his neck was broken. His semen, falling to the ground, germinated in the soil and resulted in a mandrake root.

"The plant, when dug up and treated by certain occult rituals, brought good luck to the owner but misfortune to all those around him. Many people believed this folk tale. Even Shakespeare mentioned the story in one of his plays."

"What did you mean about duplicating the legend through modern technology?" Valerie asked.

"To Braun, the earth in the legend symbolized fertility, and thus, using a string of insane logic, a prostitute. He proposed that his uncle, a doctor, obtain a sperm sample from a newly executed criminal and use it to artificially inseminate the most shameless whore he could find. The resulting child, he felt, would be the human counterpart of the mandrake root."

"The old man followed his nephew's advice," Alex said, continuing the story when Cova hesitated. "He named the girl who resulted from this unholy union, Alraune, the German word for mandrake. Needless to say, she possessed the same qualities as the mystic plant. Beneath a quiet, calm exterior lurked the mind of a sadistic maniac. Among her other pursuits, the girl enjoyed torturing little animals to death.

"A seductively beautiful woman, Alraune brought disaster to all she met. She drove a number of men to suicide, including Dr. ten Brinken, her creator. Her charms proved fatal to anyone who loved her. Finally, Frank Braun, though captivated by Alraune's spell, burned the original mandrake root that prompted his suggestion. When the plant died, so did Alraune."

Opening the cover of the book, Cova read the inscription. "To Karl Steiner—Who labors to make my wildest fancies his reality. May both our efforts help create a Reich that will last for a thousand years."

Angrily, the priest slammed the volume shut. "Don't you understand?" he nearly shouted. "Steiner dreamed of creating life just like ten Brinken. He wanted to play God. Pope Leo's treasure gave him that power."

"But he didn't need the box to duplicate Ewers' novel," Alex said. "Artificial insemination dated back to the late nineteenth century. In *Alraune,* the shock value arose from the two donors involved in the act."

"I know how he used the treasure chest," Mak said softly. "Great magic needed great power. The Germans dreamt of an army of superhuman beings fighting for the Reich. In his novel, Ewers espoused the same concept with his notion of an artificial creation unfettered by the laws of nature. Inspired by the book, Karl Steiner created a monster.

"I suspected the truth when Alex first described Vril's incredible body temperature. Purposefully, I spoke very little about it, hoping against hope that I might be proven wrong. When the German came to claim the book, I secretly probed his aura. Vril burned with the power, but his very existence fouled the air.

"Using all of the dark magic at his command, magnified a thousand times by the secret of the

Armageddon Box, Karl Steiner aged his only grandson fifteen years in only a few months. According to the *Grimoirium Verum* only a few of the greatest mages of antiquity ever dared that spell. The slightest deviation from the correct formula resulted in a terrible death for both the sorcerer and his subject.

"Steiner, aided by his nonhuman allies, directed both the growth and appearance of his baby grandson. He molded the child the same way a great artist carved a sculpture, reworking the boy into the image of the perfect Aryan warrior.

"Consider the possibilities—a new army of superhuman Nazi warriors risen to full strength only a few years after conception. Take the broadest implications of Ewers' ideas concerning artificial insemination and genetic tampering, and it leads to a monstrous scheme for a Nazi master race."

"But it never happened," Royce said. "Instead, the Nazis turned against Steiner and his project. How come?"

"Howie Rosenberg gave Alex the clue when he mentioned how Vril spared his life. The boy wanted nothing to do with the Reich. Remember, though his body aged rapidly, his mind progressed at a much slower rate. The brain of a young boy controlled the body of a full-grown man. He evidently opposed the destiny laid forth for him by his grandfather. Vril refused to follow Steiner's commands, and the old man found himself powerless to enforce them.

"Karl Steiner forgot the one danger inherent with twisting nature by sorcery. Powerful magic often backfired on the user. Through his experiments on his young subject with the darkest of magics, Steiner transferred to his victim much of the power of the Armageddon Box. Dietrich Vril absorbed the most powerful occult force in the world and bent it to his own purpose. A mere boy became a sorcerer of unmatched power. Steiner paid for his mistake with his life."

"Your theory covers quite a bit of territory," Sally said, "but it doesn't explain why Vril ages so slowly. Remember, he's well over fifty."

"Yeah," Royce said. "And that constant sweating in freezing cold weather bothers the heck out of me."

"Those strange mysteries served as the catalyst for my whole line of reason," Mak said. "Every great book of magic warned that meddling with nature often resulted in disaster. Magicians often felt a burning sensation when experimenting with powerful forces. Steiner's grandson absorbed energies beyond human ken. His very cells must have cried out in protest. The aging process destroyed his normal metabolism. The sweat signifies the eternal battle waging within his system.

"For nearly fifty years, nature has struggled against the forces of the occult. Every minute of his life, Vril pays for the mad experiments of his grandfather. Who knows the pain he endures. I don't wonder that he hated the old man with such passion. Perhaps that eternal, inner warfare slows his aging. Only Vril knows the answer."

Alex yawned. Blinking, he shook his head to clear away the sudden cobwebs. The motion made him groggy, and his eyelids felt extraordinarily heavy. Next to him, Father Cova swayed and almost fell.

"Tired," the priest muttered. "So very tired."

"Gotta sit down for a minute" Royce said, his voice sluggish. "I need a rest."

Panic-stricken, Alex grabbed the corner of his desk with both hands. Desperately, he fought to stay on his feet.

With a soft thump, Valerie dropped to the floor, her eyes closed. Next to Royce on the sofa, Sally snored softly. Only Makoto Tsuiki appeared unaffected. He stood stock still a few feet away from the others, his head cocked slightly, as if listening to some far-off voice.

"Mak," Alex whispered, hard pressed to form the words. "Help us."

"Oops, sorry about that," Mak said, noticing the condition of his friends for the first time. "I forgot you're not protected."

Waving both hands in the air, forming a peculiar pattern, he stated solemnly, *"Aegri somnia."*

A thousand tiny claws ripped across Alex's body. The sharp pain snapped him fully awake. Nearby, Father Cova jerked in agony, and his eyes popped wide open. Similar cries from the others indicated that they all had felt the sting of Makoto's spell.

"What's happening?" Royce asked groggily.

"Can't you guess?" Alex asked. "Vril didn't come back himself. Instead, he sent one of his friends to retrieve the book. We're under attack by one of the Very Old Folk."

Chapter Twenty-One

No one said anything for a moment. Then Royce broke the silence.

"Well, when does this spook make an appearance?"

"Soon," Mak answered, "very soon. He's already nearby. The way into the house stands open. The trance neutralized Father Cova's men. We're on our own."

"Great news," Royce said. "You're telling me that all we can do is sit and wait."

"Exactly," said Mak.

"Why don't we call the police?" Sally asked, pointing to the phone on Alex's desk. "We can dial 911. No reason for us to mention vampires. A report of a robbery in progress would summon the cops quick enough."

Mak lifted the receiver. There was no dial tone. "I expected as much. Vril used a simple spell to cut us off from the outside world. We're on our own."

The seconds crept by slowly. Silence again descended like a blanket over the group. Tension crackled in the air like static electricity. Then, unexpectedly, Father Cova spoke.

"I still . . ." Father Cova began, but stopped speaking when Valerie suddenly raised a hand.

"Something just entered the house."

No one questioned how Valerie knew. They were beyond doubts.

"Link hands," Mak said to Valerie and Sally. "Standing together, our magic will be magnified threefold. No matter what happens, don't break the chain."

Royce pulled out his gun and took a position next to the lamp behind Alex's chair. "Give me one good shot," he said. "Magic or not, I put my faith in Mr. Smith and Wesson."

"The Very Old Folk are material beings, not creatures of magic," Mak said, his voice calm. "As such, they are subject to the same physical laws that affect any other living thing. According to all the legends, it takes quite a bit to kill one of these creatures, but they *can* die."

"God fights with us," Father Cova said. He waved his Skorpion about menacingly. "This weapon serves as an extension of his mighty arm."

"Nicely put," Royce said. "Remind me to use

that line in one of my columns. A true expression of faith if I ever heard one. Hey, that reminds me. Will bullets even hit this thing? What about that invincibility spell Warner mentioned?"

"Most magicians use such a shield. Alex was equally correct in stating it doesn't work very well in the presence of others with the same protection. If what Crowley wrote about vampires is true, I doubt if they worry about such things. In any case, aim for its torso. Even if deflected, the bullet still might strike the thing somewhere in the body."

Alex slid into his chair. He pulled the package from Brick onto his lap and loosened the paper. He still kept the weapon hidden from view. A surprise only worked if it truly caught the target unprepared.

No one spoke. The only sound in the room was the sound of labored breathing. All eyes watched the metal door. All ears strained for some hint that their enemy was approaching.

Father Cova yawned, then Royce, then Alex. He swayed in his chair as a sudden feeling of grogginess swept over him. With a snort of annoyance, he shook himself awake. Royce muttered a curse beneath his breath. A pervasive coldness filled the room.

"The monster approaches," Mak said, through tightly clenched teeth. "I can sense its thoughts. It is alien, totally and completely inhuman. My mind aches from the contact."

The veins on Mak's forehead stood out in bold

relief. His hands clenched those of the women on his sides in a viselike grip. His breath came in deep, ragged gasps. Sally and Valerie stayed quiet, but their ashen faces reflected the drain on their strength.

"It hungers," Mak said.

Metal shrieked. The sliding door shuddered as powerful hands pounded against the panels. Alex wondered how the vampire bypassed the alarm system, but it meant nothing now.

"Shut the lights everywhere in the room, except for the hurricane lamp on the desk," he said to Royce, urgently. "If it breaks through, turn on the gooseneck. Try to blind the damned thing."

The door screamed again. The air in the attic vibrated with the force of the blows. The temperature continued to drop. Father Cova shuddered and crossed himself, reciting a quick prayer in Latin.

Mak groaned in agony, his face a mask of intense concentration. A bead of sweat trickled down his forehead and across the bridge of his nose. "Sunfire is not strong enough for a beast like this." His voice was filled with pain. "Burn is our only hope."

Royce stood poised next to the floor lamp, muttering a steady stream of curses, his gun pointing directly at the center of the doorway.

Incredible claws ripped into the steel. Alex gasped as the metal began to buckle. The paneling crumpled like cardboard. Hinges groaned under the continuous pressure. The door sagged inward but refused to give. A wave of arctic air swept into the room.

Two huge hands, immense fingers ending in gigantic yellowing nails, smashed through the wood above the entrance. The digits curled down and grabbed hold of the metal track supporting the sliding door. Exerting tremendous force, the hands pulled down hard.

The whole front of the room roared in protest as the panel gave way. Steel and wood collapsed to the floor. A huge cloud of dust swirled about and then settled to the ground.

Arms stretched out before it, the vampire stood motionless for a second in the exposed hallway. Behind it, all the lights in the corridor were out. Only the glare of the small desk lamp outlined the creature's appearance.

Based on Rosenberg's description, Alex expected a creature the size of a man. This thing filled the doorway. It stood seven feet high and four feet wide at the shoulders. Gigantic black wings rested half-unfurled on its back, like a gigantic cape outlining its torso.

Eyes the color of blood bulged out from the vampire's dead-white face. The dim light reflected off a mouth filled with monstrous yellow fangs. A thick mat of hideous black fur covered most of its body, leaving only its enormous genitals exposed in a gross travesty of male humanity.

"Sonavabitch," Royce said, switching on the floor lamp.

The bright light blazed directly in the face of

the vampire. It hissed in agony and half-turned, shielding itself with one immense wing. The monster had no eyelids. Alex ripped off the coverings on his weapon. He hesitated, wanting a direct shot at the creature's body. Behind him, Royce's gun roared, filling the room with the smell of gunpowder. Father Cova's Skorpion shrieked in response.

The vampire staggered as a hail of gunfire slammed into its body. Dozens of slugs tore through the thin membrane of its wings and pounded into its body. The thing fell back and then stopped. Slowly, it straightened. Away from the glare of the light, it rose up to its full height and again faced the door.

Red eyes glared like twin fires. Alex stared fearfully where the bullets had hit the thing. Like putty, the skin around the wounds flowed together, covering the marks. Not a drop of blood fell to the floor. In seconds, no trace of the injuries remained.

Shouting with rage, Royce threw his gun at the vampire's head. The monster made no effort to duck. The automatic smashed into its shoulder, then dropped to the floor.

The thing shuffled forward. It moved stiffly, awkwardly, like a gigantic bird trying to walk. Huge wings rustled from side to side as it advanced. A clear shot at its chest was impossible. Alex swore and gripped the barrel of his gun, waiting for the right moment.

"Burn," Mak whispered.

Alex risked a quick glance at his friend. A thin

stream of blood dripped from Mak's nose. He stood frozen, his eyes fixed on the approaching vampire. His hands held those of the two women in a grip of iron. Both Valerie and Sally stood at attention, their eyes closed, their bodies rigid with concentration.

"Burn," Mak said again.

A thin wisp of smoke rose from the vampire's forehead. The creature hesitated, drawing its wings close together for protection. Anxiously, Alex raised his weapon. It was time to ignore the legends. He needed only a few seconds to aim and fire, but he never got them.

"Enough," the vampire said in a flat, alien voice like the hissing of a gigantic snake. "I tire of these games."

As if swatting at an annoying insect, the monster waved a hand. Mak howled in pain and staggered forward, pulling free from the others. The chain broken, he dropped to the floor, unmoving. Silently, Valerie and Sally collapsed, like two balloons suddenly deflated.

Go for its mouth, Alex thought desperately, trying to concentrate only on his target.

The light bulb in the floor lamp exploded, showering Alex with shards of hot glass. A second later, the hurricane lamp flamed and went out, plunging the room into total darkness.

Immediately, Alex rolled over the side of his chair and scooted for the back of the attic. Retreat and regroup, warned his inner alarms. Once betrayed, an indefensible position was worthless. He headed for the farthest corner away from the monster. If his first shot missed, he needed time to reload.

Behind him, the vampire grabbed hold of his chair. Batlike, the monster navigated perfectly in the blackness. Wood and upholstery went flying as the creature ripped the recliner into kindling.

From the side of the room, Father Cova grunted in sudden shock and then went silent. Alex feared the worst. Only two of them faced the creature.

"Royce," Alex yelled, not worrying whether the vampire heard him or not. "Help me. You have a lighter. Burn something—anything. Hurry."

Feverishly, Alex loaded his weapon. In total darkness, he couldn't see a thing. Instead, he closed his eyes and forced himself to work by touch alone. Old reflexes took over.

In Vietnam he had trained blindfolded with similar weapons to prepare for night fighting. It took precious seconds to wind the winch of the crossbow, but finally the bowstring caught on the release. He shoved his extra shafts through his belt.

"Five seconds," he whispered to himself. "All I want is five seconds."

Royce clicked on his lighter. The inch-long flame illuminated an incredible scene. The columnist huddled close to the floor in the leg space beneath Alex's desk. In one hand, he held his lighter. In his other rested *Alraune*. Paper crackling like popcorn, the book caught fire.

Only a few feet away stood the vampire. Breath hissing like a locomotive, the monster reached down with gigantic arms and seized Royce by the shoulders. The reporter screamed in pain as deadly claws tore through muscle and flesh. Bones crunched like candy as the creature squeezed hard. Blood gushed in fountains. In a last, frenzied act, Royce flung the burning book into the center of the room.

Berserk with rage, the vampire dragged the columnist out from his hiding place. It lifted him a foot off the floor and shook him like a rag doll. Droplets of blood and gore splashed about the room. Without effort, the thing hurtled Royce through the air.

The columnist crashed into the far wall with an audible crack, leaving a red blot on the wood. He crumpled to the floor, his upper body a smashed ruin of broken bones.

Turning, the monster looked about, searching. Slowly, it reached for the burning book.

Alex steadied his crossbow, sighted and gently squeezed the trigger. With barely a whisper, the cedar bolt vanished into the darkness.

The vampire's head rocked back as if smashed by a gigantic hammer. The force of the blow whirled it back and away from the book. Hissing like a thousand snakes, the monster wheeled about to face its tormentor.

Not a mark showed on the vampire. Alex cursed. The arrow must have only grazed the thing.

Raising its arms, the creature shuffled closer.

Only 15 feet separated them, and the distance lessened with each step the monster took. It moved slowly but very steadily.

Alex's back rubbed up against the rear wall of the attic. No retreat there. He pulled a steel-headed cedar bolt from his belt and shoved it onto the bowstring. Anxiously, he wound the winch, cocking the crossbow. It only took a few seconds to load.

Unexpectedly, the vampire lashed out with a gigantic hand. The air whistled as gigantic claws missed Alex's face by inches. He ducked to the side, frantically turning the winch a final notch.

The vampire advanced another foot. Its huge wings furled open, blocking out nearly all the light from the flame. Yellow fangs flashed as if in triumph as the thing opened its mouth.

This time he knew the arrow sped true. It flashed from the powerful bow right into the creature's gaping maw. The bolt ripped right out the back of the monster's head and continued across the attic!

The vampire crashed back onto the floor. Terrible doubt filled Alex's mind as he cautiously circled around to the left. The fallen horror blocked him from the front of the room. Hands shaking, he fit another shaft into the crossbow and turned the winch.

Red eyes blazing, the vampire struggled back to its feet. Now Alex knew for sure his first bolt had made contact as well. The arrow had plunged right through the monster's body, but the wound had healed in seconds, leaving the thing intact and unharmed. Only one slender hope endured. He prayed the old legends told the truth. Everything depended on one last shot.

"Now you die," hissed the vampire, and it clawed out with both hands.

For a second, nothing shielded the creature's torso. Alex dropped to the floor and swung up the crossbow in a direct line with the monster's chest. He aimed and fired in one continuous blur of motion. The bolt shot forward like a bullet. With a thunk of steel striking bone, the wood shaft plunged halfway into the vampire's upper body and stayed put.

The impact sent the monster reeling back. Staggering, it wheeled about in mortal agony. Titanic wings snapped together on its back. Screeching, it dropped to the floor like a felled tree.

This time, the creature stayed down. Huge arms lashed out feebly as the thing tried to grab hold of the arrow and pull it out. The bolt held steady even when the vampire gripped it with both hands. Black blood bubbled up in a constant stream from the thing's chest. Beneath it, the wood floor sizzled each time a drop of black ichor fell.

Alex positioned himself a few feet back from the monster, standing just out of its reach. Calmly, he reloaded the crossbow. Holding the weapon up to his shoulder, he took careful aim.

"I am Semjaza," the vampire whispered, "first of my kind upon your world. Six thousand years of history dies with me."

"Six thousand years of evil," Alex said through gritted teeth and pulled the trigger.

The second bolt buried itself next to the first, deep in the monster's chest. The vampire shrieked, dark black blood gushing from its mouth. Huge jaws slammed shut, red eyes turned black, and the oldest living thing on Earth perished.

Instantly, a grim transformation began. In a bizarre parody of life, the creature's body twisted and turned. Slowly, it crumpled back in on itself. Only the long wood shafts of the arrows held the thing in place.

Alex gasped in shock as the monster's face bubbled and decayed as if being eaten away by acid. In seconds, the thing's features collapsed inward into its skull, dissolving into a mass of bubbling slime.

Nauseated, Alex stepped back as the vampire's corpse continued to decompose. Arms and legs crumpled into slivers of yellowed bone and decaying flesh. Its torso rotted and within minutes vanished into a heaving mass of vile black blood and gore that coated the floor. Soon even that dissolved, leaving a pool of corruption that hissed and steamed on the hard wood.

Chapter Twenty-Two

Alex turned away and hurried over to the smoldering copy of *Alraune*. Only a few charred leaves and part of the binding survived. Years before, Jake Lancaster, worried that a freak electric fire might destroy his library, had cast a spell on the floor and walls of the attic. The entire room was noncombustible. That foresight had prevented the burning volume from setting the place ablaze tonight.

Only a few sparks still burned, providing a bare minimum of light in which to stumble about. Hating to leave the room but knowing he must, Alex rushed out the door and into the hallway. The crunch of glass beneath his feet marked a string of exploded light bulbs along the vampire's route.

He tried the switches on the second floor landing with no results. The monster's passage through the house had blown every fuse.

Fortunately, moonlight illuminated the downstairs rooms, and in the parlor Alex found a box of thick white candles and a book of matches.

A minute later, the attic glowed in candlelight. Ignoring the pressing urgency of treating his wife, Alex first examined Saul Royce. A quick look confirmed what he already feared. All the magic in the world could not restore a dead man to life.

For an instant, Alex stood there, his hands clenched uselessly into fists, as a cold rage swept through his body. Then thoughts of his wife crowded out all other considerations.

He rushed over to the three bodies on the floor. Trying to maintain his composure, he lifted Valerie and carried her over to the sofa. Her pulse beat steadily, and she was breathing normally. Nothing seemed broken. Silently, he uttered a brief word of thanks to whatever powers protected her.

After propping his wife up against the cushions, he brought over Sally. He rested the redhead next to Valerie. She also appeared unharmed.

Mak groaned and opened his eyes. Spotting Alex and the two women, the magician tried to pull himself erect. After trying unsuccessfully for a few seconds, he gave up and sank back to the floor.

"We won?" he asked in a voice crackling with pain.

"Barely," Alex replied, helping his friend sit up. "Stay here while I check on Father Cova. Damned thing threw my easy chair at him."

"I survived," the priest said, rising unsteadily from the shattered remains of the recliner. Blood covered his face, and his breath came in shallow gasps.

"A piece of the frame caught me on the head, knocking me senseless. Fortunately, the sloped ceiling protected me from a direct hit, but the springs slashed my face. Otherwise, I suffered only a few scrapes and cuts."

"What happened to Royce?" Mak asked, as he forced himself erect.

"Dead," Alex said, kneeling beside the smashed body of the columnist. Hot tears welled up in his eyes, and for a moment it was difficult to speak. "He saved us all."

Voice trembling with emotion, Alex gave a brief summary of his struggle with the vampire. "The whole fight took less than a minute," he concluded, shaking his head, "though it felt like it lasted a century."

Mak wobbled over to where the vampire had fallen. Only a huge black stain marked the spot. Nothing else remained of the monster.

"Semjaza," the magician muttered. "I know that name."

"I've encountered it someplace, too," Alex said, the grief ebbing out of him as he spoke. "Time enough to track down the reference later. What do we do about Royce?"

"Before we decide, we must restore the women to consciousness," Father Cova said. He stood next to the sofa. "They fail to respond to my attempts at first aid."

"Magical backlash," Mak said. "It's nothing to worry about. The vampire proved much stronger than any of us expected. It repelled my spell and flung it back at me. I bore the brunt of the attack, but some of the effects passed through the linkage to Sally and Valerie. My yoga training brought me back faster, but they'll recover any minute. Fortunately for us, the vampire muffled its attack. It aimed to stun, not kill. The monster wanted us alive."

Alex shuddered as he recalled huge yellow fangs and the story of Aleister Crowley.

His wife groaned and stirred fitfully. Rushing over, he held her gently by the shoulders until the trembling passed. Blue eyes opened and locked with his. Wordlessly, she hugged him tight, as if afraid to let go.

"Where's Saul?" Sally asked groggily. Not receiving an answer, she straightened up, her strength fueled by panic. "Where's Saul?"

"I'm afraid . . ." Mak said, but before he could finish the sentence, Sally burst out into tears.

"Oh, dear God, no. Please, no," she cried in anguish. "No, no, no."

"He perished the way he lived," Father Cova said, "fighting evil."

The priest placed a steady hand on Sally's shoulder. Bending close, he whispered softly to her. After a few moments, she stopped crying. With an unsteady hand, she wiped the tears away.

"You're right," she said, gulping down several big swallows of air. "Saul hated tears. He told me that a thousand times. Good reporters never cry. Especially," and her voice steadied, "when there was work to be done."

She stood up.

"I need a phone right away. A lot of people owe Saul favors. Tonight, I call in the tabs. Even in death, he'll fight intolerance one last time."

"Huh? What are you talking about?" Alex asked.

"Kill a newspaper reporter and you shake loose a hornet's nest," Sally said, her voice filled with fire and rage. "It's the unspoken law of journalism. No matter what the cost, what the effort, you never let a fellow reporter's death go unsolved. With the help of some black magic and a lot of favors, I'm going to frame Brother Ambrose and the Circumcellions for Saul's murder. They already tried to silence him once. We'll use their own schemes to bury them."

Eyes filled with tears, her voice none too steady, Sally told them what she wanted done. The next 15 minutes were spent putting together a makeshift stretcher and bringing Royce's body downstairs to the basement. Only then would

Sally agree to go with Valerie to calm down. The three men returned to the attic.

"Another good man dead," Alex said grimly. "Another score to settle."

"The world is an unjust place," Father Cova said. "You could spend your entire life avenging such deaths, and in the end it would change nothing."

Alex said nothing. He knew the priest was right, but blood called out for blood.

Taking Alex's silence for agreement, Father Cova bent down and picked up the crossbow. His face wrinkled with curiosity.

"An unusual weapon," he said, raising it up to his shoulder and sighting along the barrel. "Where did you learn to use it?"

"In Vietnam. A number of scouts and Special Forces agents carried them. Crossbows killed without noise and had a penetrating power unmatched by most handguns. A supply of poison darts made them the perfect sniper's weapon.

"I used a more powerful weapon in those days, one constructed with a Springfield stock, open sights, and a two-inch Osage orange bow with a hundred-fifty-pound pull. But I left all my bows back in Nam when I came stateside. My friend, Brick, supplied me with this one. It almost proved too powerful."

He related how the arrows passed right through the vampire. "Not enough solid muscle or bone to stop them," he concluded. "No wonder the stories said to aim for the heart. It was probably the only organ of any size the creature possessed."

"An appropriate weapon against an enemy of all men," Father Cova said, as he looked down at the black stain on the floor. His features hardened into a fanatical mask. "Our quest must not fail. We cannot let Dietrich Vril or the Circumcellions gain possession of the box. Either one would mean disaster for the Church. On one side stands the heretics. On the other waits the master of evil."

As if struck by divine inspiration, the priest raised the crossbow. Gripping it where the bow joined the stock, he stepped forward until the light of the candles struck the weapon just right. As if by magic, the shadow of a gigantic cross spread across the room, blotting out the vile mark of the vampire.

"In hoc signo vinces," Father Cova declared, his voice ringing with religious fervor. "In this sign, shalt thou conquer."

Then again, his voice barely above a whisper. "In this sign."

Chapter Twenty-Three

They left for Switzerland two days later. It took more than 24 hours for Father Cova's contacts in the banking industry to discover the correct bank. Forty-five guarded inquiries finally located the institution, one of the largest privately held banking houses in the country, headquartered in Zurich. The Vatican's invisible army also arranged for their airfare and lodgings.

Meanwhile, the disappearance of Saul Royce made the front pages of all three Chicago papers. The *Post* boldly printed a full-page editorial demanding the immediate release of their star columnist by unnamed urban terrorists.

Sally Stevens, teary-eyed and gaunt, haunted

the local talk shows, describing vague threats received from a mysterious fanatical religious band. Everything proceeded exactly as she planned.

Mak opted to stay in Chicago, worried that the Circumcellions would try to silence Sally once they realized what she intended.

"Time means everything to us," Father Cova said, as they boarded their overseas flight. "Miss Stevens' bold move put Haxley and his men on the run. Hopefully, our trip also caught them by surprise. I cautioned my men about a traitor in their midst. To minimize any chance of a leak in our plans, they worked in groups of three. Only a few trusted associates know the location of the bank. I instructed all of my agents to stay away from the area.

"We travel alone and, if all goes right, unnoticed. Any publicity at this stage would be as damaging as Haxley obtaining the treasure. We must locate the box and return it safely to the Vatican without anyone learning of our mission. If we work efficiently, the prize will be ours before Haxley ever learns of our departure."

Alex had his doubts. The more people involved in planning an undercover mission, the greater the risk of betrayal. Too many secret missions in Vietnam failed due to a breach of security. Covert action required absolute trust on all levels. Cova depended on an army of underlings, some of whom sympathized with the hard line theology of the Circumcellions. And even if they managed to avoid Brother

Ambrose and his minions, Alex felt sure they had not heard the last from Dietrich Vril.

Alex, Valerie and Father Cova arrived late Sunday afternoon at Zurich's Kloten Airport. Alex rented an Avis car, and they drove the seven miles to the center of the city. Years ago he spent several weeks in Switzerland gathering data for a history book. While he only stayed four days in Zurich, mostly at the Swiss National Museum, he remembered the layout of the city perfectly. It was a gift from his days in the Special Services.

As a small precaution against treachery, they had made reservations at the Ritz-Carlton using assumed names. Still, Alex could not shake an uneasy feeling that nagged him throughout the evening.

They ate at Kronenhalle, a famous restaurant at the foot of Rami Strasse, a few blocks from the Limmat River that lazily flowed through the center of town. The fine food and good wine mellowed Alex considerably. His natural tendency to lecture about anything and everything finally overcame his fears.

"This place was James Joyce's favorite restaurant," he told Valerie, as she downed a bite of veal in cream sauce. "He often ate here, sitting at that table in the far corner, the one right below his portrait. He inscribed the painting to the original owner of the restaurant."

"Very impressive," Father Cova said, between bites of fried potato. The priest ate with a hearty appetite and radiated good cheer. "Knowing the

Swiss character, I suspect these works hanging on the walls by Picasso, Matisse and others are all originals as well."

"You bet," Alex said, smiling. "Puritan values rule Switzerland. The people like to brag about their honesty. Find me a restaurant in any other country where they would risk displaying thousands of dollars worth of rare art unprotected on the walls."

"They sure believe in large portions," Valerie said, finishing the last bit of her *geschnetzel.* "I don't know about dessert."

"Done?" Father Cova asked in mock astonishment. "But you only ate half your dinner. Here comes our waitress now with the rest. In Switzerland, they always serve your main dish in two helpings. And you hardly touched the fried potatoes and bacon."

Valerie groaned and pushed her chair back from the table. "Not in a million years," she declared solemnly. "I may be out of the modeling field, but I still want to maintain some kind of figure."

She looked around at their fellow diners in the large room. "A lot of people here obviously enjoy their food."

Then abruptly, she changed the subject. "What's the schedule for tomorrow?"

"Get up, walk to the bank, open the safe deposit box," Alex said. "Depending on the contents, we proceed from there."

"You don't expect it holds the treasure box?"

"It's possible, but I doubt it."

"Steiner opened this account long before he fell from grace," Father Cova said, waving his fork about like a pointer. "The box was in his possession at the time. I find it hard to believe he kept it in a bank. This will be only a stepping stone to the actual location."

Valerie glanced down at her watch. "Twelve hours till the bank opens. I'm impatient already."

"Aren't we all," Alex said. "I hate waiting. I learned patience during the war, but I lost it as a teacher. I probably won't sleep a wink tonight."

"Considering the time we've been alone the last few days," Valerie said, raising her eyebrows and giving him a meaningful look, "you can bet on that."

Even Father Cova blushed at that remark.

Chapter Twenty-Four

They stared at the open safe deposit box in amazement. It held the one thing none of them ever expected to find—nothing. Father Cova shook his head in disgust.

"All of this effort wasted. And Royce died for no reason."

Alex shook his head. "It doesn't add up. Steiner hid the key for a reason. He worked too hard hiding it for the box to be empty. Unless another key existed."

"No," Father Cova said emphatically. "I checked on these vaults. The bank issued only one key. Only Karl Steiner had access to the box."

"Other than the officials of the bank," Alex

said, his thoughts wandering off on strange tangents. "They could open the box if necessary."

"Violating a bank confidence carries a twenty thousand franc fine, along with a stiff jail sentence."

"A small price to pay for the prize involved," Valerie said.

Cova frowned, as he considered her words. Then, grabbing up the safety deposit box, he slammed open the door to the private booth.

"Time to stir the kettle," he muttered under his breath.

The clerk who had delivered the metal box to them jumped up from his desk and hurried over. "Is there a problem, sir?"

"Some person has tampered with this box!" Cova said angrily, his face a mask of righteous indignation. He spoke in German, the primary language used in Zurich.

A shocked look passed across the official's face. Several other clerks looked up, frowning at the disturbance. One of the armed security guards casually stepped to the main entrance of the vault and rested a hand on the alarm switch.

"Impossible," said the flustered clerk. A tall thin man with thick glasses and only a few strands of hair dotting his forehead, his whole body shook as he spoke. "You must be mistaken."

"You dare question the word of a church official?" Cova bellowed, his voice shaking the walls.

All other work in the room stopped. All attention focused on them.

"Check your cameras. I know you secretly film all transactions taking place in this den of iniquity. Then tell me whether I lied or not. This box is empty. The contents are gone. Stolen!"

"Please, please," the clerk begged, waving his hands about and trying to quiet the priest. "Let me—"

"I will handle this matter, Wilhelm," said a tall, portly gentleman with bright red cheeks and bristly white whiskers. Clad in an expensive pin-striped suit and wide bow tie, he exuded confidence. A sigh of relief echoed through the vault at his appearance. Gratefully, the clerk vanished behind his desk.

"Please, come with me," the new arrival said, pointing to a private elevator in the rear of the room. "I am Gustave Lauber, executive vice-president of the bank. Would you care to accompany me to my office."

A few minutes later, Lauber smiled pleasantly at them across a huge desk in the elegant chamber that served as his office. "One never raises his voice in a Swiss bank," he said pleasantly. "It frightens the patrons."

"And a worried depositor might never return," Father Cova said, sipping from a glass of white wine, "which would be very, very bad for business. Precisely the reason that I created a disturbance. What better way to summon the firm's troubleshooter?"

"I prefer to be thought of as a problem

adjustor," Lauber said, straightening his bow tie just a bit. "You claim someone removed the contents of your safe deposit box. I find that quite difficult to believe."

"With the permission of my two young friends," the priest said, "I will explain."

He turned for a second and winked, while otherwise maintaining a properly stern visage.

"Herr Smith's father regrettably served on the wrong side of the Second World War. Afterwards, the gentleman never spoke of his experiences in the conflict. His family always believed that the senior Smith spent those years as a common soldier in the European campaign.

"It was not until he lay on his death bed a few weeks ago that the old man confessed an incredible secret. During the early days of the war, he oversaw an important spy ring operating in England. He funded his agents through money he kept in a safe deposit box in Switzerland. The account was in his name and was well-funded with British currency and gold coins."

Cova paused for effect and took another sip of wine. "The British crushed the cell in 1943. Herr Smith barely escaped with his life. When he returned to Germany, he informed his superiors that all his funds perished with his group. He never mentioned the safe deposit box or the cache of funds it still contained. No one ever suspected it existed.

"After the war, he wanted to reclaim the money, but fear overwhelmed his greed. The war crimes trials frightened him, and he grew paranoid. In his mind, the coins and banknotes linked him with the sins of the Reich. Herr Smith suspected Allied investigators watched his every move, waiting for him to make one mistake. So he ignored the fortune only he could touch.

"Upon hearing this deathbed confession, his son, a good Catholic, decided to donate all of these ill-gotten gains to the Church in penance for his father's sins. The Holy Father himself asked me to accompany Mr. Smith and his wife on their trip to insure that there were no complications. Imagine our shock when we opened the box and discovered it empty."

Herr Lauber looked very uncomfortable. "A very interesting story," he said slowly, tapping one finger on his desktop. "Maybe the elderly gentleman imagined the whole thing?"

"We suspected the same," Alex said. "I work in the Foreign Office. Using my contacts, I obtained the official records for the period. Every detail of the story checked out perfectly. Even the amount missing tallied with the cache he mentioned leaving in the vault."

"How much?" Lauber asked anxiously.

"One hundred and ten thousand pounds," Alex said, plucking the number out of the air, "in British currency and gold coins."

"Mein Gott," Lauber said, his face turning pale. "Excuse me. I must make a phone call."

The bank official spent several anxious moments whispering into the receiver and listening intently to the party on the other end of the line.

Slowly, the color returned to his cheeks. Hanging up the phone, he stood up and poured himself a glass of wine.

"I spoke with Frau Burkhardt, a member of our Board of Directors. When I told her your account number, she recalled a difficulty with that box that occurred right after the war. Frau Burkhardt's late husband handled the transaction. She has all of his notes in her chalet outside of town. A search through them will take place as soon as possible."

"When?" Alex asked, his mind on their enemies. They could not afford a long wait.

Herr Lauber chuckled. "The impatience of youth. Not days, I assure you; merely hours. Frau Burkhardt instructed me to invite you all to dinner at her estate. It is located some miles outside of Zurich. A magnificent retreat. One of the most unique buildings in the whole country. Please agree. Her chef is exceptional."

Lauber folded both hands over his expansive middle. "My waistline offers ample proof of his skill. Eat first, then business. That is the Swiss way of solving problems. You are staying nearby. If convenient, I will call for you at four o'clock. It takes nearly an hour to reach the estate."

Reluctantly, they accepted the invitation and spent the rest of the day nervously puzzling over the scene at the bank. Sitting in their rooms, Alex put into words what bothered them all.

"They surrendered without a fight. Herr Lauber never once raised the possibility of fraud. He gave in too quickly. Swiss banks jealously guard their reputations for honesty, yet instead of accusing us of deception, he immediately called this Frau Burkhardt for instructions."

"You heard what he claimed," Valerie said. "A difficulty with the box. Maybe we aren't the first ones to express interest in Steiner's secret treasure."

"Whatever the case," Father Cova said, rising from his chair and walking to the window, "we shall learn the truth soon enough. Better to confront the devil than endure any more of this confounded stalling. A limousine has pulled up outside. Here comes Herr Lauber. Are you ready to leave, Mr. and Mrs. Smith?"

"As ready as we'll ever be," Alex said.

An icy cold wind roared as they walked out to the car. Valerie shivered and pressed up close. Dark clouds lined the late afternoon sky, blocking out the sun. A surge of doubt flashed through Alex's mind.

He suddenly realized Lauber never once asked for the number of their account. The executive had known it all along. So had Frau Burkhardt. The bankers had played it smart by not immediately pressing for a meeting. Instead, by taking things slowly, they had managed to trap Alex and the others without once raising their suspicions.

Before he could say a word, Valerie slid into the back seat of the limo. A second later Father Cova followed. Alex stood alone on the sidewalk with Gustave Lauber.

"Please, Herr Smith," the banker said, "we must make haste. Supper is served promptly at six o'clock. Though she thinks of herself as Swiss, Frau Burkhardt originally comes from Germany. Like most of her race, she believes in punctuality. She hates waiting."

Then, almost as an afterthought, Lauber added, "For anything."

Chapter Twenty-Five

They arrived at Burkhardt Hause at exactly five o'clock. Valerie happily chatted with Herr Lauber the entire trip while Alex sullenly studied the mountain scenery outside the car. He mentally kicked himself every few minutes. Outwitted by an unknown opponent without even a struggle, he felt the fool. On the opposite end of the seat, Father Cova remained silent, lost in his own thoughts.

Their journey took them off the main highway and onto a narrow road that wound around the huge peaks north of the city. More than once, Alex closed his eyes as they rounded a hairpin turn at a speed far in excess of rational driving. The driver, a compact man with a fierce mustache who answered to the name Otto, grunted from time to time as he twisted the steering wheel about like a living thing. Tires squealed as the heavy car struggled to cling to the icy road. Gustave Lauber never blinked during their journey, convincing Alex the banker either possessed nerves of steel or was blind as a bat.

All conversation ceased when the limo swung around one last turn and pulled onto a gravel drive that threaded its way through a narrow mountain ravine. The cliffs crowded so close together that they appeared to touch many feet over their heads. Tons of ice and snow rumbled ominously as they drove beneath the glacial drifts. In front, undaunted by the threat of avalanche, Otto happily whistled a few bars of an old Bavarian drinking song. It reminded Alex that the border with Germany was only 20 miles away.

They emerged from the narrow passage onto a flat plateau. At the other end, a deep gorge slashed into the earth. Beyond the chasm towered huge stone cliffs reaching for the sky. An old metal bridge stretched across the abyss to a landing carved right into the solid face of the mountain.

"Incredible," Father Cova said, staring at their final destination. "Truly incredible."

The chalet rested in the center of a man-made hollow cut from the heart of the cliff. Its bulky stone walls merged right into the rock, joining house and mountain as one entity. Huge slate slabs formed the roof of the building. Mounted there were a number of huge spotlights. Only a few tiny, barred windows broke the solid face of the structure. A tall, cast-iron fence fronted the house and effectively sealed the landing from the solitary bridge that led to the outside world. Two heavyset men, armed with rifles, watched them intently from behind a small gatehouse.

Otto honked the horn twice and slowly guided the limo onto the rickety steel bridge. Powerful winds buffeted the auto from all sides as it rolled across the creaking girders. At the other end, one of the gatekeepers pulled back the metal trellis to let them pass undisturbed.

"We are expected," Lauber said, needlessly. "Otherwise the guards check credentials very carefully. Frau Burkhardt controls one of the largest fortunes in Europe and lives in constant danger of kidnaping."

Alex murmured something proper. The manor looked more like a fortress than a country estate. The thick stone walls they passed entering the mansion did little to dispel that image.

"I gather this structure dates back a few years," Father Cova said.

"You guess correctly," the banker said, escorting them down a long hall. He obviously knew his way about the place. "The building rests on the foundations of an early border outpost constructed soon after the Treaty of Basel in 1499. The fortress housed Swiss troops until 1798, when the French invaded our country and razed the building to the ground.

"In 1939, Henri Guisan, the commanding

general of the Swiss Army, built the present manor, which served throughout the war as the regional headquarters for the Nachrichten-Dienst, our Army Information Service. After the war, Frau Burkhardt and her husband bought the estate from the government at a very reasonable price. Few people wanted to settle in such a forbidding setting, but it offered the Burkhardts privacy unmatched by any other location near Zurich."

Alex wondered about the obsession with security. Many wealthy executives lived perfectly normal lives without resorting to such elaborate precautions. Perhaps Lauber only knew part of the story.

The banker rambled on as they descended further into the mountain. Servants and guards lived in the outer shell of the huge mansion, the actual living quarters extending far into the solid rock. They finally emerged into a brightly lit reception area where a dignified butler in full tails awaited their arrival.

"Good afternoon," he said in perfect, unaccented English. "Frau Burkhardt extends her warmest welcome to you all. Dinner will be served shortly. Perhaps you would care to freshen up before your meal. Please follow me."

Once alone with his wife in a tastefully decorated dressing room, Alex pulled her close and hugged her tight.

"Hey," Valerie said, "no time for this, you animal."

"There's always time for a hug," Alex replied.

"You told me so once yourself."

Nuzzling her ear, he quickly whispered his suspicions to her. Valerie's grip around his shoulders tightened a bit, but otherwise she gave no indication of surprise.

"You think this room is bugged?" she asked, mouthing the words softly as she tilted her head close to his.

"Maybe. Why take a chance? We play dumb as long as possible. In the meanwhile, I wish I knew how the Burkhardts acquired their money. Even at bargain prices, this place cost a mint."

"Enough play," Valerie said, loudly. She stepped back and smoothed down her dress. "Maybe Frau Burkhardt will reveal some of her money-making secrets to us tonight. According to Herr Lauber, she owns a number of Swiss banks as well as the controlling interest in several major European corporations."

"How interesting," Alex said. "She comes from a wealthy family?"

"Herr Lauber never said. Evidently, she rarely talks about herself or her late husband. She prefers to concentrate on the present."

"She sounds like a shrewd businesswoman. I look forward to meeting her."

They returned to the reception room. Herr Lauber and Father Cova arrived a few moments later, followed by the butler. Together, they proceeded down another long hallway to the dining room.

The chamber was tastefully decorated in soft

shades of blue and gold. On the table rested a bouquet of fresh flowers. A blazing fire roared in the huge stone fireplace at the far end of the room. The only discordant note was a pair of 16th century halberds crossed above the mantle. The sharp steel spikes on the eight-foot-long pikes gleamed brightly in the light.

"Please be seated," the butler said, pulling out their chairs. "Ms. Lancaster here. Professor Warner, of course, at her side. Father Cova, if you please, over here. And Herr Lauber, at your usual spot. Frau Burkhardt will join you in a moment. In the meantime, would anyone care for a cocktail?"

With a heavy sigh, Alex asked for a glass of wine. While seeking anonymity, they had not gone to great lengths to keep their real identities secret. With their real names out in the open, he mentally questioned whether Frau Burkhardt had ever believed the story about the missing funds. He felt quite sure she had not. Sipping his wine, he visually searched the table for something that would serve as a weapon.

"Frau Burkhardt," the butler announced, as if ushering royalty into the room.

They all rose as their hostess entered. A tall, statuesque woman with flowing silver hair that reached almost to her waist, she walked with the simple grace of a trained athlete. Smooth skin and unblemished features betrayed no hint of age. Only her dark gray eyes seemed old beyond measure.

"She possesses the power," Valerie whispered. "I felt it the second she entered the room."

Without a word, Frau Burkhardt came directly over to Father Cova. Kneeling before the startled priest, she made the sign of the cross upon her chest. With both of her hands, she took one of his and pressed his fingers to her lips.

Father Cova looked astonished. After a moment, he managed to stutter, "Rise, my child."

"Please forgive me for this deception," Frau Burkhardt said as she stood up. "I dared not risk making a mistake. The touch of your hand was the only way I could know you came from the Church." She smiled. "I have waited so many years for this day."

"I am not sure I follow you," Father Cova said, his voice still not steady. "We have never met. Nor is your name familiar to me."

Without answering, Frau Burkhardt took her seat at the head of the table. As she sat down, servants appeared as if by magic and began serving.

"Perhaps you know me better by my maiden name," she said. "I am Magda Steiner."

It took a few instants for the words to sink in. Then instinctively, without thinking, Alex spoke.

"Impossible," he said. "Steiner's daughter died during childbirth. Even Dietrich Vril told us that his mother perished giving him life."

"Like yourselves, he confused two facts," Frau Burkhardt said, sighing. "His real mother died, but I was not her."

"Then who was his true mother?" Valerie

asked. The confused look on her face mirrored the bewilderment that engulfed them all.

"Trudie Vetter, a poor girl hypnotized by my father into thinking she was me. Trudie resembled me just enough to fool the few officials who ever visited our home during the early days of Project Alraune. During the latter stages of her pregnancy, Father kept her in complete seclusion. No one ever suspected him of using a double. Meanwhile, with the help of Herr Lauber's father, I lived a quiet life in Switzerland. When Trudie died giving birth, my name died with her. No one ever suspected father's trickery."

"But what about your affair with Rudolf Hess?" Valerie asked.

"What?" Frau Burkhardt said, choking on her wine. Her eyes widened, and she burst out laughing.

"Me and Rudy? Who told you such an incredible story? We were good friends, nothing more." She laughed again. "So much for my role in history."

"Perhaps we better compare stories," Alex said. "Then afterwards, we can ask any questions that still remain."

"Before we start," Father Cova said, looking their hostess straight in the eye, "I need to know one thing. What happened to Pope Leo's treasure box?"

"Why, I removed it from the bank long ago," she answered simply. "Sooner or later, I feared Dietrich Vril would discover the key and come looking for the relic. My father, in his last letter to me, warned of the terrible consequences if Vril ever obtained the treasure. So I made sure it was safe and secure and well-protected.

"Many times I thought to contact the Vatican, but always I hesitated. Vril was a brilliant man with unlimited funds supplied by his demonic friends. What had happened once could happen again. I dared not risk giving the box to anyone unless they came looking for it—as was the case with you.

"Gustave kept close tabs on anyone inquiring about old deposits. He alerted me shortly after your first call. Using my financial contacts, I wormed out the necessary information about you, Father Cova, and your mysterious quest. Even the Church cannot keep secrets from its bankers. Gustave and I then planned our little deception to lure you to my retreat. Your charade about stolen funds merely made his task easier."

"Then you actually have the box in your possession?" Father Cova asked.

"Forty years ago, I placed it in a safe in the next room," Karl Steiner's daughter answered. "It is still there."

Chapter Twenty-Six

An hour later, their dinner finished and the table cleared, Alex related their adventures. He again started with the phone call from Howie Rosenberg and concluded with their deadly battle with the vampire. Frau Burkhardt and Herr Lauber listened intently, not interrupting once.

"An incredible tale," their hostess said when he finally finished. "You managed to discover so much with only a few clues. Too bad your friend Tsuiki did not come with you. He almost guessed the truth."

"Almost?"

"You based your reasoning on incomplete data," Frau Burkhardt said. "Let me tell you the truth about Project Alraune and its creator, Karl Steiner.

"My father married late in life, and the union lasted little more than a year. My mother disappeared shortly after my birth. While he never spoke of her, I suspected Karl secretly murdered his wife because her presence interfered with his plans for me. A ruthless, arrogant, totally amoral man, he manipulated every person he encountered—even Adolf Hitler. My father considered himself above the law, an *Ubermensch* surrounded by a sea of inferior beings.

"Strangely enough, unlike most men of the time, he harbored no strong sexual prejudices. The sex of his child meant nothing to him. He wanted a loyal assistant with many of the same psychic powers as his own. Who better to trust than his own offspring?

"Karl raised me the best as could be expected. A cold, aloof man, he nevertheless tried in his own way to be a good parent. I never wanted for anything, other than warmth or affection. He spent many long hours teaching me the basics of sorcery and black magic, preparing for the day when I would assist him with his work.

"Most of my childhood days were spent casting spells and studying sorcery. My father never scolded me if I made a mistake. In fact, he exhibited greater patience with me than any of his disciples. In his own twisted manner, I believe Karl Steiner loved me as much as anyone in his bitter life.

"Over the course of those years, he traveled a great deal of the time. He left me in the care of trusted disciples, often for months, and in one case for several years. Those long stretches apart from my father saved my soul.

"Most of his students practiced sorcery, but they otherwise led reasonably normal lives. Staying with their families, I encountered true love and human emotion. It made me realize the emptiness in my own life, not that it mattered very much. Steiner completely controlled my future, and there was no possibility of escape.

"A lonely child, I read a great number of books. My favorites were the novels of Karl May, who wrote long novels about the American West, featuring a noble scout named Old Shatterhand. These books were all bestsellers in Germany. In fact, one of May's biggest fans was the Fuhrer himself.

"Despite their simplistic racial stereotypes, May's works awakened in me an awareness of the true nobility of the human spirit. All of the Nazi propaganda I heard for years afterward never changed my basic beliefs in the universal brotherhood of mankind.

"After Hitler's rise to power, I saw my father even less. He never finished teaching me his most powerful secrets. Instead, I spent more and more time alone at our country estate, while he traveled across Europe on secret missions for Hitler. Then, early in March, 1937, he returned home for good. It was then that he began work on his greatest scheme. He called the plan Project Alraune.

"Shortly after my father's return to Germany, a platoon of soldiers arrived and settled in the outer buildings of our estate. They served as the compound's security force, for over the next few months a steady stream of Nazi dignitaries visited our manor.

"Following my father's wishes, I acted as an informal hostess for these conferences. No servants were allowed. I often served coffee and cakes after the long meetings. Once I even prepared dinner when the proceedings lasted into the evening. None of the participants told me what they discussed behind closed doors, and I knew better than to ask.

"The Fuhrer attended three of those secret conferences, usually with Rudy in attendance. The Fuhrer always spent a few minutes talking to me. One visit he brought me a scarce Karl May novel from his own library. He enjoyed teasing me about 'devoting my life to the new Reich.' It was a line that always made me blush. I thought he referred to my helping my father. I never suspected the real meaning behind his words.

"I learned soon enough. After Hitler departed from that third meeting, Karl summoned me to his study. In a cool, detached voice, he fully outlined the details of Project Alraune and my proposed involvement in the plan. A terrible sense of doom overwhelmed me when I realized the gruesome role planned for my future."

Father Cova rose from his chair and poured

himself another glass of wine. "So I guessed correctly?"

"You deduced part of the scheme. Tsuiki recognized some of it as well. Neither of you grasped the full magnitude of the diabolical project nor of my father's actual ambitions. Looking back over all these years, I realize now that in a certain, mad way, it made perfect sense. It was the ultimate answer to the Nazi dream of the superman.

"My father actually believed in the story of the primal land and the destiny of the Aryan race. He felt destiny had chosen him to fulfill that vision with Hitler serving as his unwitting puppet. Karl envisioned a world ruled by Germany and spent most of his life working to that end.

"Though he practiced the darkest sorcery, my father was a hard-headed pragmatist. One constant worry dominated his thoughts. He realized that the future of the Third Reich revolved around one man—Adolf Hitler.

"The Fuhrer embodied the will and spirit of the Armanen superman. He was a living god to the masses, and the destiny of Germany rested entirely in his hands. Without him, all of my father's plans meant nothing. If he died, the thousand year Reich collapsed before it began.

"None of Hitler's underlings inspired the same faith among the people as did the Fuhrer. None of them could lead Germany forward to victory. Father recognized that only an equally powerful personality could replace him.

"A keen student of history, Karl closely studied the fates of earlier empires like those of Charlamagne and Genghis Khan. Those kingdoms depended on one dynamic leader. In each case, deprived of a strong, central authority figure, the realms collapsed into chaos upon his death. My father knew that one well-placed bullet, one deadly bout of pneumonia, would forever shatter his vision of a world under German rule.

"Desperately seeking an alternative to disaster, he chanced upon *Alraune,* written by his friend, Hanns Heinz Ewers. Inspired by the story, he concocted the Mandrake Project.

"Basically, my father proposed the same basic idea as the novel. He planned to artificially inseminate a woman by black magic. Once that was accomplished, he plotted to manipulate the genetic structure of the fetus while still in the womb using secrets taught to him by the Very Old Folk. This tampering guaranteed the child would be born a perfect Aryan with near superhuman abilities and powers.

"Unfortunately, the use of such powerful black magic would inflict incredible pain to the child's mother throughout the pregnancy. By the time she gave birth, death would be a relief.

"Afterwards, Karl wanted to accelerate the boy's growth by sorcery, compressing fifteen years into one. The Pope's treasure box boosted my father's powerful psychic powers, enabling him to accomplish nearly anything he desired. He promised the Fuhrer a loyal second-in-command with superhuman abilities within five years after the start of the project.

"What my father never mentioned to Hitler was that this unholy creation would be loyal only to Karl Steiner. While he never discussed this with me, I suspect he thought Hitler dangerously unstable and dreamt of replacing him with his masterpiece."

"Hitler agreed to this insane scheme?" Alex asked. "I thought he imagined treachery everywhere and trusted no one, including his closest advisors."

"The Fuhrer trusted the powers of darkness. The Very Old Folk frightened him, but he acknowledged their immense powers. Hitler consented to the project but only under one condition. He wanted to test my father's absolute dedication to the Reich. Insisting on pure Aryan bloodlines for the experiment, the Fuhrer commanded that I be used as the host mother. The whole effort hinged on my father's decision. Faced with the choice, he agreed."

"Condemning you to madness and death," Valerie said, shock and sadness mixed in her voice.

"If necessary, yes," Frau Burkhardt said. "No one, not even his own daughter, meant as much to my father as his dream. Still, after more than a decade serving the Fuhrer, he often anticipated Hitler's wishes. In this case, he guessed correctly. Resorting to a dangerous ruse, he saved me.

"Years earlier, my father realized he danced on quicksand with a madman as his partner. On one of his many trips to Switzerland, he bought a small villa. He staffed the secret hideaway with disciples of the Thule Society, men loyal to him alone. He kept the location of that sanctum a close secret known only to the two of us. It served as my sanctuary for nearly a decade."

"So Steiner replaced you with a double before he ever suggested the experiment to Hitler," Alex said. "That girl, Trudie Vetter, died in your place."

Frau Burkhardt nodded. A solitary tear trickled down her cheek. "I felt terrible knowing her fate. However, I knew the project called for a life. Despite my anguish, I was not willing to sacrifice myself in the vain effort to save another. I agreed to my father's ruse.

"Karl needed an agent working outside the Reich. For the next few years, I followed his commands, working from the secret base in Switzerland. Not until his death was I free from his eternal scheming."

Alex wondered exactly what tasks Frau Burkhardt performed for her father during those intervening years. Like a number of other unpleasant details of her story, she managed to gloss over her role in the narrative. He suspected Frau Burkhardt remembered the past in a very selective manner, one that cast her in the best light possible.

"One detail still puzzles me," Valerie said. "You said that your father used black magic to artificially inseminate Trudie Vetter. But Mak pointed out in our discussion that the technology and techniques for that operation existed long before the Second World War. He corrected Father Cova on exactly the same point."

An odd look passed across Frau Burkhardt's face. For a moment, she remained silent, as if recalling ancient ghosts. Her eyes narrowed to mere cracks. When she spoke, her voice trembled with fear.

"You asked why Hitler agreed so readily to Project Alraune. Years before, my father learned the Fuhrer's deepest secret. The all-powerful leader of Germany, master of the Reich, the man feared by half the world, could not have children. Rumors whispered the truth, but no one dared say it aloud. Hitler was impotent. Father offered him the one thing he desired above all else—an heir. The power of the treasure box made the impossible possible."

"You don't mean . . ." Valerie began, astonished.

"Exactly what you think," Frau Burkhardt said. "The man you know as Dietrich Vril is the unnatural son of Trudie Vetter—and Adolf Hitler."

Chapter Twenty-Seven

Frau Burkhardt stood up and signaled them to follow. She walked over to the fireplace. The flames had long since burned out. Carefully, she depressed a small button half-hidden in the stone. With a grinding noise, the entire chimney swung out.

Behind it was revealed a small chamber some five feet square. On the far wall hung a large wooden crucifix. Ornate decorations of pure silver capped each end. The light from the dining room candles bounced off the metal, casting strange shadows on the floor.

"The Swiss government built this manor on the ruins of an old fortress dating back to the sixteenth century," Frau Burkhardt said, as she walked into the tiny room. The rest of them crowded in after her. "The workmen found this cross when they dug the foundation for this section of the building. It has guarded the Pope's treasure for decades."

She removed the crucifix, uncovering a thin keyhole in the otherwise unmarked wall. A chain around her neck held the key.

"I spent a great deal of money having this room built to my exact specifications. Several separate teams of workmen handled each phase of the construction. Only I know all of its secrets."

Frau Burkhardt inserted the key in the unusual lock and turned it full around. Behind their backs, with the same grinding noise, the fireplace swung back across the opening. They were trapped inside the hidden chamber. An unnoticed ceiling light snapped on automatically, bathing them in a dim yellow glow. Nothing else happened, and Frau Burkhardt made no effort to retrieve the key.

"It takes a minute for the gears to engage properly. Meanwhile, a second set of switches activates a time bomb located right beneath our feet. The device contains enough explosives to destroy this building, as well as much of the mountain above it."

With a soft whirr of shifting panels, a section of the far wall beneath the keyhole folded back. In the recess stood a heavy, combination lock safe.

Quickly, Frau Burkhardt knelt down in front

of the box and started rotating the tumblers.

"The only way to shut off the time bomb is to open the safe in the thirty seconds that remain till detonation. And I am the only one who knows the combination."

Alex's mouth suddenly went very dry at the mention of 30 seconds, and Herr Lauber's ruddy complexion turned a shade redder. No one breathed as Frau Burkhardt twirled the dials. She seemed completely oblivious to their concern.

"I should replace this lock," she said in an absent-minded sort of way. "It grows old and worn, like me."

Groaning from the effort, she pressed down hard on the handle, and the ponderous safe door swung open.

"Finished with five seconds to spare," she said with a laugh. "I oftentimes wake up late at night, covered with sweat, dreaming about that combination."

Reaching inside the safe, Frau Burkhardt pulled out a large black velvet bag. It was more than a foot long and was knotted with gold strings. Her body shaking slightly, she rose unsteadily to her feet, holding the treasure clutched tightly to her breast.

"Turn the key in the lock one more time," she instructed Alex. "It will open the outer door. My aged bones betray me."

No one spoke as they filed out of the secret chamber and back into the dining room. Father Cova and Gustave Lauber headed straight for the wine rack. Frau Burkhardt deposited her burden on the table and sank down into her chair.

"I need a glass of brandy," she called out to them. "Fill it to the top."

Valerie slid up next to Alex, her eyes shining with excitement. "I can feel the power locked inside the box," she said quietly. She gripped his arm tightly. "It calls out to me with even greater power than the coins at the Devil's Auction. The rest of you can't feel it. Only Frau Burkhardt and I sense its strength. The treasure blazes with psychic energy. I understand how her father performed miracles. With that box, anything is possible. Anything!"

"Perhaps now you realize why I bought this citadel," Frau Burkhardt said, her hands trembling as she emptied her glass. "In this remote location, beneath a thousand tons of rock, not even Dietrich Vril could sense the box's call."

His wife's words bothered Alex more than he cared to admit. Frau Burkhardt's story cleared up all the loose ends of their investigation, yet he felt uneasy. He couldn't pinpoint the exact reason, but he knew that something the woman said didn't sound right.

Alex was certain that he possessed all the information necessary to solve that final riddle, yet somehow the solution eluded him. Valerie's words echoed in his mind, but he didn't understand why.

"What happens next?" Father Cova asked, his steady eyes fixed on Frau Burkhardt.

"You take the box and return it to the Vatican.

Once there, you can take the proper steps to make sure Vril never gets close to it. As for me, I finally am free to live my life in peace."

The priest stood frozen in surprise. "You are giving me the box?" he finally managed to ask.

"Of course," Frau Burkhardt said. "Why do you think I checked your credentials so carefully? I spent the last forty years guarding that cursed object, making sure that Dietrich Vril never found it. I buried it inside this mountain to make sure its aura remained undetected. Vril searched for it, I assure you. He never gave up hunting. Fortunately, with no leads, he never knew where to look. The treasure remained safe. Now I can return it to you and blot out my father's crime. You are welcome to the box. I am glad to see it gone. Please, take it."

Cova inhaled deeply, his eyes half-closed. He shook his head as if in disbelief.

"The ways of the Lord are beyond the ken of mortal man. It was my uncle, my father's older brother, who gave the box to Karl Steiner. The shame of that crime has burdened my family ever since. How ironic that the children of those involved in the original act should be the ones to set it right."

Frau Burkhardt shivered. "I, for one, do not believe in coincidences."

Another piece of the puzzle in place, thought Alex. But not the answer for which he was searching.

Valerie could not stop staring at the velvet bag. "The powers of the relic—" she began.

"I never once opened the box," Frau Burkhardt interrupted emotionally. "My father never taught me how to control such forces. The psychic energy it contains nearly killed him when he first experimented with it. I valued my life and my sanity too much to risk tampering. The box both frightened me and enticed me."

"So you lived for decades with that temptation preying on your soul," Valerie said, her eyes widening in comprehension. "No wonder you locked it away in a booby-trapped room."

Frau Burkhardt nodded. "The bomb acted as my anchor with reality. It took all my wits to retrieve the box from the hiding place. If greed ever overwhelmed my reason, I died, destroying the Pope's relic as well. The mental agony often threatened to drive me mad, but I survived. The suffering made me strong. My pledge forced me to continue on. Karl Steiner foolishly unleashed a monster upon the unsuspecting world. I swore an oath I would never let that abomination gain the one thing he most desired—the treasure of Pope Leo."

"What do you mean?" Alex asked, intent on her answer.

"Father planned carefully. Disciples of the Thule Society smuggled me out of Germany the night after our discussion. Trudie Vetter took my place. In Switzerland I stayed at a villa hidden in the mountains. Karl communicated with me by hand-written letters delivered by trusted messengers at infrequent intervals.

"At first, my father rarely mentioned the project in his notes. He usually wanted me to perform certain tasks for him and included little more than his detailed instructions. However, as months grew into years, he wrote more often. His messages reflected a growing concern with his young 'grandson.' Evidently, the child possessed powers beyond the imaginings of my father or the Very Old Folk. Soon, Vril's control of the dark forces surpassed those of my worried parent and his gruesome allies.

"Father sent me the Pope's treasure late in 1940. By then, his creation frightened him so much that he wanted a weapon held in reserve. Steiner dared not keep the relic on his estate, for fear Vril might find it. Only the mystic force of the box matched the child's occult powers. For some reason, the boy was afraid of its contents. Evidently it was the one object that held enough mystic force to destroy him.

"Father still harbored vague dreams that the child would mature and aid him in his plans, but as a precaution Steiner made me rent a safe deposit box for the treasure. I sent him the key. He hid it, along with cryptic clues to identify it, in his copy of *Alraune*.

"He gave the book to a close friend and told him just enough to recruit his cooperation. Karl dared not reveal too much. His acquaintance, a high-ranking party official, swore to hand over the book to Heinrich Himmler if anything happened to father."

"It sounds like something out of the movies," Valerie said. "The criminal mastermind always used a hidden box for insurance. He filled it with damning evidence for the authorities. But who elected Himmler as a good guy?"

"My father knew the Reichsfuhrer-SS quite well. For several years in the 1930's, Karl instructed Himmler in the dark magic of necromancy. The dead fascinated the SS commander. He strived constantly to communicate with the past kings of Germany. A small glimmer of psychic energy enabled him to perform simple tricks, but though he studied the occult with a passion, Himmler never possessed the necessary discipline which brought true power.

"I only met him a few times during those early years. He impressed me at the time with his quiet wit and mild demeanor. Himmler delighted teaching my pet dog tricks and then showing off to me. A man without imagination, he made jokes about himself and his mission, yet he changed the SS from a small band of thugs organized to guard Hitler into the most feared organization in the Reich."

"The Order of the Death's Head," Father Cova said sadly. "He based his society on the Jesuits and structured it in the same manner. That fact haunted the Church for decades."

"It functioned as a quasi-military unit reporting only to Himmler and the Fuhrer," Frau Burkhardt said. "Father considered it his best hope. The Black Jesuit, as many of his rivals called Himmler, knew the goals of Project Alraune, but not its origin. Father feared the terrible abuses possible if the Reichsfuhrer gained possession of the box, so he decided that only if he died would Himmler obtain the prize.

"Father was confident the SS chief would figure out the hidden message and retrieve the box. Using its power and the vast resources of his organization, he could destroy Vril."

"What happened?" Alex asked.

"I never found out what went wrong. Hess witnessed something monstrous at father's estate and panicked. He flew immediately to England to beg for peace at any price. Hitler exploded in anger and blamed it all on the project. He declared father a non-person and an enemy of the Reich. The Gestapo placed him under house arrest, and I never heard from him again.

"Hanns Heinz Ewers suffered a similar fate. A number of other important party officials dropped out of sight. Evidently, the Fuhrer decided to isolate all those who knew the truth about the project. All records of the experiment vanished.

"Meanwhile, Dietrich Vril escaped from the estate and vanished. The Gestapo and SS hunted for him for months without success. Hitler instructed them to capture the child alive, but all their efforts came to naught. Vril disappeared until after the war. When he surfaced in West Germany in the late 1940's, it was as a powerful though mysterious industrialist.

"My father's friend never gave Himmler the book. Probably, with Karl's arrest, he feared that any link with my father would result in his own imprisonment or death. Such events were commonplace in those mad days. The officer died during the Battle of the Bulge, and the book never resurfaced."

Alex sorted out the events in his mind. Nearly everything fit together now. It all made sense. Vril wanted the box because he feared it held enough power to destroy him.

Yet Alex found it hard to believe that anything frightened Dietrich Vril. They still were overlooking something. The puzzle lacked one piece to make it complete. Only then would all the facts mesh into a unified whole.

"Excuse me, Frau Burkhardt," the butler said, hurrying into the room. "They need you up front. It seems that several carloads of unwelcome visitors demand entrance."

"Damn," Frau Burkhardt said, rising to her feet. "When you told me your whole story, I worried that perhaps my snooping alerted your enemies to my location. I suspect the wolves are howling at the gates."

"How dare they threaten you?" Herr Lauber said, his florid features puffed up in anger. "You are rich."

"Unfortunately, that fact means very little to certain people," Frau Burkhardt said with a grim smile. "In fact, it annoys them a great deal. Fanatics hate money, especially when it belongs to someone else."

Chapter Twenty-Eight

From small peepholes in the stone walls of the courtyard, they stared out at their enemy. Powerful spotlights illuminated the plateau as if it were broad daylight.

On the other side of the metal bridge were parked a dozen cars. Big, powerful machines, their chassis rode low to the ground, indicating to Alex that they were reinforced with steel shielding.

Nearly 50 men knelt behind the armor-plated automobiles. Each of them carried an automatic weapon, aimed at the manor. Stocking masks hid their features, but Alex recognized one figure instantly. He stood behind the car parked directly across from them. In one massive fist he gripped a bullhorn. Nothing could disguise the huge form of Brother Ambrose nor muffle his booming voice.

"We wish you no harm," he bellowed. "Let us have the treasure and we will leave in peace. Do not force us to use violence."

Frau Burkhardt shook her head in disbelief and made a clucking sound deep in her throat. "Tch, tch, tch. He probably means what he says. If I hand over the box, he will take his men and leave. Unfortunately, I find the notion of surrender inconceivable."

Father Cova breathed a sigh of relief. "If he obtains the Pope's treasure, he will destroy the Church."

"I strongly doubt that," Alex said. He wondered what motivated Father Cova more—the health of the Church or his family honor. It didn't much matter. In either case, the priest was dedicated to returning the treasure box to the Vatican. He did not look like he would give up without a fight.

"The Catholic Church survived the Reformation. I suspect that charges of aiding the Nazis would prove painful but not fatal."

"Who cares about that," Frau Burkhardt said. "If this fool outside gains possession of the box, then Dietrich Vril ultimately triumphs. Do you think Haxley could keep the treasure safe for long? Only we understand the power of that monster."

She snapped her fingers and one of the guards came running forward with a loudspeaker. A wiry, middle-aged man with graying hair, his calm features betrayed no hint of worry. He carried a submachine gun slung over his back. In his free hand, he gripped a snub-nosed revolver.

"We fight?" he asked politely.

"Probably, Franz. It depends on the idiots outside. Go alert the others."

The guard trotted off to warn his comrades.

"Despite Hitler's efforts, the Thule Society still exists. Loyal to my father, the members serve me as well. Six of them guard this fortress. Like me, they will die if necessary protecting the treasure."

Frau Burkhardt raised the loudspeaker to her lips. "You are trespassing on private property. I order you to leave at once. If not, I will summon the police."

Brother Ambrose laughed heartily. "Please, no foolish threats," he yelled back, not bothering with the amplifier. "We cut the telephone lines on our way through the mountains. You can expect no aid from the outside. Besides, such publicity would subject you to intense media scrutiny.

"People whisper behind your back, Frau Burkhardt, about your checkered past. How did you accumulate your mysterious fortune? My friends in Zurich speculate that you collaborated with the Germans. Did you build your financial empire on the blood of innocents. Dare you risk an investigation?"

"Wait," Frau Burkhardt said, a note of deep

concern in her voice. "I need time to think."

"An hour," Brother Ambrose shouted, sounding very satisfied with himself. "One hour to decide your fate."

Switching off the loudspeaker, Frau Burkhardt shrugged and smiled faintly. "At least I bought us a little time. We can set our defenses. Fortunately for us, these conspirators see the worst in everyone. That fool actually believes he worries me with his reference to my fortune."

"Where did the money come from?" Valerie asked.

"You forgot why Karl Steiner originally came to Switzerland," Herr Lauber said. "Working with my father, he opened a large number of secret bank accounts for top Nazi officials. All of them maintained emergency funds here in case of disaster. None of them ever suspected that their trusted messenger made duplicates of all their keys and kept a journal with all of their account numbers. He passed that information along to Frau Burkhardt."

"I never touched the money during the war," Frau Burkhardt continued. "But after the Fuhrer committed suicide, I looted all of the trusts. Much of the money I donated to war relief funds. The rest went into a holding company that invested the funds in privately held Swiss banks. Herr Lauber Jr. and his partner, my late husband, Wolfgang Burkhardt, handled all of the purchases. Wolf specialized in such transactions. He swore to me no one would ever be able to untangle the multiple transfers involving the purchases. In all the years since that time, nothing has happened to make me doubt his word."

The minutes ticked by slowly. Franz provided Alex, Father Cova and Herr Lauber with pistols and automatic weapons. While checking the sights on his rifle, Alex tried to persuade Valerie and Frau Burkhardt to return to the safety of the dining room, but both women refused.

"My place is with you," his wife said, "especially in situations like these. Besides, if I stay close enough, my warding spell will shield us both from bullets."

"I was born German," Frau Burkhardt said, carefully loading a small revolver, "but the ensuing years made me Swiss. And in this country," she declared firmly, "we fight for what we believe."

It was nearing midnight by the end of the appointed hour. As if to protect them from the spotlights across the gorge, the Circumcellions had switched on the bright lights of their vehicles. Shining off the snow, the headlights formed a glaring barrier behind which they stood invisible.

"We await your decision," came the booming voice of Brother Ambrose. "What do you chose? Life or death?"

"Death," Father Cova cried, "to heretics," and opened fire with his machine gun.

Glass exploded as his bullets hit a half-dozen headlights. The next instant, the entire canyon roared with the sound of automatic weapons. Guns chattered wildly, sending brick and stone jumping off the ancient walls of the manor.

Alex held his fire, while Father Cova and Frau Burkhardt's guards sprayed the plateau with bullets. Actually, all the shooting served no purpose. As Alex suspected, the Circumcellions' cars were armor-plated. The gunfire did little damage to the vehicles or the men behind them. The thick walls of the manor house worked the same for Alex and his friends.

After a few minutes, both sides realized the futility of their actions and firing stopped. Now, the waiting began.

"They outnumber us nearly ten to one," Alex said. "In most battles, numbers like those spell easy victory for them, especially in a few hours when we grow tired. But the intense cold works in our favor, as does the crevice with one narrow bridge. Unless they cross it, we hold all the cards."

"It didn't take them long to reach the same conclusion," Frau Burkhardt said. "Here they come."

Motors roared as the Circumcellions revved up their cars. Four vehicles pulled out of line and headed for the bridge. Each auto carried several men who blazed away with their guns, creating a nonstop barrage aimed at the manor. The hail of gunfire served as a near-perfect shield as the cars barreled towards the narrow trestle.

"I'll handle this," Alex said coolly. "They left their tires unprotected."

Carefully, he stuck his rifle out a tiny crack in the wall. Squinting, he picked his shots, then whistling softly to himself, he gently squeezed the trigger. Every bullet counted. Shooting with uncanny accuracy, he punctured the front tires of the lead car. Several more rounds shattered the auto's window, wounding a man and sending all of the passengers scrambling for safety.

A return volley buried itself in the thick walls of the manor. Ignoring the fire, Alex methodically disabled the second car in the caravan, then the third. The fourth vehicle turned and roared out of range.

Total silence descended as the renegades regrouped behind their machines. The attack was over.

"They'll try crawling across the bridge soon," Alex said. "Unimaginative, but that's the way most battles are won. Not tonight, though. Tell your guards to let a few of them make it halfway across before opening fire. Less chance of them missing any targets from that distance. Nothing destroys confidence like seeing several of your friends lying dead in plain view."

Alex yawned. "God, I'm tired." He yawned again. "It must be the night air."

Father Cova nodded in agreement as he stifled a yawn with one hand. "I feel pretty sleepy myself."

The priest closed his eyes and within seconds started snoring.

A few feet away, one of the guards carefully rested his rifle on the ground. Leaning up against the outer wall, he rested his head on his crossed arms. In seconds, he was asleep standing up.

The sight of an unarmed man with a rifle at his feet shocked Alex awake. Groggily, he realized the terrible truth.

"Vampires," he managed to croak, as he forced himself unsteadily to his feet and staggered over to Valerie. She rested with her back up against a wall, eyes closed, her breathing slow and even. Like everyone else, she was already lightly asleep.

"Wake up," Alex said, his voice no more than a whisper. He grabbed her by the shoulders and shook as hard as he could. Valerie's head wobbled back and forth, but she remained asleep.

Desperately, Alex drew back a hand and slapped his wife sharply across the face. Valerie struggled sleepily, trying to escape the pain. He slapped her again and then a third time. With the fourth attempt she caught his wrist angrily.

"You son-of-a . . ." she began and then saw him staggering about, trying to keep his balance. Her gaze swept across the enclosure and sudden understanding sparked in her eyes.

"Aegri somnia," she said, snapping her fingers.

The spell worked its magic instantly. The compound echoed with howls of pain as their comrades returned to consciousness.

"The Very Old Folk!" Alex shouted, forestalling any questions.

A deathly silence reigned beyond the walls of the fort. No one moved on the other side of the ravine. Then, out of the night sky, came the sound of huge wings. Eerie shadows passed in the moonlight.

"I see Hell on Earth," whispered Frau Burkhardt, and no one raised a voice in disagreement.

They drifted down out of the dark night sky. The creatures flew with an easy grace that proclaimed them masters of the air. Nearly a dozen of the vampires rode the winds, their giant wings blotting out the moon. Monstrous yellow fangs gleamed in the near darkness. Red eyes burned with unholy fire.

Faintly, Alex heard a human voice raised in wild, maniacal laughter. The ghoulish howling of Dietrich Vril echoed through the canyon as his minions settled among the Circumcellions and landed to feast.

"We are doomed," the old woman said, her face ashen. "No force on Earth can stand against the Very Old Folk."

"I killed one," Alex said defiantly.

"A single monster, in a confined space and unable to fly," Frau Burkhardt said, unconvinced. "Listen," and her body trembled as she spoke, "they feed on human flesh."

From across the crevice came faint, unidentifiable sounds. The vagueness of the sounds made them all the more terrible. In the moonlight, huge shapes ripped and tore at human flesh and drank warm blood.

"Better that we destroy the box than let Vril gain possession," Frau Burkhardt said. "Imagine a new Hitler, armed with the foulest of black magic and aided by the Very Old Folk."

"A thousand years of evil," Father Cova said, crossing himself. "The Antichrist arisen."

Alex cursed as the truth eluded him again. For a bare instant, he sensed the answer—then nothing.

"The box," Valerie said slowly, almost as if in prayer. "Bring me the box."

"What?" Frau Burkhardt said.

"Hurry," Valerie said, without explanation. "Hurry."

The old woman looked at her for a moment and then, without another word, rushed off. Father Cova hesitated and then followed.

Frightened, Alex gripped his wife by the shoulders.

"Are you crazy?" he shouted. "You heard Frau Burkhardt say the relic nearly killed her father the first time he tried to use it."

Valerie shook off his hands, the expression on her face unreadable. It was as if she was listening to a voice that only she could hear. Alex stepped back, frightened by the strangeness that possessed his wife.

Father Cova came running back, carrying the black satin bag under one arm. Frau Burkhardt trailed him, her breath coming in short, hard gasps.

"I lead too easy a life," she said, groaning. She tugged off the covering from the box. Huffing and puffing, she handed the ornately carved chest to Valerie.

It was 12 inches square and four inches deep. Four small legs protruded a half-inch from the bottom. Carved on its lid was a detailed picture of the Crucifixion. The sides of the box were decorated with scenes from the life of Jesus. The work was incredibly detailed, obviously the work of a master craftsman. Precious jewels were everywhere—diamonds, emeralds and rubies. Though the box dated back to the time of Pope Leo, the polished surface glistened like new in the pale light of the enclosure. Without a scratch showing, it looked as if it had been carved yesterday. Not a crack broke its smooth surface, giving the box the appearance of a solid block of wood.

"My father told me to press both hands of the Lord simultaneously," Frau Burkhardt said. "Only doing that releases the secret lock."

Father Cova held the box as Valerie followed the instructions. With a gentle sigh, the entire top of the treasure chest swung open. Valerie and Frau Burkhardt both gasped as if in sudden pain.

"The power," the old woman whispered. "The power."

The box was lined with thin layers of silver and gold. Resting undisturbed at the bottom was one fragile item.

Valerie said nothing. Her face appeared blank, as if under a deep hypnotic trance. With trembling hands, she reached into the box and pulled out the treasure placed there for safekeeping by Pope Leo many centuries before.

A soft glow surrounded the fragile circlet formed by a few supple thorn branches. Two thousand years old, it remained unbroken. No one among them doubted that it dated back to a moment when for an instant, time stood still. How it had survived and come to Rome was a mystery buried in the sands of time.

Father Cova's eyes grew very wide, and he murmured a prayer. Alex could only stare in astonishment at the amazing relic his wife held in her outstretched arms. Outside, from across the ravine, a human voice howled both in anger and fear.

"Dietrich Vril senses the power," Frau Burkhardt said. "He knows the treasure is here."

"Too late," Valerie said, her voice distant and serene. Carefully, she placed the crown of thorns on her head.

Chapter Twenty-Nine

Tears filled Valerie's eyes, and her face twisted in agony. The air whistled between her teeth as she sucked in great gasps of air. Her whole body shook in pain.

Helplessly, Alex grabbed hold of his wife by the shoulders, trying somehow to pass some of his strength on to her. She bit her lower lip as she choked down a scream. Her hands clenched into fists so tightly that the nails drew blood. Then, slowly and painfully, she forced herself erect.

As she straightened, an incredible transformation took place. Her breathing eased, and her body relaxed. A soft yellow glow spread around her body, bathing her in a dim light that clothed her in a cloud. Alex stepped back, realizing Valerie no longer needed his support. Her body pulsated with energy.

"The vampires!" cried Franz from across the compound. "They have finished with the Circumcellions. We are next!"

Instinctively, Alex reached for his revolver.

"No need for that," Valerie said quietly, in a voice not entirely her own.

She reached out and touched him on the shoulder. For a brief instant, he felt some small measure of the immense occult power that flowed through her body.

Suddenly, it became very clear to him that, in some incredible manner, his wife personified 6000 years of relentless destiny. An orderly universe strived for balance. Tonight, Valerie served as its agent.

"Come. Follow me."

She spoke as if in a dream. Her feet appeared to hardly touch the ground as she walked to the entrance of the enclosure. White fire circled her hands as she pointed to the barred doors.

"Let me out," she said, and no one thought to disobey her.

The guards unbolted the huge steel gates and pushed them open. Confidently, Valerie stepped forward into the ice-cold darkness. All followed, their guns held high in a futile gesture of defiance.

Only a few headlights still burned in the autos across the ravine, but the searchlights on the chateau provided ample light. Alex's muscles tightened as he spotted the Very Old Folk. They stood clustered by the metal bridge, their red eyes burning like coals. Not one of the creatures moved. As Valerie strode forward, they drew in on themselves, huge wings wrapping around their bodies like protective cloaks.

"They fear her," Frau Burkhardt said, her voice filled with awe. "The most evil things on Earth *fear* her."

The scene held for a moment, with each group staring at the other. Alex tried in vain to spot Dietrich Vril, but he was nowhere to be seen.

Then, as if obeying some unspoken signal, the vampires launched themselves into the air. A dozen pair of wings cracked open and pounded the winds. Up, up, up into the night flew the monstrous horde. The Very Old Folk glided forward, exhibiting all the ruthless grace of the most savage, winged predators. In seconds, the creatures halved the distance separating them from the small band of humans.

Franz and the other guards blazed away with their guns, but the monsters ignored the fire. Valerie shook her head, as if lecturing a child.

"Bullets cannot harm them. Only two things will kill a vampire."

The terrible jaws of the Very Old Folk split open to reveal gigantic yellowed fangs. Even in mid-flight, their taloned hands clutched and tore. Black wings darkened the night, pounding the air like giant drumbeats.

No one retreated. There was no time left to

hide. Instead, all attention focused not on the approaching horde but on the slender young woman wearing the crown of thorns.

Raising her right hand, Valerie spoke the one necessary word.

"Sunfire."

Out of nowhere, a whirling, twisting ball of white fire materialized and settled over her head. Six inches across, it blazed with all the fury of a star. Bright fingers of incandescent energy reached out in a deadly embrace.

One long tendril lashed out and touched the nearest vampire. Fire crackled and roared.

The vampire shrieked and spun away, a black line burnt deep along its torso. Its companions hesitated in mid-flight. Suddenly, understanding their peril, they tried to turn and retreat, but it was much too late. Normally, the sunfire spell was not strong enough to harm the monsters, but the crown of thorns multiplied the magic's power a thousandfold.

"Sunfire," Valerie repeated, louder this time.

Above her, the miniature star expanded and expanded. It rose high up into the night sky and grew as it moved. Waves of incredible heat rippled from its core as searing brightness flooded the valley.

Hot tears engulfed Alex's eyes as he tried to follow the fireball's path. The intense pain finally forced him to lower his gaze. It felt as if he stood in the center of a roaring furnace.

Gasping, he dropped to one knee. A wave of dizziness swept through him, leaving him weak.

Sweat poured from his body and evaporated into steam. Then, from behind, strong arms grabbed him and pulled hard. Reluctantly, he retreated.

Valerie stood alone, untouched and unharmed by the second sun she had created. The rest of their group clustered at the edge of the manor, desperately trying to shield their eyes from the light. It hurt to watch the fireball. All around them, winds howled as waves of superheated air collided with the frigid cold of the mountains. The entire valley filled with mist as ice and snow vaporized into steam.

"Behold" Father Cova said, gripping Alex's arm tightly. His voice rose to a shout to be heard over the roaring thunder of the fireball. Religious awe filled his every word. "Behold the power of the thorns!"

Shielding his eyes as best he could, Alex watched the final destruction of the vampire horde.

At the edge of the crevice he spotted several of the Very Old Folk pressed close to the ground. The wind held them pinned to the earth, and they huddled together, limbs raised high over their heads in a vain effort at protection. It did them no good. As he watched, their wings burst into flames. He imagined their final screams of agony, for the roaring whirlwind blotted out all other sounds. In seconds, their bodies shriveled and blackened into dry husks. Even then, the relentless fire continued, until only piles of black ash remained.

Desperately, a solitary vampire flew high into the sky. For a time, it seemed to have escaped. Then, like a living thing, a long tongue of fire lashed out and wrapped itself around the fleeing monster. The creature exploded into flame, its dust drifting to the earth.

Everywhere, the remaining monsters fought a futile battle against the heat and light of the midnight sun. One by one, the vampires perished. Fingers of energy coiled about the strongest monsters, consuming them with a touch. The fury of the fire was overwhelming, and not one vampire escaped. The death the Very Old Folk brought to so many others came full circle and claimed them at last.

For several minutes afterward, the fireball rotated high above the ravine, as if hunting for further victims. Nothing stirred on the plateau. Of the vampires, only black piles of ash remained.

Finally, as if sensing the completion of its purpose, the sun contracted, dissolving even quicker than it formed. Darkness reclaimed the valley.

Valerie stood alone on a scorched mound of earth. Her hands were still raised in the air, as if not comprehending what she had done. Half-turning, she dropped her arms wearily to her sides. Then, without a sound, she crumpled to the ground, unconscious.

Alex rushed forward and lifted her in his arms. As he did, Frau Burkhardt tugged the crown off Valerie's head. Quickly, as if holding a burning torch, she dropped it back in the box and closed the lid.

"Do not worry," she said reassuringly, patting Alex on the shoulder. "The backlash of the forces she controlled drained her strength. It happened to my father many times. She needs only a good sleep to recover."

Then, as if sensing Alex's unspoken question, she continued. "The crown throbbed with energy when I took it from her. Your wife barely touched the power within it. Remember, my father used it for years without seriously diminishing its strength. Now you fully understand why I feared what would happen if Vril obtained the treasure box."

"He died in the conflagration," Alex said, hoping he spoke the truth. "Let's get Valerie inside."

Chapter Thirty

An hour later, Alex and Father Cova returned outside.

Valerie rested in a deep sleep in one of Frau Burkhardt's spare bedrooms. Their hostess and Herr Lauber waited in the manor's study, soaking up the warmth of the fireplace and indulging in old memories. Neither of them indicated any desire to brave the night air.

Alex still worried about the fate of their enemies, and Father Cova indicated he was also troubled by the same concerns. They both required more than suspicions to satisfy their fears. Bundled in heavy parkas and armed with pistols and flashlights, they searched for mental peace.

Other than a few warped beams, the trestle bridge stood firm. They crossed it cautiously, staying to the center of the structure. Powerful winds swirled about them. The icy surface forced them to inch their way across, one step at a time.

"This crevice drops straight down for hundreds of feet," Father Cova said when they reached the other side. "Tomorrow, Franz and his cohorts will drop the remaining bodies over the side. Not much of a Christian burial, but good enough to forestall any questions for months, if not forever. A brutal end, even for a man like Haxley."

Despite Cova's pronouncement, Alex detected a note a grim satisfaction in the priest's voice. He was not sorry to see the end of the heretic and his followers.

The wide beams of their flashlights played across a scene of absolute carnage. The sub-zero temperatures had frozen everything exactly the way the vampires had left it. Dozens of torn bodies lay scattered throughout the plateau. Each of the corpses bore the distinctive signs of the vampires' attack.

Alex pointed his flashlight at the nearest corpse. Gulping hard, he swung the beam away. The victim looked like a monstrous jigsaw puzzle with several pieces missing. Large chunks of muscle and bone had been ripped out of his chest and shoulders. The Very Old Folk lived on both flesh and blood and evidently had been very, very hungry.

Silently, they forced themselves to search the ravaged bodies for the remains of Brother Ambrose and Dietrich Vril. All the while, they found not one trace left of the vampires. The blazing sun had burned the creatures to ashes. Only black markings on bare rock indicated that the Very Old Folk had ever existed.

After a short while, they decided to split up. Otherwise, their search would take all night. Father Cova hunted among the autos, while Alex tried the area closer to the mountain pass. Ten minutes later, he discovered Ambrose Haxley in a sheltered gully far from the ravine.

A cold chill swept through Alex when he spied the Circumcellion's smashed remains. Unlike the other bodies, Haxley's corpse appeared intact. Instead, Ambrose's arms and legs dangled at impossible angles from his torso. They had been twisted with such incredible force as to almost rip them clear off. Muttering a half-remembered prayer, Alex walked closer, and then felt himself grow terribly queasy as Brother Ambrose opened his eyes.

"The devil left me here to perish slowly in the cold," the giant whimpered, his breath coming in short, desperate gasps. "He tortured me but refused to let me die. Finally, he dragged me here to protect me from the wind. Vril wanted me to suffer."

"What happened to him?" Alex asked, stepping closer to the broken man.

"Kill me," Brother Ambrose begged, ignoring the question. "In the name of God, please kill me. Grant me release from this smashed form. Let me join my maker."

Alex drew his pistol and waved it in the air. "Tell me what happened to Vril and I'll grant your wish," he said anxiously. A feeling of panic gripped Alex. "Talk."

"I last saw him a few hours ago," Brother Ambrose said, desperate to be believed. "He departed soon after the fireball disappeared. He never returned."

The huge priest squeezed his eyes tightly shut from the pain. "Quickly," he gasped. "The pain grows worse."

"After the fireball," Alex said, horrified yet somehow not surprised.

He took a step closer and raised his gun.

"Beware, Professor Warner," Haxley muttered, as if remembering something important. "Vril is one of the giants of the Earth."

When the gunshot echoed through the still valley, Father Cova came charging across the plateau, gun drawn. His eyes widened at the sight of Alex standing over the bloody body of Brother Ambrose.

"What happened?"

"No time for explanations," Alex said. "Back to the fortress. Vril is still alive, and he's after the box."

They sprinted for the bridge. As they made their way back across the steel girders, Alex related Brother Ambrose's final words.

"Those few words jolted my memory. He called Vril one of the giants of the Earth. The term originated in *The Book of Enoch* in the same chapter that mentioned Semjaza."

"I remember," Father Cova said, a look of horrified understanding crossing his face. "The immortal watchers mated with human women, who gave birth to the giants. Half-mortal, half-divine, nothing harmed them. They terrorized mankind, living on flesh and blood, until God sent the flood to destroy them."

Alex cursed. "That was the one discrepancy in Frau Burkhardt's story that gnawed at my subconscious. If she wasn't Vril's real mother, then his tremendous psychic gifts weren't inherited from her. They had to come from his father!"

Reaching the end of the bridge, they raced for the manor house. The front door stood wide open, light pouring out into the night. Alex leapt over the smashed body of Franz and rushed down the long hallway to the study. Sweeping through the open door, he came to an abrupt halt.

Dietrich Vril stood in the center of the room. In one corner sprawled Frau Burkhardt, either dead or unconscious. On the floor at Vril's feet lay the lifeless body of Gustave Lauber. His throat was ripped out, but not a drop of blood stained the carpet. Only a thin red line trickled down one side of Vril's mouth. In his huge hands, the giant held the Armageddon Box.

Chapter Thirty-One

Vril laughed with pleasure. "How perfect. The eternal circle draws to a close. The first is now the last."

Alex backed away from the door, his mind racing from one mystery to another. All of the clues tumbled into place. A frightening picture emerged of a hideous occult experiment that merged man and monster. He finally understood the secret of Dietrich Vril's unholy birth.

"Steiner double-crossed the Fuhrer," Alex said. "Hitler never fathered a son. The magician used Pope Leo's treasure to create a devil in human form."

"You flatter me," Vril said with a chuckle. "I prefer to think of myself as the first member of a new order. Why do you think I named myself Vril?"

The giant held the box straight out like a prize possession. "My grandfather dreamed of a Reich lasting a thousand years. He envisioned a reborn Thule, ruled by true Aryan supermen. From the very start, Steiner realized that Hitler offered only a means to that end, not a solution. The Fuhrer lacked the necessary vision to understand Project Alraune.

"So Steiner tricked him. Capitalizing on Hitler's obsession with virility, my grandfather promised him a son. A few parlor tricks and a little mystic gibberish embellished the hoax. The madman never guessed the ritual meant nothing."

As he spoke, Vril twisted and turned the box. His fingers pressed at the decorations, and his hands tugged and pulled at the sides. Clearly, the giant feared damaging the contents. Equally obvious was the fact that he did not know how to open the box.

Alex clung to a slender hope, and it all depended on him keeping Vril talking. The longer he stalled, the better his chances. He knew he could not defeat the giant on his own. On the other side of the room by the fireplace Frau Burkhardt stirred. She still lived.

Meanwhile, Father Cova had not followed him into the room but lurked outside the door. Hopefully, even now, he was rousing the other guards. All fighting together, they might overcome Vril.

A roaring fire blazed in the fireplace. The flames cast weird shadows on the floor, reminding Alex of the curious jacket illustration on *Alraune*. The thought awoke vague memories of the finish of the novel. His mind racing, Alex tried to recall how Frank Braun defeated the invincible seductress.

"Ewers was in on it from the beginning," Alex said, trying to start Vril bragging. "The inscription he wrote in the book bothered me from the first. I never guessed the true meaning behind the words. I hunted through the book for the truth, never realizing that the dedication spelled it out in bold script right before my eyes."

"His tale provided the inspiration for the experiment," Vril said. His voice reflected his growing annoyance as he struggled with the wooden block.

"My grandfather read it as a young man and never forgot it. He struggled for years to transform fiction into fact. When he stole the crown of thorns, Steiner acquired the power source necessary to make the impossible possible, and the Very Old Folk provided the final ingredient to create a true super race."

"The vampires tried before to crossbreed with humanity," Alex said, shuddering. As he spoke, he started to slowly circle the room. He needed a weapon. "*The Book of Enoch* described one of their earlier attempts. Their children were the giants of the Earth, creatures who lived on human flesh and blood, beings like you."

"Not like me," Vril said angrily. "Semjaza told

me of those disasters. Thousands of years ago, the vampire conspired with renegade priests of Atlantis to create a new race of mixed heritage. Their combined magical efforts proved unequal to the task. The resulting offspring were grotesque horrors that mindlessly attacked all living things. Fortunately, the creatures died quickly. Mankind never forgot the giants. Their brief reign of terror inspired legends for many centuries afterwards."

Vril's eyes narrowed. "The Nazis wanted me to lead their troops into battle. Hitler expected me to prove myself worthy of him in combat. My grandfather insisted that I seize control of the Reich in accordance with his master plan. The vampire demanded that I use my occult powers to reopen the gateway to their dimension. They all sought to manipulate me. I agreed to all of their demands, but I honored none of them."

"What do you mean?" Alex asked. Like most megalomaniacs, once he started talking, Vril continued to gloat with only the slightest stimulation. His tremendous ego betrayed him.

"The vampires underestimated the force of my will. I possessed all of their strength and none of their weaknesses. Being half-mortal, sunlight never bothered me. My psychic gifts dwarfed theirs. After a few graphic demonstrations of my power, they learned to obey me. I rewarded them with gifts of blood for their cooperation."

By now, Alex's maneuvering positioned him so that he faced the entrance of the study. Vril stood directly between him and the door. The giant's back was to the entrance. Thus, he never noticed the figure emerging silently from the dark shadows of the hall or the other men who followed.

"What frightened Hess?" Alex asked, focusing all of his attention on Vril.

"He stumbled on me feasting," Vril said. "Caught by surprise, I reacted too slowly to prevent his escape. I sent the vampires after him, but he eluded them and fled to England. Hess saved himself by becoming a valued prisoner. Only the drastic security measures enforced by his captors insured his safety from my allies."

Vril shrugged his shoulders. "Hitler immediately suspected the worst. He never fully trusted Steiner, and my powers disturbed him. A small army of SS troopers descended on the estate with orders to arrest my father and kill me.

"Fortunately, the fools underestimated my strength. I managed to escape. Fleeing to the high Alps, I took refuge with the vampires of that region. Nearly immortal, time meant nothing to me. Secluded from my enemies, I plotted my next move."

Father Cova moved carefully, not making a sound. In his hands, he held one of the halberds from the dining room. The sharp steel head glowed blood red in the reflected light of the fireplace. Slowly, he turned the pike so that it pointed at a spot directly between Vril's shoulders.

Behind the priest, Otto studied the vampire's every move as he gripped a heavy crowbar from the limo. Next to him stood Gerhart, another of the guards. He balanced the other halberd like a spear on one shoulder. All three men watched and waited for the right moment to attack.

"Listen, Warner," Vril said, taking a step forward, "I know you are stalling, hoping for some sort of divine intervention. Only fools believe in miracles. Give up that foolish notion. I am willing to bargain. Your life means nothing to me. Cooperate for a few moments, and I will let you and your wife leave here in peace."

Alex hesitated as if considering the offer. Vril probably meant what he said, not that it mattered. Only fools or politicians made deals with the devil. A compromise with evil always ended in disaster.

"Tell me what you want before I decide."

"Naturally," Vril said, taking another step closer. He held out the Pope's treasure chest. "The crown rests inside this accursed container. I lack the necessary knowledge to open it. Smashing it will destroy the relic. You must know the secret. Reveal it to me, and you can go free."

In the corner, Frau Burkhardt groaned and forced herself into a sitting position, but Vril ignored her.

"Cooperate or die," he demanded harshly, advancing to within a few feet of Alex.

In the doorway, Father Cova nodded his head

up and down in an exaggerated motion that Alex couldn't miss.

"Faced with that choice," Alex said, "I agree."

He reached for the Armageddon Box.

"No," Frau Burkhardt cried, rising shakily to her feet. "If you give that monster the crown of thorns, mankind perishes. He offered me the same choice, but I guessed his secret. He plans to father a new race of human vampires, living off the flesh and blood of humanity. Imagine an army of his children ruling our world. Fate caught him unawares. Like most crossbreeds, Vril is sterile! He needs the crown to duplicate my father's experiment. Without it, all his schemes mean nothing."

"Ignore the old woman," Vril said. He extended the box to Alex. "If you refuse, it merely delays my work. Away from this place, I can pay an expert to open the box."

Arms outstretched, the giant presented a perfect target. Alex stood absolutely still, his body tense with excitement. Behind Vril, Father Cova raised the halberd and edged closer. The other two men followed.

"Your *father*," Vril said, the implications of Frau Burkhardt's words suddenly hitting him.

He half-turned as he spoke, wheeling about to face the old woman. His unexpected motion caught Father Cova by surprise. Vril's eyes widened in shock as he spotted the ambush.

Desperately, Father Cova thrust the pike up and in with all his strength. The steel point slashed through the air in a straight line for the giant's back.

Vril moved with inhuman speed, leaping to one side and flailing out with both arms. One huge hand grabbed hold of the pike and wrenched it close. The added force sent Father Cova flying forward. Vril, still gripping the treasure box with his other hand, slammed it into the priest's head. Cova dropped to the floor, blood gushing from his scalp.

The giant whirled to confront his other attackers. He acted without thought, a deadly fighter working entirely on instinct. He spun the pike around like a twig and hurtled it at the astonished pair before they could react. It connected with terrible force, sending them sprawling.

Panic-stricken, Alex lunged forward and hit Vril with a flying tackle in the stomach. They crashed to carpet, Alex using Vril's body to cushion his fall. The giant grunted in pain as his head cracked down hard against the floor. The Pope's treasure box went flying across the room.

Veteran of innumerable fights, Alex relied on his instincts, battling in close. He butted his head into Vril's ribs. That blow normally knocked the breath out of an opponent and broke several bones, but not with Dietrich Vril.

With a bellow of rage, the big man flung his arms around Alex, trapping him in a crushing bear hug. Laughing madly, the giant started to squeeze.

Alex arched his back and wrenched his knees up hard. The move caught Vril squarely in the groin. The giant's laughter turned to curses, but he continued to apply pressure. A few seconds more and Alex's back would break.

Gnashing his teeth in pain, Alex dug his elbows into Vril's chest and pushed with all his might. For a second Vril's grip loosened. In a blur of motion, Alex hugged his arms close to his body and slid out of the giant's grip.

They both regained their feet at the same instant. Alex whirled and kicked, aiming for Vril's neck. The giant reacted equally as fast. Crossing his arms in a perfect block, Vril caught Alex by the ankle and with a powerful heave sent him staggering back across the room. Alex hit the far wall and slumped to the floor, dazed.

A gun boomed from the doorway. Vril staggered, as shot after shot rocketed into his upper body. Hurriedly, Gerhart pulled Alex behind the sofa while Otto blasted away at Vril.

Incredibly, the giant's wounds healed in seconds. Bullets ripped through him and left no trace. Only the force of the explosions kept the monster at bay.

Angrily, Vril grabbed a nearby endtable. Picking it up with one hand, he flung it across the room at his tormentor. Otto jumped to the side, but the few seconds gave Vril all the time he needed. The giant raced across the floor and grabbed the chauffeur by the neck. Otto shrieked in agony as Vril swung him around like a stuffed toy.

Growling like an animal, Vril slapped the man's head back and forth. Blood spurted from a dozen wounds. In seconds, Otto's face was reduced to a featureless ruin.

Finally, as if tiring of the spectacle, the giant tossed the broken man to the floor. Savagely, he followed with a knee to the chest, crunching bones to powder.

That murderous assault gave the rest of them time to regain their strength and they attacked. There was no talk now of bargaining. It was kill or be killed.

Holding a halberd with both hands, Gerhart jabbed at the giant's chest. At the same time, Father Cova swung the tire iron in a crippling blow at the big man's knees. Neither attempt connected.

Moving quicker than humanly possible, Vril ducked and deflected the halberd harmlessly over his shoulder. At the same time, he reached down with his other hand and caught the heavy crowbar only inches from his legs. No mortal man could stop a swinging metal bar, but Vril was only partly human.

The crossbreed straightened, ripping the tire iron out of the priest's grip. Continuing the motion, he slashed the bar into Gerhart's face. The guard's features exploded in a shower of blood and gore. He collapsed to the floor, dead before he touched the ground.

Vril swung around, still gripping the iron, looking for Father Cova. He never found him.

Timing his thrust perfectly, Alex rammed the other halberd into Vril's chest. Shoving with all the power in his body, Alex plunged the pike's steel head straight through the monster, pinning him against the wooden doorframe.

Vril shrieked in pain. Relentlessly, Alex twisted the halberd's shaft, driving it as deep as possible into the monster's chest. There was no way it could be pulled free. The giant twisted in agony as black blood hissed down the wooden haft of the pike, boiling like acid on the floor.

Satisfied, Alex turned away and joined a shaken Father Cova standing a few feet away.

Behind him, Vril's struggles lessened and then grew still. The giant's eyes closed, and his breath grew weak. He sagged onto the pike, his arms limp at his sides. Alex sighed with relief. Totally exhausted, he dropped on to a nearby couch.

"He isn't dead!" Frau Burkhardt screamed.

Shocked, Alex raised his eyes. The giant had been merely gathering his strength. Features contorted with pain, Vril wrapped his arms above and below the shaft holding him pinned. Powerful legs dug into the floor for leverage. Then, in a frightful display of sheer, brute strength, he jerked his arms together and twisted. The wood pike snapped like a toothpick.

Grunting with exertion, Vril wrenched his body forward. Inch by inch, he struggled, tearing himself free from the section of pike that pinned him to the door. Roaring with defiance, he pulled free. A huge, open hole in his chest dripped black blood and gore.

Horrified, Alex and Father Cova retreated

back across the room. Vril's glistening white flesh regenerated as they watched. Turning, the giant grabbed the bloody portion of the pike embedded in the doorframe. Jerking hard, he ripped it loose and raised it over his head.

"My will is stronger than death," he bellowed. "I am immortal and unkillable. Darkness lives within me. Give me the crown. It belongs to me."

"Never," Frau Burkhardt answered. The old woman stood directly in front of the fireplace. The flames roared as if in agreement, sparks dancing with her every word. "Better that it be destroyed than in your grasp."

At her feet sat the treasure box with the lid open. Reaching down, Karl Steiner's daughter pulled out the crown of thorns. Energy pulsated through her body. Something akin to terror flashed across Dietrich Vril's face.

"Stop," he shouted and threw the bloody spearhead at the woman.

Frau Burkhardt raised her free hand. The blade froze in place, then dropped harmlessly to the carpet. Vril's features twisted in fear. He quickly began to chant in a language older than mankind.

"All these years," Frau Burkhardt said, her words cutting like a knife, "I suspected the truth, but I never knew for sure until this very instant."

Then, turning, she carefully tossed the crown of thorns into the flames.

Vril screamed once.

The fire blazed, and black blood erupted in a thousand fountains from Vril's body. It spurted out of every pore. At the same time, his skeleton exploded, sending shards of bone and cartilage ripping out of his flesh like a tiny million spears.

Skin, muscle and brain dissolved. Dietrich Vril collapsed into a formless, seething puddle of living tissue. A vengeful nature claimed its due.

"Frank Braun burned the mandrake root to destroy Alraune," Alex whispered, finally remembering the end of Ewer's novel.

"Vril's existence outraged natural law. The crown of thorns gave him life, and only the power of the crown kept him alive. Destroying it shattered the unholy truce between his human and vampire heritage. No longer bound by dark magic, his body literally tore itself apart."

"My father lied to me," Frau Burkhardt said, shaking her head in dismay. "No wonder he wanted me out of the country. I never once encountered Vril. If I had, I would have immediately sensed his true heritage."

Eyes filled with tears, Father Cova closed the lid of the Armageddon Box. "Only we few know that the Pope's treasure box contained the crown of thorns," he whispered, his voice filled with sadness. "Let it be our secret."

Then, drawing in a deep breath, the priest announced, "It was God's will."

Standing there, in the midst of the blood and death, Alex felt strangely at peace. In *Alraune,* Frank Braun questioned whether God existed, whether good triumphed over evil. After tonight, Alex had no doubts, no doubts at all. And that, in itself, was true peace.

Of all sinners the greatest is he who arrogantly tears the eternal laws from their appointed brazen grooves!

. . . He may create to his own wilful desires. He may break all the rules, turn nature inside out and topsy-turvy. But let him beware, for the creations of his pride are naught but fabrics of lies and deception.

from *Alraune*
Hanns Heinz Ewers

Author's Note

Unlike most secret religious orders featured in recent novels of horror and suspense, the Circumcellions actually existed. Interested readers are referred to the history of the Donatist movement for more information.

The author is indebted to Professor Robert M. Price for his information about the group.